# NEVER

# IS

# NOW

## TIMOTHY L. RODRIGUEZ

Copyright © 2022 by Timothy L. Rodriguez

ISBN: 978-1-957723-68-6 (Hard Cover)
         978-1-957723-69-3 (Soft Cover)

Rodriguez. Timothy L..
Never Is Now

Edited by: Karli Jackson

Published by WARREN Publishing
Charlotte, NC
www.warrenpublishing.net
Printed in the United States

*I'd like to thank two of my recurring characters—Boggs and Tinnin. They have given me many good stories, one even published in the* Dead Mule Society of Southern Literature.

# CHAPTER ONE

"Was a moccasin in the dang commode," said Shine Walker, repeating himself for the sake of the new arrival, Coonie Pride.

"Ain't signed no papers," announced Coonie. He was one of the more pitiful members of Random, a hamlet barely more than a crossroads in the southern part of Dinwoodie County.

Its hub consisted of Shufflin' Sam's store, Shine's Quonset garage, a brick post office, and a blinking yellow light. For the past two weeks, Coonie had faithfully traveled forty miles south to visit his wife at the Southside Mental Health Institute in Chesapeake. She had come down with a case of the nerves. Dinwoodie County welfare people had her committed.

"And I ain't payin' on none of them bills neither," said Coonie. However pitiful, Coonie was singularly consistent. He always kept his gray hair as short as the greasy stubble on his dirty face. He always wore the same rumpled cap that always retained the same sweet-sour odor of alcohol when distilled through the pores.

Coonie plunked himself down on the long-worn bench in front of the darkened store. The old men of Random gathered there most nights. From the time the dogwoods bloomed until the mums lost their color, they had their places assigned, worn smooth. Some even brought sitting pillows.

Coonie pushed back his cap and scratched his head. "Damndest woman I ever seen. Who ever heard tell of a woman puttin' on twenty pounds given only hospital food?"

Shine let the question stand and resumed his story. "So Agnes, she comes on this moccasin in the commode. Heard a noise like something was swimmin' in the thing. And she goes in and sees them steady, cold eyes restin' real easy against the white bowl. She don't holler or nothin'. She just reaches over real careful and throws down the seat and lid. And Will, now he's got hisself one of them cushioned rubber seats. Says it's a proven yardstick of affluence in all the catalogues and such. Though I ain't never seen one 'cept over at his place. But that there rubber seat liked to worry Agnes to death. She figured the moccasin would get good and cool 'fore too long and slide under it. So she weighted it down with a laundry basket but weren't satisfied with that and goes and gets some bricks. Well, in no time she had the lid so weighted down that if the snake had a mind to use dynamite, it couldn't blast its way out."

Shine paused and stretched his long legs, crossing them at the ankles. He rivaled a scarecrow for height and weight. The bulkiest, most formidable part of him was the pair of thick, black-rimmed glasses that made a saddle slump on the bridge of his thin nose. "So with them bricks to hold the snake down, Agnes runs and gets in the truck and drives right up into the parade to fetch—"

"Now you tell me what sense there is in having a Fourth of July parade four days after the Fourth of July," said Coonie at once scornful and confused.

"Said it was a right big success," said Shufflin' Sam. Sam had thick gray hair, a wood block for a chin, and a jutting nose separating ore-deep iron eyes.

Coonie said, "But here it is, a full four days after the Fourth of July."

"I can't rightly say it's progress, but we come a ways," said Sam, who was known for the bits of light he shed on the damn fool things men were liable to do even though they were forewarned and armed to the teeth with all manner of sworn testimony, solemn prayer, and sacred oath.

"Maybe next year they'll have it four days 'fore the Fourth," said Shine. "Then we'd be ahead of everyone else."

Plans for the belated parade materialized after the local American Legion sold only a dozen barbecue dinners at its holiday pig picking. Legionnaires then conceived of the parade as a rallying point for the community and a second chance to sell their high-priced pork. Because it was a weekday event sanctioned neither by God nor government, the participants nearly outnumbered the spectators. Of the two dignitaries, Chief District Court Judge John Hardy had to cancel. Court was in session. But Sheriff J.B. Harris took the time to march. He wore a bright red Christmas ribbon for a sash. Ten yards ahead of the sheriff was Deputy Carson Tinnin in his patrol car with the blue light blinking. Every so often he'd give the siren a whoop. Behind the sheriff came Random's peewee championship team, a depleted Greensburg Junior High marching band (many of whose members were away on vacation), six cheerleaders, a tanker from the county's volunteer fire department, and four legionnaires dressed as clowns. Because the three-man color guard from Fort Jackson arrived late, it pulled up the rear.

Milt Allison said, "'Less they fly our flag up there in front for all to see, we ain't gonna be ahead of no one." Milt straightened his square back. "Puttin' the flag in the back is disrespect, plain and simple. Disrespect is what it is." He bent down to pick up the rusty tin can he kept under the bench. He spit tobacco juice and settled back, letting the can rest on his flat stomach.

After a moment of silence, Shine rushed into the breach. "So here come Agnes drivin' Will's smelly old pickup. Them cheerleaders musta believed she was part of the parade cuz they made room for her. 'Cept they didn't know what to make of her on the running board hollerin' for Will. And he got in such an all-fired hurry, he never did pay for his barbecue. But he got the truck turned 'round, though by this time what part of the parade was ahead of the cheerleaders had done finished walking. No one minded none, 'cept maybe Will. He told Agnes to watch the rest of it and went on back to the house only half believing an ole moccasin was sitting in his fancy commode. But he weren't taking no chances cuz he got his twelve gauge, and sure enough under all them bricks was a four-footer. Just having a high ole time. Well, Will just kinda eased the barrel in under the lid and let loose.

"Now, all this time Agnes is up yonder at the parade frettin' that Will got bit or maybe ate, so just as soon as them boys from Fort Jack—"

"Disrespect, that's what it was," said Milt. He spit.

Shine nodded and quickly continued. "So when them boys passed, Agnes picks up them little feet of hers and runs faster than that girl we seen runnin' the roads 'round here. And it don't take no time 'fore she's back and come to find Will sittin' on the porch like he was lettin' a toddy settle. 'Cept for one thing. He looked like he done been swimmin' or sweatin'. But 'fore Agnes can say anything, he informs her right quick he's taken care of the snake and got everything cleaned up like new. Well, Agnes she knowed it was a lie and marched off to the bathroom when Will calls out for her not to use the commode. That stopped her right dead in the doorway. Reckon she couldn't half believe her eyes. Cuz it was like Will said, all clean and shiny. But then she musta smelt gun powder cuz she slides on up and careful as care lifts the lid. Will said she didn't scream or put up a fuss when she seen how he blowed out the back of the commode and half the wall."

Shaking his head as if to shake off his grin, Sam said, "That Will always been quick on the draw."

"I s'pect I'll have to fix it," said Coonie.

"Shot the whole damn thing to pieces," said Shine, laughing.

"But if they ain't had the thing four days after the Fourth, then maybe none of this would a happened," said Coonie.

Milt said, "Hear tell the Braves is gonna get shut of Chief Noc-A-Homa."

"I mean, shot all to hell," said Shine, his laughter on its second wind.

A minute later Coonie asked, "Ever any of y'all cut down what they call a locust tree, them with the three-, four-inch thorns?"

And so it went under the white writing of the stars.

# CHAPTER TWO

The sounds of the night hid from the howling sirens. Agnes Blake drifted through the supper dishes, lost to all but the photo of her son on the sill. She looked at it until she could no longer see it. She saw Andy, not the picture.

She saw Andy as whole, not missing in Vietnam. Andy was complete, not missing an arm or leg. He was walking with that careless grace, his big bare feet shuffling through the dust of the drive, his smile forever cleansing his face. He was laughing. She cocked her head and smiled, hearing his three-beat chuckle. He was telling the story about having two dates for the senior prom: one girl in the parking lot, the other on the dance floor. Neither knew about the other, and neither was suspicious when they reversed positions. That Andy could sure enough talk his way in or out of anything.

If she had to pick one word to describe him, Agnes chose the word "smart," not clever and not only school smart but also horse-sense smart. Until Vietnam, he enjoyed tacit consent from the future to rise without restrictions to a height Agnes had built so high in her mind that she couldn't see the top.

In the window, Agnes saw herself smile. But the smile died at the sight of itself. The story was true, but not the thought. The thought was barren, sickened by the hope that so richly inspired it. Wicked though it was, she prayed against hope, prayed that the army would let her son die. The army told her it needed a body. A wound would help too. Her wound? No one thought about that. Her wound had been festering for thirteen years now. Hope would not let it heal.

Agnes was already a tiny woman and in that time seemed to have shrunk, somehow gotten smaller, to the unspoken astonishment of those who knew her. Hers was the body of a teen perhaps a year away from menstruation. Her face had a neat, almost pert, cut with down over her lip. The still-lively arches over her blue eyes suggested wonder and a capacity for surprise.

Despite her size, she was packed. She possessed not so much power but might, not strength but the might of one friendly smile in the face of many angry blows. Agnes's smile once came often and easily, instantly soft and genuinely persuasive, an altogether resplendent match for the traveling light in her eyes. But the comfort taken in meeting her smile sometimes withdrew at the sight of the mark, the hellish mark of time, a time beyond any measure or count. Cruel lines around her mouth and eyes left a pattern that resembled the radials of a clock. Agnes accepted these lines, as she believed in the biblical passage about time; there was a time for work and a time for pleasure. Her pleasures were so simple they never had to be deferred, like sitting on the porch in the cool of the night with nothing more pressing than sleep. By the same token, her pains were simple. The loss of her oldest boy was a simple pain; there was no need to complicate it. Likewise, there was no reason to stop it mainly because there was no way to stop it. The pain only went deeper each time she sought relief.

"It's the trailer!" shouted Will from the porch.

Agnes heard the yellow dog bark at the sirens. She heard Will's pounding steps and then a plate crash.

Agnes dried her hand with the towel looped through the cabinet handle below the sink. She stepped over the shards of the plate she'd dropped and headed down the darkened hallway. Creaks spread through the floorboards at well-known points. She passed Billy's bedroom, an empty hollow ever since he moved down to the trailer. Seven more steps took her past Andy's room, which she kept as neat and clean as any in the house.

With her two boys gone, the household diminished, but the size of the house itself seemed to enlarge. She could readily recall when it took no time to reach the screen door. Now, just getting past the bedrooms seemed an interminable journey, a labor that came with a usurious cost. She felt she had paid in full when she finally stood on the front porch.

She was not really alert to the reason why she had come all this way until she saw Will streaking through intervals of moonlight at the south edge of the pond. She discovered the kitchen towel in her hand and dried her already-dry hands. Set off by the pale light, Will looked suspicious, a fleeing criminal.

But then Agnes noticed the reddish-orange light mounting and muscling the breezy black night. That light was the criminal; that was the crime.

By the time Agnes reached the trailer, it was hissing rubble. The clearing had as many lights as a city. She looked for her boy. The mechanical voice spitting from the fire engine cabs made her search all the more intense, sweeping her gaze over the firemen, none of whom seemed to have faces. She looked over the ground where thick hoses snaked, so fat and corrupt. She looked for her husband, but a flashing red whipped all her thoughts into its vortex. She walked toward its berserk spin as if entranced as the brilliant light within the ambulance suggested a celestial opening.

Agnes stopped.

Will came clambering out of the rescue unit. At once, shadows engulfed him.

As he walked toward her, he took a form she knew and suddenly hated. She resisted his hug, attentive to the ambulance doors closing. She bit into Will's chest as life started to leave her, feet first.

Deputy Carson Tinnin worked his way around the puddles and over the hoses toward Will and Agnes. In the intense light, he was a shadow that Agnes had seen coming months ago, about the time Billy first took up with that Trollinger boy. She knew this shadow, or one similarly outlined, would come.

She was convinced, totally, bodily, that Billy and David Trollinger had been drinking to such excess as to sicken themselves and their minds. No pleasure was gained from their drinking, only escape. From what, she wasn't sure. Maybe from a crazy urge to break out or cut loose. But here again came the question—from what?

She also believed, without ever having or needing proof, that Billy had been taking drugs. What kind was beyond her grasp. In her day, drugs were something one read about in the lives of the truly wicked. But all that changed somehow. Somehow, the heart and mind of her boy, of all the children, seemed to change so that none of them cared for or about themselves, about how they saw themselves, or about how others saw them. Billy, all the children, didn't have a long view, let alone a short view. They just stopped looking.

Maybe Billy was her fault. Yes, she was to blame. She was looking for Andy all these years, looking down the drive on a chance. She was looking so hard for her oldest boy that she never thought to look at Billy. Now she was to be punished; now was the time for retribution.

A new light caught the approaching deputy. Agnes focused on the brown uniform and the wide black belt with all its attachments and appliances. Here came the penalty imposed for setting Andy's picture on the sill. Here came not the law or justice but the imperious claim to punishment. Agnes glowered at Tinnin, thinking he should be carrying a handgun or a rifle instead of a pad and pen. Although she knew Tinnin as well as her own children, his baby-fat face suddenly repulsed her. It wasn't a man's face. A man would look serious, not sad.

Tinnin said, "Will, we want to do an autopsy. We just can't say what happened. It was the fire more than—"

"Weren't no fire."

"Believe these firemen would say otherwise."

"What started it?"

"We don't know just yet. We'll know more—"

"When?"

"When we get time to investigate, that's when." As soon as he heard his raised voice, Tinnin considered apologizing. He didn't. He couldn't say why until Agnes broke in.

"Carson Tinnin, you and Billy went to school together. You've knowed him all these years, and this is all you can say to us." She stepped closer to the deputy. "And here all this time I believed you was from better stock. Well, ain't I the fool."

The deputy stood at some semblance of attention, his fingers flicking the black stripe running down the side of his uniform trousers. He opened his mouth, but no words were available.

Will said, "You best get on with your investigatin', son."

Will slung his arm around Agnes's shrunken shoulder. Together they turned and left.

# CHAPTER THREE

"Now there ain't one of us willing to swear to it, but them detectives, they got a feeling they're getting close," lied Deputy Tinnin. "Least to where they can get a general idea. They can pretty much reconstruct what all happened out there." To temper the lie, he added, "But then reconstructing it don't really tell us who done it. But it does tell us a lot. It kinda cuts down on who might could have done it. You get that far and 'fore too long …"

Will looked at the fat-faced deputy without seeing him. He knew what the officer was saying was a trick. All the setbacks in Will's life were tricks, not necessarily magic or evil tricks, but tricks potent enough to yank the hardscrabble ground out from under him. He was at a loss to explain these machinations and had to resort to the loser's prayer—the hosanna of if-only—if only he could slip behind the scenes to where he could see why these tricks were played on him. That he never found an answer left him certain of one thing: neither weakness of the flesh nor the dissipation of the blood could lay a man low. No, a man could always fight such afflictions. But not the tricks—especially one as lowdown as never knowing. There was nothing to confront, to strike out at, or even to accept. There was only a nothing at the center of everything. It seemed so simple—a simplicity that was powerful and shattering.

As undetectable as it was, anger etched its way into his expression. His was not a face of a feeling man, one apt to be shaken, but of a massive stone plunked down in the earth—a mystery, a monolith, completely impenetrable. Only a twitch now and then along the twin cuts running deep from high cheek to jaw suggested life in the weathered stone. Even when he spoke, normally a word or two and no more than a sentence or two at a time, his voice sounded too grave, too deep to have an emotional register. Most mistook it for anger because they had seen Will flare up against innocent words or harmless deeds. Such behavior went without explanation or apology. If blame be cast, no one looked further than the bottle. Will was one of Shine's steady customers. A terrific need answered best by drink, but even then left wanting, preyed on Will in spells. None ever lasted long because nothing that Will ever said or did could break the desperate inertia of work.

Work was a state of motion to which Will had been born fifty-seven years ago. Since he was an only child, the family's ninety-two acres went to him. So the farm remained large enough for him to escape the fate of working in a textile mill.

From the start, Will was a step ahead of the others. He was the first to double-crop, the first to raise chickens under contract, the first to leave the tillage in the field and employ ridge-till, the first to listen to the ag-extension office and plant cotton. Despite his lead, Will sometimes seemed to fall behind, fall behind himself. He was the last to realize that something awful had happened—to him, his crop, his land. These were tricks too. There was no earthly way to anticipate them. Sometimes there seemed to be answers for them, but the answers never answered anything, like the answers about Andy that the government sent in envelopes that didn't require stamps.

Why the government just didn't come out and say Andy was dead remained as much a mystery to him as why he ever hoped his oldest son was alive. Hope counted time much slower than a clock, and Will's resolve began to rot. The stench was so unbearable that he finally relented and told himself Andy was dead. In time, his time, he came to believe that the nation's body count was one shy of a load. Proof was not needed.

Billy's death was different. Proof was the trick. The crater the .38 caliber slug left in Billy's head wasn't proof that David Trollinger pulled the trigger. Neither was the body burnt beyond decency proof of anything other than a fire. The fat deputy said that neither a weapon nor an accelerator such as gasoline was found at the scene. Even if they had been found, linking one or the other to Trollinger was too much to expect.

Though they didn't find a murder weapon or even a whiff of a motive, the sheriff's department still considered Trollinger a suspect. Billy and Trollinger ran together: drinking, gambling, and whoring. On that fact alone, detectives brought Trollinger in for questioning. The two-hour session revealed something intangible but invaluable: Trollinger was scared, running scared even though he had an alibi. Questioning Mary Jane Henson, the girl Trollinger was supposedly with that night, produced another revelation: she too was frightened, but not of the law. That no one on the street claimed Trollinger as a friend suggested another law was at work. A grave had more to say about a person than what was being said about Trollinger.

Will slapped his hand down on the wax tablecloth. "Just what is it you're trying to tell us, Carson?"

The deputy warily eyed Will's .38 revolver 6, a chrome piece with a rubber grip. Even though its cylinder was out and a rag wound around the rear cylinder opening, the barrel pointed at him. Beside it were bottles of solvent and gun oil, new and used patches, a bore brush, and a cleaning rod. His gaze passed over the weapon and confronted Will. "Just that there ain't no proof Trollinger done it. It might coulda been someone else, and it might coulda been for reasons bigger than a fight between drunks."

Will's dark eyes constricted to thin lines. "You tellin' me you ain't gonna have the boy arrested?"

"We can't." He sidled his left hand across the table to nudge the barrel in another direction.

"Why? This some kind of trick? Everyone knowed he run with Billy. The boy told me hisself he'd been drinking with David. He said he was fixin' to have a card game. Come up here lookin' to borrow some money. Damn fool said he'd pay me back twice what he borrowed. But then I don't reckon you found any money on him?"

Tinnin refrained from mentioning that the body was burned beyond recognition, burned down to the bone, a fact that shamed even his sorrow. In his mind he knew there was no possible way he could have prevented this tragedy. He nevertheless languished under an inchoate sense of guilt and isolation.

Blame reared up almost immediately as if it had always been there waiting, just waiting, for an identity to assign itself to and to take the assignment not for a day or weeks but for a lifetime. All at once Tinnin had become an outsider in Random. He was looking in when, throughout his life, he had been on the inside, born and bred—so inbred that Sam, sole proprietor of The Store, had let the preteen Carson handle one of the sacred knickknacks Sam kept on the shelf behind the counter—The Chief.

The Chief was a wooden toy Indian who hid his nakedness by standing inside a barrel. Sam had told Tinnin to lift up the barrel, which Tinnin did and saw the Chief's skinny ass and enormous erection. Everyone laughed, not at The Chief but at Tinnin who jumped backwards.

Fighting against his fear of provoking Will, he asked, "Even if we had, what would it prove?"

Will examined the dirt embedded in his cuticles and wiped his hands down the chest of his V-neck T-shirt. He splayed his fingers atop the table and pressed down. A moment later he snatched up an old toothbrush and began cleaning the muzzle and the flat sides of the cylinder.

Tinnin was silent, watching and waiting for Will to turn his attention to the extractor rod. But Will ignored it. He set the brush down and held up the revolver, aiming down the front sight at an object between Tinnin and Agnes at the sink. Without the slightest hesitation, the O of the barrel suddenly swung onto the surprise in Tinnin's face. Just as quickly the gun came to rest on the yellow and white squares of the tablecloth.

Without looking up at the deputy, his fingers twitching beside the trigger guard, he said, "Carson, I been knowing you since you was a pup. And I ain't never done you or your daddy thisaway, and I ain't expecting you to do me like this."

Tinnin watched Will's hide-like hands, which now gripped the edge of the table. The deputy's eyes shot between the hands and the barrel. So intent was his vigil that he felt he had to do something with his own hands. He dropped them below the table, his fingers twiddling. "Will—Will, the law ain't … well, we just can't be locking folks up for no good reason. We—"

"My boy's dead, ain't he?"

"But there ain't no proof Trollinger done it."

"That David's mean as a snake."

"It don't make no difference what he is. We don't know what he done." Tinnin added, "Leastways for sure."

The dark glint of his eyes on Tinnin, Will snared a cloth already moist with gun oil and wiped down the weapon. After a while he looked up and said, "Ain't we got a body?"

Tinnin bowed his eyes. "Yeah, we got a body."

"That's right. You do." Will nodded as if he had settled the dispute. He ripped off the tied rag and snapped the cylinder back in place. With a clean cloth, he wiped the gun down again to remove excess oil.

"That's right. You do."

Tinnin looked to Agnes on the chance she would turn and offer some explanation as to what her husband was trying to say. Her back remained a wall. At a loss, Tinnin said, "So?"

"So!" Will grunted. "So the trick is this." Without warning he brought the barrel up and took dead aim at Tinnin, cocking an eye as if to fire.

"Goddammit, Will. Get that damn thing outta my face." After a moment, he apologized to Agnes for his language.

Will obliged. Acting as if scolded, he folded his arms and stared at the floor. Suddenly, he drove the fat side of his fist against the table top. "You got a body. My boy didn't take his life. Trollinger took it."

"But you don't know for sure."

Will bowed his head and threaded his hand through his peppered hair. After a time he spoke. "I don't need to know it. Like I don't need to know what I got to do tomorrow. I do what needs to be done. There ain't no knowin' for sure about it."

"But, Will, there is," pleaded Tinnin.

Will seized the weapon and pressed the cylinder latch. From a small box he took out one bullet and loaded it. The loading process was painstaking, seemingly taking five minutes to fill the five chambers. Looking up at the deputy, he pressed the cylinder back into the gun's frame until it locked.

Holding the loaded gun up but not aiming at Tinnin, he said, "Boy, you ain't got—you don't know the first of it." He paused and let the barrel sway as if a divine rod. "Like who was he playing cards with if not Trollinger?"

"Trollinger never said nothin' 'bout no card game."

"Well, Billy did."

"But Billy didn't tell you who all was there, now did he?"

No answer came. Tinnin followed the loaded gun, back and forth, back and forth. At last he screamed, "Goddammit, now. I done told you to get that thing outta my face."

Tinnin was about to apologize again, but Will did not respond.

"I said—"

"I heard ya."

"You want to shoot me. Is that it?"

Will lowered the gun and his eyes.

"Put the dang safety on." He added to no one in particular, "Honest to God … ain't got a lick of sense than to point a loaded gun …"

Will complied.

No one said a word for several minutes. Finally, the deputy said, "Will, I know you want—I come here on account of my knowing you. If you want a detective down here to explain all this, I'll get one tonight. You—"

"The onliest reason for a detective to come down here is to take Trollinger off to that jail of yours and to stand him 'fore a judge for what he done." Will added after a moment, "Course, whatever they do won't be near enough."

"Maybe not," said Tinnin wearily. "Maybe not." He rose. He was about to say something but stopped. He looked to Agnes at the sink. "Night, Misriz Blake."

"Night, Carson."

The deputy opened the screen door but let it close. He turned back, almost shamefaced. "Misriz Blake, you ever seen Billy with drugs?"

"Night, Carson."

The deputy left.

After a while Agnes asked Will, "More tea?"

When Will didn't answer, she took his plastic tumbler and refilled it with ice and tea. She resumed her dishwashing, the water by now long cold.

Will closed his hands around the sweaty glass. He peered into it as if it were as clear as a crystal ball. The law seemed to be saying that Billy was murdered, but there wasn't a murderer. The longer Will thought about it, the more he sensed decay, the rotting of his patience, his hopes, and dreams. All befouled. The law or what passed for the law conspired with the unseen to play tricks. Never mind that the law was meant to protect, was meant to solve crimes. Will called the law his enemy. He gripped his glass tighter and tighter and then flung it against the wall. He stood and announced, "Them sheriffs don't know shit."

# CHAPTER FOUR

Not long before dawn on Saturday morning, the morning after Deputy Tinnin told the Blakes there wasn't evidence to arrest David Trollinger, a '54 Chevy pickup took the turn at Garner onto McKenney hard, almost balancing itself on two wheels. The truck went about a hundred yards north and glided to a stop on the grassy shoulder.

When the passenger door opened, no light shone inside. A song by the Police, "Spirits in the Material World," came out of the cab along with a modestly built man with a severely hooked nose. He tugged on his Pride in Tobacco billed cap. Although the man pushed the squeaky door closed, it didn't shut. Unconcerned, he went to the back, letting his open hand ride the fat, flared fender. He dropped the tailgate by unhooking inner tube-coated chains. Before he made another move, he put on a pair of leather gloves. He reached in and removed the bricks that held down the army blanket. He grabbed the exposed running shoes on the body lying on its back on the warped plywood bed. He yanked as he stepped back, taking no notice of how hard the shoulders and head smacked the ground.

"Need any help?" came from the open driver-side window.

"I got it."

The man had his reason for wanting to do this job alone. He dragged the body away from the road and across a shallow ditch, at the top of which he stopped to adjust the blanket. It had gathered around the corpse's head. As he entered the well-spaced corn rows, he had to yank and tug from time to time because the arms got caught on stalks. He stopped at the third row. The sky was beginning to lighten; even so, the dark mustered among the tasseled corn. But the man didn't need the light.

He dropped to his knees, removed his gloves, and tossed aside the annoying blanket, most of which had collected about the neck. He stretched out his arms and cupped his hands on the doughy breasts and tender nipples. He just had to have one last feel. He pressed, his eyes closed, and released a soft groan.

"Let's go, man. We ain't got all night."

He cursed. "Lost the blanket. I can't—"

"Forget it. Let's go."

The hooked-nose man snatched up the blanket and ran back to the idling truck.

Not long after first-light, buzzards found the girl's body and pointed the way for Shine Walker to make the discovery. While on his way to his Quonset hut, he felt compelled to adjust how his glasses sat on the bridge of his nose. He squinted through the thick lenses. At last he came to a stop because he had never, in all his years, seen so many vultures in one place and most of them on the ground and hopping mad at each other. The way some hooded their wings as they charged each other reminded him of Lon Chaney when he spread his Dracula cape.

When he went to see what caused the commotion, the birds turned ornery, refusing to make way. He hissed and hollered at them, but only when he went to kick them did they make room for him. He smelled the decay before he ever saw what caused it. The sight of the corpse made him drop to a knee and hold his fingers to his temples in an effort to stop a dizzy spell. It took a moment to regain his balance; by then his composure was a lost cause.

Shine staggered back to his truck. With two hands gripping the wheel, his bony chin jutting out close to the windshield, he struggled to steer. He drove up to The Store, half the time in the wrong lane. Breathless, he stumbled inside and told Sam to call Tinnin.

Deputy Tinnin, just home from third shift, missed Sam's call, but he did answer the call to report back to work because a body had been dumped in his territory while he had been on patrol. Excuses were easy to make but impossible to articulate. An even greater weight than his remorse was that no one, not the sergeant nor the lieutenant, blamed him. They were well aware that the community of Random was the largest area the department patrolled. Because it was the least populated, the sheriff assigned only one car, and he didn't expect his deputies to cover every rural mile of road. All the sheriff asked for was that his men maintain a presence. And that was what Tinnin did last night. Still, he felt a suffocating responsibility for the girl's death, although the sergeant said she was dead long before she was tossed.

Buzzards still hovered overhead as Tinnin stood at the far end of the ten-acre field. He, along with ten others, had been told to look for evidence. Since no one told him what exactly to look for, he looked without really seeing. In a cornfield such as this, so beguilingly still on the surface, a man was liable to come across anything.

Tinnin remembered driving his daddy's combine and how it seemed as if Noah had just opened the ark's doors. The field was a veritable back alley of critters on the tear—snakes, rats, birds, cats, and sometimes deer and coon, although the deer and coon were partial to Silver Queen corn rather than the silage corn his daddy grew. But often as not Tinnin never saw enough of a shape to say whether it was a rat or cat, just dark dartings without legs or fur, no bigger than the moment it took to run from the six-row swath he cut.

To search for something in particular in this underworld seemed downright foolish, so Tinnin relied on his eyes in a general, unthinking way, hoping they would alight on something meaningful to the solution of this, the second murder in the county in four days.

Tinnin was grateful that this crop was of the kitchen table variety; otherwise, the rows would be so dense that he would have to sidle with his chin and gut tucked tight. Beholden as he was to this Silver Queen crop, he didn't like the looks of it; in fact, it chastened his appetite for corn, and he usually possessed a hunger capable of consuming a half dozen ears at a sitting. Although never one to complain about corn once it was on the table, all swaddled and steamy, he certainly didn't like the looks of this crop. It looked buggy, and the silk was reddish, which could be the result of some hybrid seeds mixed in at sowing. Gray tracks etched on the leaves told him flea beetles had dined there—and God knows what else.

The sight reminded him of Coonie's son, Loonie, and the story told about his love bugs. Red-eyed and clear-eyed witnesses told of how stink bugs and beetles had found their way up to Loonie's shoulders, there to fornicate without regard to the onlookers. Since the boy smelled no better or worse than the next person, the reason why his skinny shoulders made for satin sheets drew a big crowd, but one not given to sober reflection. At first, meals at the Pride homestead were deemed the culprits because Mrs. Pride was a legend for pickling everything from plain cucumbers to wild weeds. Then it became known that the family ate much like a pride of lions. Because the sight of dirty dishes made the missus vomit, they didn't use plates. Instead, she simply slung the food on the table. Soap was the next suspect, but all eleven family members used the same bar.

At the close of the second summer of her son's affliction, Mrs. Pride became hysterical. She insisted it wasn't Christian for her boy to walk under the eyes of the Lord with a veritable brothel on his shoulders. To assuage her, Coonie reached for the one thing that was usually within reach, Shine's white lightning. The boy gulped down a Mason jar full. The next day he was hungover but healed. From then on, father and son stayed about half-drunk, referring to the moonshine as "the cure."

Loonie tippled constantly until the army drafted him. He was sent to Vietnam where he died in a place no one in Random could pronounce, much less point to on a map. Ostensibly, he was the only one from Random to die in that war, and Random had actually produced a bona fide hero in Gurney Liddle who returned with a chest full of medals and ribbons and hidden scars. During the parade the Legion held for Gurney, he wore a black armband to honor his friend, Will Blake's boy, whose fate was somewhere between dead on paper and dead in the ground.

Tinnin couldn't recall ever hearing stories about the Blake boy like the one still told about Loonie and the love bugs. For the life of him, Tinnin couldn't even remember the boy's first name. He knew for a fact that the Blake boy was never declared dead, still missing somewhere—either in Washington or Vietnam.

To declare death struck Tinnin as odd. Either a person was dead, or he wasn't. Not to be dead and at the same time not to be alive posed an impossible picture. It was as if the Blake boy had never been, so he couldn't die and couldn't live the way Loonie still did. At least Billy Blake would be remembered, and so too would be the girl they found in this field this morning.

Tinnin's self-reproach was unbounded because this was the second killing in four days in Random, the territory that he tried to guard as if he were law and order personified. What he could have done to prevent either one he didn't know, but somewhere under the brooding was the judgment that he was responsible.

According to the shift lieutenant, the authorities found her body not two hours ago. She lay among purple and white morning glories. They said all manner of bugs infested her open mouth. They said she was still wearing her peppermint jogging britches. They said that she had been raped. They said that it looked like the work of a long gun, not a man. They said she had definitely been shot. Aside from dried vaginal bleeding, there was blood, black as a bullet, in her abdominal cavity. They said it was the usual amount of blood, although Tinnin didn't know what "usual" meant. He had seen only two dead men in his life: one crushed by an overturned tractor and Billy, burned beyond recognition.

No one wondered why her hands were in the shape of claws after seeing rope burns and bruises on her wrists. No one mentioned the neck and ankle contusions. No one had much else to say about anything, either out of respect for womankind or out of guilt for mankind or out of a sense of place.

No one spoke about a girl from a rich family. No one talked about the rich the way they talked about the poor, those poorer and commoner than they were. The only time they denigrated the rich was when a wealthy person stooped to the ways of the poor. Even then, they didn't talk about a woman the way they talked about men.

They said this girl, the one they had been looking for ever since she disappeared three days ago, was the daughter of Dr. Allen. He was the last man to serve as county coroner, back in the day when doctors and lawyers weren't so common, back when the county needed less than a handful of each. Because she was Allen's daughter, they didn't say anything about catching the man or men who raped and killed her. They knew they had to catch someone, or else people would have their say. It would be far harsher than the current criticism about the department's incompetence in stopping sex and sin, in the vice squad's inability, its numerous arrests notwithstanding, to interdict drug trafficking.

They said the girl was beautiful. They said she died with her blue eyes open. Tinnin wondered if they thought to look into her eyes on the chance the image of the killer was still there, fixed in the dark sphere of the distended pupil.

Baby blue eyes. Peppermint short shorts. Tinnin could only imagine … a pretty girl who probably never heard, much less understood, such words as *no* or *can't* or *don't*.

Thoughts of her raised the question of how long it had been for him, never mind all the nos endured or the nots spoken or the don'ts as arms pushed him away. The answer was—painful as it was to admit—it had been a while. Only now and again, and "agains" were fewer since high school six years ago, the last time he had a steady girl. He lost her when her graduation gown couldn't hide the belly bump, and she left the ceremony with the father of her baby. Talk now was about Tinnin being twenty-four years old and unmarried, without even a piece to knock on every now and then. This unsolicited chastity was not a virtue in Tinnin's eyes. He wanted to sin—but discreetly. He saw himself as a casualty of circumstance. Because of the swing shifts he worked, he had little time or occasion to meet and greet.

No sense denying it—the perennial matter of obesity and his ambivalence to do something about it was also in play. He accepted it, albeit reluctantly, even though he knew it lessened his chances for passion.

A third prong to this celibacy: Carson had heard his father, and even muleheaded men like Will, invoke the word "trick." Usually they spoke of broken machinery or weather forecasts or nitrated hay. But the word and its altering meanings cast a shadow over him. Long ago, he came to understand that love was a trick, a fiddly one at that.

A pretty face, prettier than pretty, would appear. Before too long the words spoken between him and the pretty face begot caresses, irresistible caresses that had him begging, *More … more … evermore.* Then the exchange of whetted whispers lulled him, and torched touches lured him onto its treacherous ground where the inevitable happened—the pretty face fell away to be replaced by the dung heap of humiliation.

However chagrined, Tinnin held out hope like a carrot on a stick. It gave him a forward vision that included a white clapboard home with a wife and children inside. Until that happened, plain old sloth allowed him to ignore the japes about being overweight or the dry spell with women, unless they were clearly meant to be within earshot. Then he was forced to stand and challenge.

After the first few violent encounters, the jokesters left him in peace. And peace and quiet summed up his life's ambitions. But these killings demolished his well-established routine. He remembered—and it seemed strange that he should at a time like this—when he was ten and his mother dismantled his bed, coated the boards with vinegar, and burned the mattress out back behind the work shed. She had to use a chunk of an old tire to keep the mattress and bedbugs burning, and she had to buy on time a new mattress, one on which he could sleep in peace.

Here lately, no peace was found. No sooner had he finished third shift and settled into bed than the lieutenant called and ordered him to this field—not only him but also the entire shift. Tinnin knew that if any evidence was in the cracked clay, it would be the only thing not to up and run, and it would probably be the one thing to elude them. As Shufflin' Sam often said, a man is apt to find all sorts of things he isn't looking for. But then Sam was talking about hunting around the house, not in a cornfield whose rows held the silence and shame of a story only half-told.

The other night, Sam had told Tinnin and Shine about killing, not about Billy Blake's but killing in general. He said the life you took somehow became the life you led. He explained how the old you died with the killing and how the world you knew was never the same. The world was different because you saw it from different eyes. The world came closer and watched you just as carefully as you watched it.

Tinnin considered the man who killed this girl, wondering how he could ever live out his life, let alone hers. Two lives, a new life, seemed too much to bear. But if the man murdered again and again, he might lose himself in the many lives he took until there was no longer any semblance of the original man; until he was neither one man nor many but everybody and everybody's burden; until he was killed, as he surely would be, and then a new man in a new world arose. The progression, the burden, seemed endless.

Tinnin reached the end of the row. He looked up for buzzards. Seeing none, he checked on either side. No deputies were in sight. Rustling leaves told him the others had proceeded on down a new row. He absently snapped off the horn of a trumpet vine. He curled the red cone in the fat of his hand. In an instant, a bee buzzed against his palm. The sting followed.

# CHAPTER FIVE

A breeze approached like a stranger. It hit the very foundation of the now-rising heat with a low, sloughing blow, then died suddenly. The dry spell, establishing itself ten days ago and claiming more and more ground ever since, produced an identical cycle of blazing white haze in which nothing but buzzards stirred and stagnant night in which the dark stood as thick as water. Though there was no relief to be gained, Will and Agnes took to the ends of the tattered couch on the front porch. Bugs butted against the screen door in their senseless desperation to reach the kitchen light. No lights were on the porch to attract them, only Will's Camel cigarette that crackled as he took a pull.

The static and stillness worked against Agnes. She was helpless not to stare at the twin ponds. Their flat, oily surfaces captured the first-quarter moon, rendering a picture of reptilian eyes such as those glinting things in her commode. Those eyes, so charged with evil, refused to quit; their steady, slimy beads drew down on her so that her skin crept and bubbled. At the sound of Will gulping a beer, she turned and slowly released the breath she had been holding. The beer drinking was a reprieve, in more than one sense.

Will's switch to beer signaled an end to his heavy drinking. For three days, he had laid up drunk while Agnes bided her time, letting even her understanding steer clear of his destructive path. Will sought to destroy himself. The guilt consuming him was not hers. It was his alone. There was nothing she could do to share its crushing weight. So she continued as she knew Will eventually would. From the chicken feed at dawn to the dog scraps at night, she hadn't a moment's rest. It was better that way. Idleness would have set her to thinking. Under such a maddening sky, liquor made it harder on Will, fevered him so that he took a shotgun to the buzzards. They soared too high, escaping range without so much as a flutter. Will flung the rifle and stormed back to the porch. "Won't even come down. Like we ain't fit for 'em."

Three days was a long time to be idle. The seventeen cows Will bought in the spring needed to be moved to a new pasture; the chicken house needed a new layer of litter; the waterer and feeder need to be cleaned; the light bulbs needed to be inspected; the irrigation pipes needed to be fitted between the north pond and the thirty acres of corn; and those were just the more urgent matters. But Will had just walked off, leaving the tractor's unrepaired fuel line on the ground. If not for Coonie, the tractor wouldn't have been ready for tomorrow.

Coonie had called about dinnertime two days ago and stayed the afternoon, fixing not only the tractor but also the commode. The only thing Agnes ever asked him was to sit and eat Will's dinner, and not because she was lonely and in need of conversation. At her table there was always more than anyone could ever eat. Coonie ate as quickly as a bachelor and then went to work seeking no more approval than when he helped himself to more butter beans. While Coonie worked, Will drank. His binge was a godsend for Agnes because it gave her something in the here and now to worry about.

"Now quit," said Agnes quietly, looking down on the ponds.

Will clipped a jet of smoke short. "What?"

"Oh, nothing. Just thinking."

"About what?"

Agnes didn't have an answer. About the time Will walked off to sit and drink, she discovered that behind any comment, no matter how simple or matter of fact, resided a question mark. Like the time she said, "I believe it's near four …?" That dreadfully silent mark popped up out of nowhere to taunt and bedevil her so that the only thing she was really sure about was that she could be wrong. Chances were that she was wrong. She was wrong to think she was right about David Trollinger, and she was wrong to think Will was right about the sheriff. It was wrong to be right. A person wasn't entitled to be right anymore.

After a time she asked, "You reckon the people what stopped for the funeral cars, pulling up 'longside the road out of respect and them not even knowing Billy or us … or even them what brought all the food by way of respect to us … you reckon they could kill another?"

Will flicked the butt. "S'pect so. It's got to where it don't take much." Will tapped the .38 revolver on the ragged seat between them.

"You believe Jesus—there is a Jesus?"

Will folded his hands over the rivulet of hair on his belly and stretched. "Hard tellin'."

"I don't believe," Agnes said flatly.

"In Jesus?"

"In none of it." After a moment she added, "Leastways not like I done."

"Just as well. Jesus only get in the way 'round here."

Will fell silent as the V-line between his eyes deepened to crags. He had no quarrel with Jesus and fully intended to argue his case on judgment day. For now, though, he carried a flesh-for-blood grudge against—against whom? The local draft board? Andy's lieutenant? The Pentagon? President Johnson? Nixon? David Trollinger? Sheriff Harris? His deputies? His detectives? To avenge the death of one's son required a target. Will had so many he couldn't decide where to aim.

Agnes said, "See where the sheriff's got hisself another murder."

"That doctor's daughter," said Will.

"Paper said she was raped and throwed up 'longside Leland Jackson's land." After a while she said, "Got no clues, paper says."

"S'pect they'll leave off Trollinger seeing as how Billy ain't no doctor's boy." Will flicked a stick match with his thumbnail and lighted a cigarette. He smoked it halfway down.

Agnes said, "Maybe we ought to get a Rockford?"

"The guy on TV?"

"Somebody like 'im … maybe? That Rockford's all the time solvin' murders."

"This ain't no TV. Ain't no solvin' going on 'round here."

"Got nothing to lose, do we?"

"That's the truth."

Agnes glanced back at the ponds, and the oily eyes stared back at her. Without Will ever noticing, she took the revolver, aimed it at the snake eye on the pond, and fired. The dimple and then the ripple in the white surface told her she hit it square.

"You aimin' at that?"

"Yep."

"Damn. That's fifty yards or better. You're not s'posta do that with a .38." He drew on a cigarette. "Good shootin'."

"It still ain't dead yet," she said, referring to the snake eye.

# CHAPTER SIX

When the phone rang, private detective Boggs was in his Greensburg office on Tabb Street, which overlooked the new courthouse complex. He had the answering machine on to allow him some quiet time to put together the parts of the night before.

He awoke to find his wife asleep beside him. No sooner had he raised his head off the pillow than he dropped back as if kicked by a heavy boot. Where he was last night and what he did were rumors obscured by the hammer of a hangover. In any event, whatever had happened was now meaningless. Over the years Boggs had come to accept that his history repeated itself: call the wife to say he was working late, drinks with a women who wasn't so strange after two or three Jack 'n' gingers, and slip out the back door in the early a.m. to drive home.

Hardly an advocate of Socrates' examined life but on occasion given to wondering why this or why that, Boggs sometimes asked himself what women saw in him; he really had no idea. That he was big might give the impression that he was big elsewhere, but he wasn't. He assumed he was normal. That he was less than handsome suggested women would shy away from him, but they didn't. At any given time he had one (sometimes two) on a leash, and every so often he'd throw in a stranger for spice. Unlike his wife, these women clamored for his time, his attention, their time in bed. Why, he couldn't say. He never set the bar very high in terms of looks, which expanded the field. And he never tweaked or tinkered with any of the particulars of his demeanor. He was what he was.

Boggs rested his forehead in the cool of his palms. He scarcely listened to the caller announce how he wanted a first-rate detective, one as sharp as that "feller Rockford on the television." Boggs split his fingers covering his eyes and peered at the answering machine. The caller said he wanted him to investigate his son's murder and left a number. There was a click. No goodbyes or thanks. Just a disconnect. After ingesting four aspirins, Boggs returned the call.

Will pressed for assurances that Boggs was as capable as Rockford. He drilled all the way down to what kind of car he drove.

"A '78 Malibu Landau Coupe." He added, sensing the caller wasn't impressed, "A V-8."

"What, don't like the Firebird?"

"I'm a big man, Mr. Blake. Be like sitting in my bathtub."

There was a moment of silence before Blake asked, "You ain't black, are ya?"

The question confirmed what Boggs already knew: that Blake was from the country because townsfolk would never have the nerve to ask such a question, even though everyone, the Realtors in particular, would sell their souls to be able to ask it.

"Last time I was black was when I slopped tar on roofs for a summer."

That apparently satisfied Will, who went into the details of Billy's murder.

Normally Boggs would have balked at a murder investigation since it took too much time and brought in too little cash. But Will's remarks amused him, so he agreed at least to discuss the matter that afternoon.

When Boggs first set eyes on Will, he developed serious reservations. The Blake murder was gruesome enough to capture the front page of *The Herald Chronicle* for three days. As reliable as the newspaper was, he usually gained better insight around the courthouse. The unofficial word circulating through the corridors of crime and justice was one of bafflement—no clues, no motive, just slaughter. If that wasn't enough to dissuade him, one look at Will told him he faced a closed door, one bolted from the inside.

Blake's wife was haunted by a different narrative, a tender story that spoke of considerable injury. She was such a tiny woman. Boggs was helpless before her, before that expression that rose from inside where something unchecked and intractable tormented her. The moment he met her blue eyes, he agreed to take the case out of some fool notion of endearment. He was even reluctant to take the two-hundred-dollar retainer, which she counted out on the kitchen table. So deliberate was she that he thought the twenties weighed twenty pounds. Will grabbed the cash and thrust the ball toward him, saying, "C'mon. I'll show you."

When Will stood, Boggs was surprised by his height. The farmer was only an inch or two shorter than Boggs's six-foot, three-inch frame. The contrast between the two occurred in their weight: Will was a wiry 170, and Boggs a stout 236. Their faces were different too: Will lean and sunburned, and Boggs thick and washed-out. Their attire clashed as well: Will shirtless in overalls and brogans, and the detective in khaki trousers and a dress shirt.

They walked down the drive between the ponds, crossed the paved road, and tramped into the woods. The click of the cicadas was so forceful that it seemed a malefic presence prevailing over the land. Will was far more agile than Boggs in negotiating thickets of pine limbs, spider webs, and prickly vines. He stayed a step ahead, mentioning buzzard so often that Boggs assumed he was talking about the killer.

At a glance the case seemed simple enough, requiring Boggs to find that one person. Nine times out of ten, a murderer confessed to someone, and with a teenage girl involved, finding the confidante seemed that much easier. Boggs staked his less-than-prestigious seventeen years as a cop and PI that maybe not Trollinger but certainly this Mary Jane Henson had talked to someone, maybe not about the murder but certainly her whereabouts and maybe his on the night of the killing. Somewhere in Dinwoodie County or in the city of Greensburg was a person just as frightened as Henson. All Boggs had to do was pass around some cash, maybe a drink or two, maybe a little reefer, and that person would have a name, then a place, and then an appointed time.

No, finding that someone wasn't what made this case difficult. What made it difficult was Will. Boggs had no use for guns, not since a lunatic stripped him of his and fired one shot into his ankle and four shots into his partner's gut. Guns were for events as big as war, and from the looks of it, Will had already made his declaration.

Near the intense light of a clearing, Will slammed his arm against Boggs's chest. "Wait here, Rockford."

As Will moved off, Boggs objected. "What're you—"

"And hush."

With a .30-06 rifle held almost as if a balancing pole, Will crept toward the light, carefully determining where and when to set down or pick up his boots. To Boggs it seemed to take an interminable time before the man reached the border of the field. In the shadows of the tree line, Will settled slowly on his right knee, eased the rifle into position, and scanned the brownish field and then the white sky. His whipsaw smile vanished. "Durn buzzards," he said to himself and waved for Boggs to come.

As they crossed the field, Boggs was startled to see a dog staked to the ground spread-eagle on its back; the legs had been rent from their joints, so they lay flat. Its maggot-infested innards oozed from a belly slit in its yellow hide. Will walked past it as if it weren't there baking a stench.

"Yours?" asked Boggs, unable to stop staring.

"Was."

"What ya kill it for?"

"Buzzards."

"Got something against them?"

"Actin' like we're none too good." Without warning, Will swung the rifle, causing Boggs to flinch and duck. Boggs next saw the barrel when it rested on Will's shoulder.

"Careful now."

Will's whipsaw smile emerged. He had never seen anyone quite like Boggs. Everything about the man said big. Despite the great bulk, he looked sturdy. His hands were large enough to palm a pumpkin. His face was wider than the blade of a shovel. Certain features were downright memorable, such as the hunk of a nose that had enough dents to appear chewed or the earlobes crinkled like lettuce leaves. What really amused Will was the sweat staining not only the Sunday shirt but also the pants along the waist and in the seat.

Squinting, Will said, "Safe's on."

"Don't like guns." Boggs took out a folded white handkerchief and dried his pocked neck and pitted face.

They walked through a line of trees that served as a windbreak and into another field. "That there's it," said Will, pointing to the lower end of the field by the road.

As they approached Boggs said, "Ain't much, is it?"

"Wanted you to see it."

The only thing Boggs could see with any clarity was the dead dog. He had heard stories of cruelty and abuse, but none ever described killing your pet just to lure buzzards. Had he not set eyes on Agnes and her quiet sorrow, he would have tossed the money down and left. But he had seen her, and he could see her now. Looking at nothing in particular, he said, "Reckon the fire marshal went over it good." He turned to let his squinting eyes follow the rutted road through the field and a break of pines. "That the only way in?"

"By car."

"Any houses nearby?"

"Ours."

"Down the road?"

Will pointed east over a hill with the barrel. "Yonder's Shine Walker."

"Nothing in between?"

"The sky." Sensing a lack of interest in the ruins, he said, "Ain't ya gonna look around?"

"What might could've been here ain't here now." Boggs added, "What the fire didn't get, the law contaminated." He pointed to the charred recliner ten yards away from the wreckage. "This place has been sifted through, trampled on, and tossed about so what evidence might have been here is gone, long gone."

"What you trying to say?"

"Look, Mr. Blake, I'm going to have to look at the fire marshal's report and the sheriff's."

"Shit ..."

Will moved off toward the dirt drive. Boggs fell in behind him. Every so often Will stopped short to survey the relentless sky, causing an unsuspecting Boggs to bump into him. They followed the S of the lane to the hard-surface road. Boggs stopped abruptly, exhaling as if exhausted and moping his face with the handkerchief. After a moment he said, "Ya know, you could use table scraps or bad meat. It would work just as good as anything else."

Squinting fiercely, the farmer said, "The dog was running 'em off."

"Why not tie it up 'stead of killing it?"

"You want to see anything else, Mr. Boggs?"

Boggs dried the back of his neck. "Yeah, there any place where a man could park and the car not be seen?"

"None 'cept for the old wagon road thisaway."

In the midafternoon sun, the burning road almost adhered to their shoes. The heat was a haze of drunken air through which they seemed to wade, not walk. After a quarter of a mile, they turned onto a wide path that was soft on the feet, and the trees pushed back the spreading sun. In the mottled shade, gnats buzzed their ears and lunged for their eyes.

Boggs didn't need to inspect the foot-tall grass for tire impressions. He was standing in one; the bent-back grass was a clear indication a vehicle had been down this path.

Boggs asked, "Who uses this?"

"Don't know anyone did."

"Well, someone drove down here." He added, "And not too long ago."

Both men knelt for a closer look. The dry ground dashed Boggs's hope of lifting a print of the tire tread.

"Judging from the width, I'd say it was a Jeep or a pickup."

"I'd say so too." Will added, "Might could be those knobby things the kids like."

Boggs asked, "You show this to the deputies?"

"Didn't know to."

"Bet they didn't find it." He stood. "Let's look around and see what we see?"

Each took a track and inspected the ground, hunched over and parsing the groundcover with sticks.

"Hey, what's—well, lookee here." He picked up a quarter, holding it high for Will to admire.

"What's it tell us?"

"Someone's missin' a quarter."

They resumed the search. Within a minute Will discovered a square of foil, the kind used in a cigarette hard pack. He smelled it. "Menthol. Don't women mostly smoke menthols?"

"Shit, I used to smoke 'em."

The tire impressions stopped after fifteen yards. They found nothing else.

"Damn," said Boggs. "I was sure we'd find a cigarette butt."

"Doubt there would be if they had gas cans."

"You—Don't ever underestimate the stupidity of a criminal."

"Ain't so stupid what the sheriff can find him."

Boggs looked down the path. "How far back it go?"

"A ways."

They trekked a half mile finding nothing out of the ordinary, only the simple order of nature reclaiming lost ground.

On the way back Boggs, speaking more for Agnes's sake, said he planned to set up surveillance on Trollinger's trailer. "Say it's … what … about a mile down the road?"

"Better than a mile cuz it's about a mile past The Store." He added, "But it ain't much more than a mile. It's set off same way Billy's is and don't look much better than Billy's does now. He rents it … from Milt Allison."

Boggs nodded. "Well, we know someone was down here, someone who had to know this part of the county, because that road ain't easy to see. And we know this person is a smoker, and—"

"Everybody round here smokes."

"I just got to get that girl to talk. Where's she from?"

"Mary Jane Henson?" Without waiting for an answer, he said, "Ain't from 'round here." He added after a moment, "Far as I know."

Boggs told him that in a week he should have something positive to report.

At the house Will invited him in for tea. They stepped up on the front porch but found the screen door locked. Will hollered and kicked the baseboard. Agnes plodded down the hall and unfastened the latch.

"Trouble 'round here?" asked Boggs.

"Naw, she just took to locking everything up."

# CHAPTER SEVEN

"That's it?" said Will in a baleful tone.

"For now," replied Boggs.

"And here we ain't seen ya in … what? Better than a week. Don't know if you run off with our money or—"

"I've been—"

"Been doing nothing," cried Will. "You's crooked as the rest of 'em. Shoulda never paid you till you come back with some proof. But then you didn't have to do nothing, did ya? What with your pay already in your pocket."

"Now listen here, Blake. I pulled more hours than I'd like to think."

Will cut his eyes toward Agnes. "And you was all for gettin' a Rockford."

Boggs said, "It ain't like what they make it out to be on TV."

TV was an infectious lie that Agnes had depended on for years, without ever understanding her dependence, without ever realizing how open and vulnerable she was. But now she understood that for her unquestioning belief in the box, that instrument of magic in which she saw life as she really wanted it to be, she deserved more scorn than she could summon. To see herself smile at the happy ending after an hour of dark trouble seared her with disgust, and she felt nothing so much as just for feeling that way. Now she knew what justice meant. It wasn't meant to redress; it was meant to scorn.

Agnes looked to Will, who hung his head between his hands, his greasy hair gray as an old coin. She looked out the kitchen window, and in the halo of their outside light, she saw the buzzard strung from the water oak. She saw through her memory the bird's small, disproportioned head, red as wrath; its face, wrinkled and old as age itself; its look, fierce and penetrating as much now as when it was alive. From the moment Will strung it, with its shadow companions circling overhead, she had a premonition.

"Just don't seem likely that it's anything but drugs," said Boggs, breaking the silence that was breaking the room. Though Will didn't appear to be listening, he went on, "Everything is shut down. No one's talking."

Will locked his narrowing eyes on Boggs. "Thought you said this was gonna be easy?"

Still drawn to the bird outside the window, Agnes asked, "Just what is it you do figure, Mr. Boggs?"

"'Member the other day I was thinking it had to be someone who knew this part of the county? Well, now, I think that whoever done this had scoped out the place. And that makes it premeditated."

"The fire done told us that," said Will.

"Yeah, but … do you think Trollinger is smart enough to plan this thing out? Plan a fire so there's no sign of an accelerant? Don't know the boy like you do, but I think it's highly unlikely. No, the more I think about it, the more I'm convinced this is drug related, a deal gone bad. Billy double-crossed his dealer and literally got burned. What Billy do for a living? Who'd he hang with other than Trollinger?"

From her post at the kitchen sink, Agnes looked at him blankly. Will said, "Worked at Henry's Tire in town. Least that's what he used to do. Don't know when he stopped working there. But he never asked us for money," he lied. "Paid the rent on the trailer like clockwork."

"How long did he live in the trailer?"

Will looked to Agnes. "What? Better than two years?"

She said, "Give or take."

"And did you know that about a year and a half ago your boy got busted for possession?"

"Of what?" asked Agnes.

"Marijuana. It was simple possession, and they eventually dropped the charge. No reason given."

"Who arrested—"

Agnes interrupted Will. "We knew Billy done drugs, but it never seemed as harmful as what the liquor done to him."

"D.L. Wynne," said Boggs in answer to Will's question. "He's the man that runs vice." He paused and glanced over at Agnes. "Where Billy get his liquor?"

Will replied, "Shine, the ABC store, wherever."

Boggs made a mental note to talk to Shine. He wanted to ask why these people were so unfamiliar with their son's life. He refrained.

A silence chafed against all of them.

Her back now to the window, Agnes said, "Mr. Boggs, it might seem like we don't know much about our boy. But when he moved out, he coulda been a hundred miles away, not no five-minute walk, and we'd still not see 'im. Billy, he was a growed man of twenty-four. He needed to be out on his own. And we wanted him to be shut of us. He wasn't a boy no more."

Agnes fixed a doleful look on Will. "Now we know we didn't know much about what Billy was up to. And I'm wonderin' if his brother, Andy, wasn't the better parent. He looked after that boy like no mother ever could. They was eight years apart, and Andy mother-henned Billy like … no harm was ever coming to that boy. No, sir. No harm. Not ever."

Boggs studied her, waiting for her eyes to tear. They didn't. The silence returned.

After a minute Boggs fumbled through his briefcase and retrieved a folder, which he tossed on the table. "Here's some of the pictures I made while surveilling Trollinger's." He paused. "It's like I said. This is all about drugs. Too many cars coming and going at Trollinger's."

"On account of him having callers?" asked Will, incredulous.

"He's the street dealer. With Billy out of the picture, it reverts to Trollinger."

Agnes asked, "We get any more for our two hundred plus expenses, Mr. Boggs?"

"Ma'am, it ain't Trollinger. The arson report said it was a professional. And David Trollinger might be a lot of things, but he ain't no professional arsonist."

"But a right good shot," put in Will. "Know it for a fact."

"Well, I don't know about that. But look—"

"Well, damned if I don't." His voice raised, he added, "Know it for a fact."

Boggs kept quiet. With his index finger he slipped photographs out of the folder, twirled them, and let them come to rest in front of Will.

Instead of examining the photos, Will read the expressions his wife and the detective wore. Fact or no, he was mistaken. His error resided exclusively in him, in his feelings; there was no place for his feelings, his thoughts, his beliefs. No place anywhere.

"Boggs, we waited near thirteen years now for them to say our oldest is dead, and now if I'm hearin' you correctly, you're sayin' wait another thirteen 'fore someone up and confesses. Waiting two weeks like we done gets to a man. Waiting years, now that's—"

"Won't be that long," said Boggs.

"I know," said Will, coming to his feet. "Got me one buzzard. Reckon I'll get me another." He headed for the door.

Boggs looked to Agnes for answers. In the background, the door slammed, and pebbles crunched.

"Stop him," shouted Agnes, as if awakening.

The pickup door clanked closed; its inline-six whined and then erupted.

"Call the sheriff," said Boggs, stomping out the door.

He sprinted to his car and cussed thunderously when he couldn't immediately find his keys. His Malibu caught on the third try. He jammed the column stick into reverse, its tires spitting dirt and gravel while he swung wildly. He yanked the stick down into drive and punched the pedal. He fishtailed down the drive. His chassis slammed into the edge where the dirt road met the paved road. He whipped the wheel to the right and struck out for the red taillights ahead of him.

Both vehicles ignored the blinking yellow light at the crossroads.

Boggs was four car-lengths back when Will swung onto Trollinger's driveway. Boggs shot onto the rutted road. He punched the horn. He flicked the lights through the short tunnel of trees. In the clearing, his high beams flooded Will, who loosed buckshot at the lock and kicked in the door.

The Malibu rocked when it came to a complete stop. Boggs never bothered to shut his door as he raced up the molded concrete stairs.

The inside of the trailer was black.

"Blake?"

There was no response, not a sound. Inside the doorway he frisked himself for a match and found a cigarette lighter belonging to last night's tryst. He struck it and held it high. The room was empty of furnishings, any signs of habitation. "Blake?" He moved cautiously through the kitchen on his left and then down the short hallway to the bedroom. A draft knocked down the flame. "Blake?" He flicked the lighter and stepped up to the doorway.

Will stood in the middle of the deserted room, still as a preying cat. "Blake, he ain't here."

Will wheeled, the shotgun level with Boggs's gut. "Like he ain't never been here. Thought you was watchin' 'im?"

"Put it down, Blake."

"Like he ain't never been here," Will said in a slow monotone.

"He was last night." Boggs edged toward the twelve-gauge shotgun.

"Like he ain't never been here."

Boggs slid the light away, hoping Will would follow it. His free hand inched toward the firearm.

"Like he ain't—"

Boggs jumped into the intervening space, pushing the barrel. As it swung wide and high, Boggs kicked Will in the groin. The gun blast heaved Boggs against the wall. With a groan, he slid to the floor and muffled his ears against the delirious roar. He saw a whirling blue light through the window. For some reason, it reminded him to get the gun. He crawled. A flashlight reached it before he did. First, Boggs saw shiny shoes, then dark-brown pants with twin black stripes, then a nickel-plated revolver, then a smile, then Carson Tinnin.

"Y'alright?" asked the deputy.

Boggs saw the fat-faced deputy's mouth move but heard only the ringing. He shook his head hard.

Will sat on the floor nearby, his head fallen against his raised knees.

Tinnin holstered his piece and kicked away the shotgun. He knelt between the two. "Ain't either of you hurt, is ya?"

Boggs stared blankly and after a moment asked, "Where is he?"

"Trollinger?"

Will lifted his head, his slobbered mouth unhinged.

Boggs shouted, "Where is he?"

Tinnin leaned toward Boggs and mouthed, "The county jail."

"Fer Blake?" he yelled back.

"Mary Wanna."

"What?"

Tinnin pretended to smoke a joint, although it looked as if he were blowing a tiny whistle.

Smiling, Boggs said, "Marijuana?"

A second and then a third chin emerged when Tinnin nodded back.

"He talkin'?"

Tinnin shook his head no.

Will's shoulders collapsed like a marionette cut at the strings.

# CHAPTER EIGHT

H is back against the bolted door, David Trollinger seemed to be loitering, posed as the timeless tough on the street corner with eyes the width of wire. He appeared to be hanging motionless from hidden strings. His spindly shoulders sagged; his angular jaw, dotted by the outcroppings of a dozen moles, was taut. His long hair, matted by the bunk, drooped. He was silent. Only the occasional pull on the cigarette butt slung between his lips betrayed any sign he was even breathing.

"This here's your boy," said the jailer to Deputy Tinnin. All of a sudden, the jailer slammed a forearm across Trollinger's chest and jerked the cigarette out of his mouth. He tossed it on top of his ward's brogan and stomped it out, twisting and grinding the inmate's foot. The butt in shreds, the jailer clutched Trollinger's throat and hoisted him high up against the gray steel door, which was the entrance to the cells. "Boy, you ain't right. Judge Hardy will set you straight." Still maintaining his choke hold, he let Trollinger slide back to the floor. He snapped his hands away as if he had just touched something revolting. He turned to Tinnin, took court papers from his wide belt, and handed Tinnin a bond order and an affidavit of indigency.

"Why hasn't he been taken 'fore now?" asked Tinnin. It was three days since Trollinger's arrest. Normally, a first appearance in district court was scheduled the morning after a felony arrest.

"Reckon he's special," said the jailer, leaving the anteroom and returning to his desk and a copy of *National Enquirer*.

Tinnin led the prisoner away by the arm, feeling a tension with as much pull as a hunting bow. The spring door continued to bang after they came out onto the stoop. Trollinger jerked his arm free and stepped recklessly off the steps. Such bravado tickled Tinnin because he expected it from someone reputedly mean as a snake. Tinnin remembered the high school halls where Trollinger and Billy and their gang strutted, their thick heels tapping a signal to get out of the way. Everyone did.

"Now, just as a precaution, Mister David, case you take a notion to outrun me in them irons, let me remind you how much I resent having to exert myself. Long as we been knowin' each other, you know I scarcely give it 80 percent, much less 110." For some inexplicable reason, the constant regret he carried about for Billy Blake eased; thanks to this unexpected reprieve, he breathed easier.

They came out from under the shade of twin maples and into the glare of the afternoon sun.

Tinnin continued, "Runnin' a car in this heat is too much like work. Even sittin' seems a whole lot like a load."

The deputy pushed Trollinger's shoulder to indicate he should step off the curb. Trollinger reared back, forgetting he was cuffed.

"Now, now, David, let's not forget where you are."

The man's silence amused Tinnin. Trollinger had made a show of clicking the taps on his heels as he and his gang cruised the high school halls. Now he clanked his chains.

Cars stopped for the prisoner. Once safely across the street and on the sidewalk, Tinnin asked, "So how much was you and Blake sellin'?"

Without moving his lips, Trollinger said, "Enough."

"Heard you had near one pound."

Trollinger loosed a glower. "Try fourteen. And twenty pokes of MDA."

"That much, huh?" He laughed to himself. He would never understand why criminals thought that the bigger their crime, the bigger they were. "I s'pect that's a right big chunk of money there."

"More than you'll make in a year." Through a thin smile he added, "Innerested?"

"Nope, sure not. This drug business looks a lot like work."

"Make thirty grand, man."

"Naw, a monthly paycheck suits me just fine." He paused to reflect. "Be nice, though. Take me near three years to see that kind of dough."

Tinnin opened the glass doors. They passed through fetid air hazy with cigarette smoke. In lieu of the elevator, the deputy chose two flights of stairs.

Tinnin asked, "This your first time?" Trollinger was too involved with each shackled step to answer.

District court, the lower of the two county courts, was held in a long room divided in the middle by a polished rail. On one side were twenty rows of hard seats where the unwashed and undisciplined, the accused and accuser alike, took their places. On the other side of the rail, where the business of justice was transacted, were plush seats, shining linoleum, varnished tables, and the awesome mount of the judicial bench. From the relative luxury of these confines, prosecutors and lawyers called up defendants and clients, respectively, without ever looking upon the bedraggled assembly that watched the unhurried march of the law in utter confusion.

Before entering the nearly empty courtroom, Tinnin undid the shackles but not the cuffs. He was down on a knee when he heard, "I'll take it from here, deputy." He looked up to see Captain D.L. Wynne, chief of the vice squad.

Wynne had a narrow build for a six-foot-tall man. His hair recalled the '50s when men combed their hair back in a thick wave. Now, his was thinning and tinted reddish to ward off the gray. His long face and short forehead made his mouth seem wider and his nose seem longer. His graying eyebrows pointed up toward a deeply furrowed brow. He smiled often, his teeth too-perfectly white. No one could ever remember him laughing though. He wore a light, short-sleeve cotton shirt, sharply creased trousers, and polished loafers. His gold badge was clipped to his belt. He had no weapon.

"Sir?" said Tinnin, rising.

"I'll take it from here."

"Suits me," said the deputy, handing over the shackles, the key, and the paperwork. He watched as Wynne led the man to the far side of a sequestered pit behind the defense table. He shrugged, telling himself he didn't have a dog in this fight. Still, he had to wonder what a captain of vice was doing here for a case that seemed of little importance. Or was it? Tinnin couldn't be sure. Shadows followed all men, usually just one. In this instance, and perhaps many others, Wynne was the exception. Wynne was responsible for so many grave and egregious incidents that Tinnin wondered if the Trollinger drug arrest and the Blake killing weren't new shadows gathering about the captain.

So many contentious events had occurred during Wynne's controversial reign as vice captain—like the three serious accidents in which Wynne, had he been a civilian, would have been charged with driving under the influence, or the time he nearly sparked a riot in the Halifax ghetto by shooting a dog dead for no apparent reason.

For a time, he was a cause célèbre, making headlines in all the state newspapers for the Frye case in which he gave a service revolver to an informant who then shot and killed two suspected drug dealers. The district attorney's office considered itself lucky to get a manslaughter conviction against Frye.

Whether he was famous or infamous, Tinnin didn't know. Either way he seemed to be too important a figure to be involved or concerned with the Trollinger case. Then again, why worry about something that was now out of his hands? Tinnin shrugged and left the building, glad to be getting off work early.

Judge John L. Hardy lacked that look of general disinterest most jurists acquired. For one who spent so much time indoors, he had a surprisingly hale and alert mien. Fifty-four years had hardly cut a line into his fine face. His thick, curly hair, dark as his robe, added to the overall youthful impression. So too did his broad frame that looked capable of strenuous work. And work was something for which the judge was renowned. He had put himself through college and law school, working nights at a textile mill and commuting during the day. Upon his admission to the bar, he worked his way up from assistant solicitor to district attorney in a remarkable five years. In less than half that time, he was appointed to fill a vacancy on the bench, and there he remained, rising to chief judge. In his twenty years overseeing the court, he gained a reputation for being the toughest yet fairest and for having the uncanny ability to make a defendant or witness whom he knew to be lying recant. While the law insisted he punish those who told the truth of their crimes, he all but rewrote the law when evidence proved a defendant to be a liar.

Before the judge called the Trollinger case, he waited until the last of the spectators in an assault case left the room. Finally he said, "Call your next case."

Wynne escorted Trollinger to the defense table and shadowed his left side.

The assistant district attorney, the ADA, was a well-dressed man who kept pushing his glasses onto the bridge of his nose whether they needed it or not. "Your honor, in cases CDC 1891 and 1892, David George Trollinger is believed on or about July 18 to have willingly, knowingly, and feloniously had in his possession approximately two pounds of marijuana and five tablets of a Schedule 1 drug, an amphetamine-based hallucinogen commonly known as MDA. Mr. Trollinger, how do you plead?"

Bewildered, the defendant looked from the judge to the ADA. "Y'mean did I do it?"

Hardy said peevishly, "Are you innocent of these charges or not?"

"I ain't done nothin'."

Wynne jabbed Trollinger in the ribs, telling him to say "Sir."

"Now, your honor, with respect to bond," said the ADA, "this is a vice arrest. Mr. Trollinger was attempting to flee the county when he was apprehended on Highway 1. He had a trailer with all his belongings hitched to his vehicle."

"All right," said Hardy, without a moment's deliberation. "Let it be noted that the court orders the defendant's bond to remain at $55,000 secured. Now, Mr. Trollinger, do you have a lawyer, or are you asking the court to appoint you one?"

"Can't afford no lawyer." He added, "Sir."

The ADA passed to the bench the affidavit of indigency and said that the defendant's possessions and 1972 Plymouth had been impounded.

"Who's next on the list?" Hardy asked the clerk at his right side.

"Wesley Craven, sir."

"So be it." He looked at the defendant. "Mr. Trollinger, your attorney, Wes Craven, will be meeting with you shortly. Any questions?"

"Sir, I didn't have no two pounds—"

With a sleight of elbow, Wynne rammed Trollinger's ribs. Trollinger keeled over, using the table for support.

"Mr. Trollinger, please do not address the court until you have had the benefit of counsel. Court adjourned." He thumped the gavel.

# CHAPTER NINE

The lone requisite for becoming a Dinwoodie County deputy was what attracted Tinnin to the job. Contrary to his father's expectations, Tinnin wasn't asked to lose weight. At the time, he still rode his reputation as the clean-up slugger for the Dinwoodie High School Generals and appeared in passably good shape. Throughout his childhood, he rivaled a balloon for definition. But as a high school junior, he turned to sports, encouraged by a coach to try out for the football team. He replaced the starting right tackle by mid-season and followed what seemed a natural progression to baseball, where he became a star catcher. During this time his weight dropped from obese to stout to sturdy. Not long after graduation though, his chin, neck, and gut once again developed deep folds.

Yet sports rebuilt him in another way. It freed him from a perpetually sullen expression and allowed him to acquire a more natural image, one that made—nearly demanded—that others smile. His Bambi eyes and innocent veneer compelled others to pardon him for whatever he did or didn't do. Tinnin hadn't many cares. One thing in particular he truly didn't care for was work. So when told all he had to do to become a deputy was register as a Democrat, he saw only one problem—getting up before noon, the hour the registrar closed. The most arduous part of his training proved to be learning not to spill coffee and doughnut crumbs while the shift corporal put the 422 patrol car through NASCAR-type maneuvers.

Because Tinnin was a decent speller and printed neatly on his reports, Sheriff Harris assigned him a territory after six months: Random, his home hamlet in the southeast corner of the county. The major drawback to the assignment was that the Burger King was in town, and even though a twenty-minute run sometimes left his stomach burning in anticipation of a Whopper, he had no real complaints. Random was quiet. Tinnin was there to assure votes. What crime there was usually involved property. In looking for a thief, Tinnin never went far, usually to a neighbor or kin. Until the Blake murder, the only death Tinnin investigated was when Pumpkin Hawks, drunk as a coot, rolled his tractor over on himself. The one shooting that ever amounted to anything was when Betty Foust flicked off her husband's right hand. The couple insisted it was an accident. Tinnin classified it as a domestic.

The only trouble spot was a biker bar on Highway 1 near the community of Dewitt, a place called the French Quarter. It received the attention of a two-man car on the second and third shifts Friday through Sunday. Sometimes Tinnin was called to assist, but the Highway Patrol always reached the scene before he did. He made sure of it. A believer in the path of least resistance, Tinnin took the long way by heading west to go east.

The Blake murder did more than just ruffle Tinnin's set ways. For the first time, folks looked to him as a deputy, not as one of their own. Somehow, he had lost his membership in Random. By virtue of his position—but more important by virtue of the fact that there had been two killings, something he had been sworn to prevent—he was now an outsider.

To say people treated him differently was inaccurate. At no time was he the subject of bad behavior or an unkind word. There really was no discernible difference in the way anyone acted. But now folks awoke to a nuanced apprehension. They knew more than they ever wanted to know, not necessarily about Tinnin but about what people were truly capable of doing. And that is what Tinnin represented to them; he was the messenger who brought the underside of life to the fore. When he greeted people he had known all his life, they extended a hand to shake, but the true hand, the real hand, the one that held their true feelings, they kept behind their backs. They didn't even know they were doing it, he told himself, feeling all the more downcast.

These people expected him to do more than nothing, and he felt both pointless and powerless. All along he knew that upholding the law meant power, but he never considered himself powerful, unlike some deputies. The true test of power was how long the peace prevailed. A broken law meant the possibility of no law at all, the prospects of which frightened people and, most of all, Tinnin. All of a sudden, he became their answer, and he couldn't even begin to imagine their questions.

"Thirty-four, what's your twenty?" came over his radio.

"Preacher Holmes Road."

"Proceed to Rock." The Rock meant headquarters, a boulder of a building that Sheriff Harris heaved up at the corner of East Tabb and Madison. While constructed in the same granite motif as the new law enforcement quad, it stood apart and for that reason seemed to dominate the landscape. That it sat at the edge of a bluff produced a fortress effect.

Since it was suppertime, he thought he caught a break. "I have time to—"

"Right now," said the dispatcher, adding that a female subject asked to speak to him.

"So I got to go all the way up there for that?"

There was no reply.

Tinnin fingered the open pack of peanut butter crackers on his lap, popped one in his mouth, and chewed as if it were sour. Then he drove the cruiser to the Rock.

Mary Jane Henson met him in the parking lot beside the magistrate's office. She had the shape and the bones to be an attractive blonde. What she didn't have was the time or the inclination. Her outfit was identical to what Trollinger wore yesterday, only her jeans and T-shirt were clean. She had come to the sheriff's department to claim her furniture but learned the trailer and its contents had been impounded.

"Ain't nothing I can do," said Tinnin. "'Sides, it's a vice arrest, not mine."

"But David only had it cuz we was fixin' to meet up when he got to Florida."

Tinnin rolled his tongue along the inside of his right cheek. "A judge might could help ya."

"Won't deal with none of them." She added, "Can't."

He leaned back against the patrol car, crossed his ankles, and folded his arms. "Y'know there's something I just can't figure out. David didn't kill Billy, so why'd he run?"

"You would a too if they had a contract on you."

He delivered a wide smile. "Mary Jane, this here's Dinwoodie County. Only contracts we have is them for building and such."

"But David and Billy done ripped off the ..."

She cast her dark eyes down and after a moment flung them straight at the deputy. "The franchiser. Leastways Billy did."

"The franchiser? What in the tar's a franchiser? Like Burger King?"

Mary Jane seemed to weigh the silence. Her slight shoulders rose and fell with a deep breath. She began slowly as if trying to recall where to begin. She said the franchiser was the supplier. He designated who could sell what and where. As far as she knew, the franchiser took control of the county and the city after a supply shortage a year and a half ago. As a result, the market changed completely. The sale of weighted ounces of Colombian had run its course, and "sense," always in demand (especially the increasingly popular Asian variety) but not in supply, became the drug.

In response to Tinnin's question, she said, "Sense, it's like the bud. Real potent and real expensive."

She indicated that Billy and David had a twenty-five-pound franchise. Their $30,000 deal called for $2,500 payments every two weeks for six months. David and Billy anticipated clearing $30,000 apiece. At first, they sold quarter pounds for as little as $600 and as much as $1,200. Making payments posed no problem until Billy started using cocaine. To compound matters, their customers began to balk at their prices. A week before Billy was killed, they were short $5,000. They argued about lowering their prices. David wanted to sell whatever was necessary to raise the cash. Finally, they agreed to sell two pounds at cost, $2,400. They hoped it would buy them time. It didn't.

Billy went to the beach and sold two more pounds but returned with only $1,900. David knew there had to be more and that Billy probably pissed it away on cocaine. To try and recoup the loss, David scored a hundred hits of MDA at 75¢ each. He sold eighty for $3 apiece. Even so, they didn't have enough to satisfy the debt. So the night of the murder, David took five pounds to Greensburg, but the deal never materialized.

"We was waitin' on this turkey there at the convenience store at Washington and Crater when Billy was killed."

Astounded as much by the amount of money as her ability to do arithmetic so quickly without pad and pencil, Tinnin asked, "How come you're tellin' me this?"

"On account you won't bust me."

He stared at the plasticized shine of his brown shoes. Memory urged him not to trust her, not because of what she said or the way she acted but because of the way she looked. She reminded him of Melinda Sue Faucette, an eighth-grade classmate who never participated in the attacks on him. Such standing jokes as using Tinnin for the ball smarted all the more when in the company of girls. But Melinda Sue didn't so much as giggle in consort with the others. One day toward the end of the school year, Tinnin followed her home. As soon as she was a safe distance from campus, he called out to her. She waited with her books clutched to her small breasts. He ran up and in a breathless gush asked her to the class dance. She smiled and said, "With you, you fat creep?" Later, Tinnin learned that the older boys were punching Melinda Sue as if she were a time clock.

Tinnin said, "How do you know I won't bust you?"

"Heard talk."

A deepening arc at the right side of his mouth wore away his firm expression. "So where'd he get the cocaine?"

"From the franchiser," she replied as if it were obvious.

"What for, to sell?"

"No," she whined petulantly, "to use. They couldn't sell cocaine. MDA neither."

"How come?"

"Someone else had the franchise."

Tinnin scratched his brown, matted hair. "All this talk of franchises …"

He looked across the street at the brick house the vice squad used for its offices. If not for the yellow light burning at the front door, he would have assumed the place was unoccupied as all the windows were blackened. Rarely did any deputy or office personnel encounter a member of the vice squad because they worked the long part of the night. "So who's this franchiser?"

A weak laugh caught in her throat. "Wouldn't tell ya if I knew. David and them never would say. They was afraid, but like they'd laugh sometimes and say I'd never believe it anyways."

"Can't hardly believe it myself. David and them selling drugs in Random like it was the Piggly Wiggly." He added after a reflective moment, "Never heard tell … weren't none of them causing no trouble till Billy up and got hisself killed."

"And David's next."

"He's in jail."

"Don't mean nothin'."

"You wanna tell vice about all this?" He added, "Seems a whole lot to remember."

"Ain't tellin' nobody. And I'll deny I ever told you."

"Have it your way then." He paused for a moment. "Hey, Mary Jane, there's this private detective the Blake's hired, a guy named Boggs. Maybe you ought to talk to him."

"I already talked to him—well, it was more like he talked to me."

"Still, he might could help. Ain't nothin' official about him."

"Like I said, I ain't talkin' to no one no more." Mary Jane turned to leave.

"'Fraid this furniture of yours stays put. Won't nobody bother it none though."

She said thanks and stepped off.

"Hey, uh, how much did David have when he was pulled?"

She stuffed her small hands in her front pockets and shrugged. "A bunch, a whole bunch."

"Two pounds?"

"A bunch more than that."

Tinnin nodded as if he already knew.

# CHAPTER TEN

At the precise moment the second knock struck, a thick-set man snapped back the lock and yanked open the door. His appearance surprised Tinnin. He had long dark hair and a longer beard. He wore a basketball jersey, worn-out jeans, and black, paint-spotted sneakers. The beard, perceptibly rimmed with age, choked off much of the fleshy face so that there was little to see: a long, slightly warped nose and small trolling eyes under which were heavy scimitars of bulge. The yellow exterior light lent a waxen sheen to his skin. The way he stood like a stone in the doorway, his large hairy hand gripping the edge, stated he was ready to challenge anyone because no one warranted a free pass.

"Yeah?" he said in a voice that surprised Tinnin because it wasn't gruff, but a tone used when answering the house phone.

"I'm Deputy Tinnin." He tried to conceal his wince because he realized he was in uniform and didn't need to tell the man he was a deputy. "Seen the light on, so I thought I'd call."

The man looked Tinnin up and down and narrowed his eyes. A deep-set inverted V imprinted his brows. "Got no time for visitors. Whaddya want?"

"Got some information. Wanted to tell you guys 'fore I forget."

The man walked away without a word. Tinnin stepped inside, asking, "And you're who?"

"Sergeant Shorter," he said without turning back. He passed through the small reception area and headed down an unlit hallway.

The vice squad was a separate, almost clandestine outfit over which no one but the sheriff had control. Seldom did any deputy or patrol commander ever see the three agents and their captain. They never attended departmental functions such as the Fourth of July picnic, and their nocturnal hours created something of a mystique about them. Aside from his encounter with Captain Wynne the other day, Tinnin had only seen one agent before now, and if not for the search warrant the man was returning to the magistrate, Tinnin never would have believed he was vice. That agent looked worse than Shorter, like something that crawled out from under a rock. Whether it was on purpose or not, the ponytailed officer had bumped into Tinnin, driving his shoulder hard. Such ill-mannered behavior went a long way in explaining why none of the agents ever appeared in court, why Wynne, the respectable-looking one of the bunch, saw to it that he was at every raid, and why he personally took charge of the evidence.

"Don't remember ever seein' you before," said Shorter.

"I work down around Random."

Shorter stopped at a lit doorway, the first office on the right. "Well, close the door, Tinnin."

The deputy went back and, while pulling the door to, swatted away a moving blob of flying insects. He turned back and paused to scrutinize the office. Behind an empty reception desk was a rail, similar to the one in district court. The first items to score an impression were the black window shades; they were all drawn. Next came the generic green walls; they were blank—no paintings, photos, or framed displays. The room seemed overly large and nearly empty as a result. A large mailbox, painted gray and marked Evidence, stood in the far corner behind the rail. Staring at it, Tinnin realized he was standing on carpet. He smiled.

"Through lookin'?"

"How do y'all rate carpet?"

"You said you had some information?" Shorter walked into his office, which consisted of a gray desk and a gray file cabinet. On the shelves of a gray bookcase was an assortment of pipes, roach clips, small scales, and tiny spoons.

The narc took a seat and lit a Kool cigarette. Tinnin looked for a chair. There wasn't one. What he did see, though, were a half dozen plastic bags of pot, fat as ticks, neatly aligned across the front of the desk.

"The captain seized it last night," said Shorter before Tinnin thought to ask a question. As he exhaled smoke, he asked, "Now what is this information?"

Standing at a lazy at ease, the deputy said, "What're y'all fixin' to do with all that?"

"Burn it."

"Worth much?"

"Fifteen."

"As in thousand?"

"What's this information?"

Tinnin gave a brief account of what he had just learned.

Shorter stabbed his cigarette out in an ashtray already filled with jackknifed butts. "How'd ya come by this information?"

"A person what knows."

"The person got a name?"

"Can't say."

"Why not?"

"Confidential." He added, "You know how that works, right?"

Shorter was about to answer when the telephone rang. He went into the office across the hall to answer it. The conversation lasted a minute. Shorter asked two questions: "How much?" and "When?"

As soon as he was seated again, Tinnin asked, "So tell me, just how does this franchise business work?"

"On a need to know, man."

"C'mon, man, we're both on the same team."

Shorter delivered a piercing stare before he said, "No, we're not."

Tinnin blinked once. "So does it operate like a, uh … like a Burger King? That kind of a franchise?"

"I'll tell ya one thing, Deputy Tinnin." Shorter lit a cigarette. "Put your damn franchises aside. What we need around here is a new DA. Know how many—we've brought fifty-two felony cases to court this year. Know how many made it to superior court?"

Tinnin shrugged. "What, five?"

"Zip, none, nada. All plea-bargained down to misdemeanors. And I'm not talking just weed."

Tinnin nodded as if in sympathy and understanding and grimaced out of allegiance.

The mention of the district attorney resurrected frustration and failures, not necessarily Tinnin's but nearly every other law officer in the city and county. The DA was a drunk. Perpetually disoriented, he sequestered himself in his office, leaving only for lunch and then seldom returning. His gross incompetence attracted incompetence. His three-man prosecutorial staff barely survived from one day to the next under the avalanche of backlogged cases. The ADAs were just as liable to lose important records as the track of time, just as willing to continue a case as to dismiss one, just as likely to infuriate victims as well as cops. Still, the Democratic Party saw to it that the DA won all three of his reelections.

"So, uh … Blake and Trollinger, they have one of these franchises? I mean, I patrol down that way. I'd like to know what's going on."

"Let me gaze into my crystal ball." Shorter pulled open a desk drawer and studied its contents for a minute. "Says here … says all's quiet."

"You get this franchiser, and it should stay quiet. Know who he is?"

Shorter sneered. "Wouldn't tell ya if I did."

"Mean you don't know?"

"I mean let's just say I ain't ready to make an arrest." He crushed his cigarette.

"Heard y'all's involved in that girl's murder? That a drug thing too?"

"Who told ya that?"

"Hear all kinds of things when you're on patrol."

"You don't say." He paused and then in a raised voice said, "Listen, Tinnin, I want the name of the person who told you all this shit?"

"The shit about the dead girl?"

"No, the shit about the franchise."

"Can't. Done promised."

"Well, unpromise."

Tinnin looked down at him, beating back the edges of a smile. After a moment he said, "So the dead girl ain't any of vice's business, huh?"

"I ain't talking about the girl."

"Talk at The Store was your plainclothes captain was down my way."

"Captain Wynne can go anywhere he damn well wants." He rose and pointed a finger at Tinnin. "You tell anybody about this, and I'll have your fat ass in a sling. Understand?"

Tinnin saluted and snapped out a crisp "Aye, aye, Sergeant." As he turned to leave, he asked, "Say, uh, when y'all's ready to burn that stuff, can I watch?"

"Why?"

"Curious."

"Don't be."

Upon leaving, Tinnin blazed a nonstop trail to Burger King. Since it was long past suppertime, he felt hollow and parked in the back of the lot, there to consume his Whopper, large fries, and supersized orange soda without interruption. He wasn't halfway through when dispatch radioed, asking for his location. He denied the urge to lie and say he was on patrol. His mouth full, he answered, "Eatin' supper. Why?"

"You're to head to the Rock. The—"

"I was just there."

"Car thirty-four, 10-3 and call dispatch."

The message troubled Tinnin. It was code telling him to use a pay phone to contact dispatch so they could talk without anyone listening.

By now the burger was of a manageable size. He drove with one hand and ate with the other. He went west on Washington and then turned south on Sycamore. He knew the hospital parking lot had pay phones.

The dispatcher answered immediately but put him on hold. Through a straw Tinnin sipped his RC Cola.

"Okay, thirty-four, I'm back. And you ain't gonna like what I got to say. The sheriff was just in here raising all kinds of hell—"

"What's Harris doin' there at this hour?"

"On account of you, man. Did you go over to vice?"

"Yeah. Had some information for 'em."

"Shit, you done done it now. You gotta get your sorry ass in here A-S-A-P. The captain's gonna put a sermon on you, boy."

# CHAPTER ELEVEN

The sight of a battered pickup with three in the cab and four straddling mounds of bagged garbage and household junk in the bed reminded Tinnin of the time Shufflin' Sam saw an overloaded vehicle and remarked that hell was being moved because he just saw the first load go past. If hell was relocating, Tinnin thought, it was putting down roots in Random, what with the early morning sun already burning the sky clear to the blue. The very idea of the impending swelter needled him because he had answered the 0700 alarm without any thought given to the hot, hard labor ahead.

He palmed the wheel of his blue-and-white Cougar XR7, admiring how effortlessly it spun. He dropped off Stiff Branch Road onto the dirt road leading to what was left of the Blake trailer. He maneuvered slowly lest the dust mar the car's showroom condition. He would rather have suckered tobacco than waxed the car any time soon.

Since he was on second shift and not on duty, he wore jeans, but in his rush to get to breakfast at Mahone's, he forgot to bring the tools of his trade, including his pistol. Why he pushed himself remained as inexplicable as why he wanted to take a look at the trailer. He assumed the detectives and arson experts had been thorough. He presumed that what they had been unable to find doubtless would elude him as well. Still, he felt compelled to meddle, to try and find a plausible theory, if not an answer, to why the killer torched the place. There didn't seem any point unless there was something in the house the killer had to destroy. This whatever-it-was seemed merely elusive but then became lost to time when a new timeline began nineteen days ago with the Wendy Allen murder, the heinous account that pitted kidnap and rape against wealth and beauty. It so alarmed the right people that their raised voices had to be heard or else the sheriff would suffer at the polls. Accordingly, Harris assigned every available man to the case, reducing the Blake slaying to the status of a second thought. Even Tinnin, as caught up in the tragedy as everyone else, came to view the death of the doctor's daughter as more important, more urgent because a white girl had been raped and killed. But Saturday night's conversations with Mary Jane Henson and Sgt. Shorter infected him with something akin to doubt and suspicion yet never wholly resembling either one or the other. Nothing important ever seemed to happen to Tinnin, and given his druthers, nothing ever would. But the butchery on the scale of the Blake murder made solving it of the utmost importance. The meaning of the law was at stake.

Tinnin used to think of the law in general terms. You had little laws that sprung from *the* law. *The* law was finished while the little laws were just that … little. Some unnecessary, some so undercut by the way officers enforced them that they heckled *the* law. What rattled Tinnin was whether he actually knew what *the* law meant, whether as a deputy he stood for *the* law or just the chickenshit little laws.

The clearing was ablaze with white light. The dazzling light reduced Bogg's eyes to the smallest of squints. He parked on the beaten grass, turned off the engine, and lingered in the cool car. With an "aw, hell," he opened the door and pushed himself out of the car. The heat and humidity immediately clung to him. Shading his eyes, he looked to see what was left of the wreath of morning clouds and saw buzzards circling, their funnel drifting toward the northeast edge of the field. Tinnin shoved his hands in his pockets for the lack of something else to do with them. He sauntered over to the black and twisted rubble, asking himself what he expected to find. Since he had no immediate answer, much less any hope of finding one, he turned his thoughts to Will. He wondered if Will ever intended to remove the ruins, recalling how Clint Dempsey left the tornado-strewn remains of his chicken houses in the trees, seeing no reason to collect them. Tinnin shuffled his brogans and kicked aside the various objects he encountered. In the back of the charred perimeter, he bent down to take a closer look. There was nothing to see but burnt materials.

He delivered himself of a sigh because what he was about to do went against every tenet he held dear—hard work. He decided to pull back the fallen walls and went to his car for a tire iron and work gloves. A niggling shadow that had been dogging him compelled him to undertake this task, foolhardy as it seemed. He still blamed himself for the two murders; after all, they happened on his watch, on his turf.

As soon as he reached into the trunk, he heard a gunshot. He swung instantly toward the sound of a bullet ripping through the woods on his left. Grabbing the tire iron, he threw himself on the ground. A second bullet whistled past, almost the moment he heard the crack and concussion of its report. He judged the rifleman to be hidden somewhere in the east rim of the clearing. He crawled along the passenger side to the front of the car and peered over the hood. A third report dropped him. He yelled loud enough to punish his throat, "I'm with the Dinwoodie County Sher—"

Another shot speared the sound of "sheriff."

He remembered the white bag that contained the two chicken biscuits he had earlier. He slid down to the door, cracked it open, and retrieved the paper. He spiked it on the iron and waved it over the roof. Half-expecting to draw fire, he heard not silence but his own labored breathing. In a minute's time the black iron became heavier than he ever imagined. He lowered it and hunkered back on his heels. His thoughts raced for a clue as to who was firing at him—and why?

One by one, reasons—be they good, bad, or ugly—fell by the wayside.

"Git up."

Sweat smeared Tinnin's eyes as he stared at a .30-06 rifle. It took a moment to see beyond the barrel.

"Blake! Blake, you son of a bitch! You're under arrest." He sprang to his feet, but his buckling knees almost felled him. Once balanced but not quite plumb, he screamed, "Just what in the Sam Hell you doin'? Firin' on a deputy! You coulda kilt me."

Will settled the rifle in the crook of his arm. His small eyes were steady, leveled against Tinnin's.

"Blake, if you so much as put a scratch on this car I'm taking you in." He hesitated when he heard what he said. "Hell! I'm taking you in anyways. Firing on an officer of the law. Just what—Blake, if you even had a half a brain you'd fly backward."

"What're you here for?"

"You puredee crazy?" Tinnin hollered. "You forget this here's the scene of a crime?"

"The crime's that sheriff of yours." Will shrugged.

Pointing a finger, Tinnin said, "Now you ain't got no call. We's workin' on it. Leastways when we ain't bein' shot at. Just whaddya doin' shootin' at me? You out of your mind?"

"If I was shootin', I'da hit ya."

His cursing loosed, the deputy stepped back and then wheeled back quickly, snatching the rifle and heaving it to the ground. "You … you just … you just committed attempted damn murder."

Will gave a once-over to the place in the grass where his rifle landed. "How's I s'posta know it was you?"

"The hell you say." Tinnin took a deep breath, sensitive to the downcast eyes in Will's rock-lean face. "All right, Will. All right. Listen, I'm fixin' to … well, I'm looking for … for evidence. You want to lend a hand? I could sure use it."

"How come they sent you? Where all them detectives? Working on the doctor's daughter?"

Tinnin flushed. "They sent me on account of—I sent me. Mean … look, I'm not gonna argue. You want to help, go get a crowbar or something. I'm turning back these walls."

Will inspected his folded arms for a moment and then looked up at the burning sky. "Reckon they won't come down nohow." He left, retrieving his rifle on the way.

Fifteen minutes later Will returned with Coonie Pride. Each had a three-foot pry bar. Tinnin slouched in the driver's seat with the door open. Coonie called out, "The work ain't gettin' done what with you sittin' down." Tinnin laughed and pushed himself out of the seat. The smile he wore in greeting faded the instant it confronted the grimly drawn expressions of the two men.

Coonie asked, "So what is it we're lookin' for again?"

Tinnin said, "Hair on the wall."

"Huh?"

Will asked what kind of hair.

"I don't know," said Tinnin. "Just something I heard on TV."

"TV?" said Will, shaking his head.

"What's it mean again?" asked Coonie.

Exasperated, the deputy said, "Whatever it means, it don't mean nothin'. Now let's get to work."

With few words, the three worked through the morning like a practiced team and, as a team, quit when it occurred to them that whatever it was they were looking for wasn't there and probably never had been. They stopped within seconds of one another and moved away. Coonie went off a ways to piss. Will strode to the middle of the field to hunker down and gaze at the sifted debris. Tinnin went back to his car and let the rev of its engine say goodbye. The Cougar tore down the dirt road, its driver heedless of the dust and gravel.

On the hard-surface road, Tinnin turned south and accelerated. He didn't stop for the blinking light at The Store. He didn't brake until he reached Trollinger's trailer. In what could be called the front yard, he found cigarette butts. He picked up the longest and rolled it over in the palm of his hand. Its markings were clear: a Kool cigarette. He bent to examine the others. Only the one he held was a Kool cigarette, but it wasn't crushed or jackknifed, just stanched. He lifted his open hand up and with a flick launched the butt into the air. About halfway back to the car, he turned with the intention of retrieving the filter. He stopped upon realizing that his fingerprints had probably smeared any others.

# CHAPTER TWELVE

The detective division was empty. A wisp of smoke looped from an ashtray. The silence accentuated the tick of the clock; it was a half hour before his patrol meeting. Tinnin looked up and down. He listened for sounds from nearby offices. A desk drawer closed. An electric typewriter hummed. Tinnin started to shut the door behind him but then thought better of it. He eased over to the investigative file cabinet and slowly opened the drawer marked B–D. He flicked through the folders, unable to locate Blake's. He tried A and then E–F. Almost five minutes passed before he located it under R. Probably for Random. He snorted, thinking the detectives wouldn't know how to pour piss from a boot with the directions on the heel.

The report was thin. Its first sheet noted the basics:

**Date:** 7/10/82

**Time of Death:** On or before 2130. Exact time undetermined. Victim burned beyond recognition.

**Cause of Death:** Homicide.

**Place:** Stiff Branch Road, three-tenths of a mile north of Garner Road, a single-wide trailer owned by William (None) Blake Sr., Rt. 2 Box 345, Random.

**Victim:** William (None) Blake Jr., 3/1/58, white. Shot with a .38 caliber. Right ear. Close range. Body found on right side, six inches from couch in living room. Unable to determine signs of a struggle due to fire.

Skipping past the parents' statements since he had written them, he read Mary Jane's. Drugs weren't mentioned. Trollinger's first interview likewise contained no reference to marijuana. The most revealing part was the lab analysis, which showed no similarities between the voice on the 911 tape and Trollinger's. A second statement, taken after his arrest, clearly implied that Trollinger remained a suspect. Yet the interrogation focused on drugs, not murder. The last line was capitalized: "REFUSES TO DISCLOSE SUPPLIER; EXPRESSED FEAR FOR LIFE."

As soon as Tinnin turned to the fire marshal's report, he glanced past the name Wynne. He was unable to find it again amid the thick, single-spaced text. He had to read from the top. His lips moved as he went down the page. Midway, he placed a finger on Wynne's name. Apparently, the captain had been called in to assist. There was no explanation. The deputy assumed Wynne was trained in arson investigations. After all, his resume was legend, both in the military and law enforcement. His completion of a prestigious course at the FBI Academy five years ago virtually assured him of becoming the next sheriff. Why he stayed in vice confounded everyone.

The clock told Tinnin to hurry. The report indicated that the fire started shortly before 2130. The trailer was "fully involved" when Station #12 arrived. That it ignited so quickly pointed to an accelerant. However, investigators found no trace of flammable material or containers at the points of origin: the living room and bedroom. The fire marshal initialed the conclusion: that there were two sources left no doubt the fire had been set "by an expert."

Tinnin was the last to arrive for the roll call or, as the captain referred to it, choir practice. He was about to take a seat when ordered to report to the sheriff. "N-o-w."

Sheriff's Harris's office was in the rear of the long building. It was small, even smaller when the six-foot-three, 230-pound man occupied it. Though paneled and carpeted, its real recommendation was the private entrance. No one ever knew if the sheriff was in, but the safest course was to act as if he were.

Despite his size, Harris had a reputation for moving quietly, springing on unsuspecting deputies at all hours. He made his presence known with a voice that boomed. Some were so startled they had a hand on their weapons before realizing it came from their boss man. This quiet approach was a method Harris mined and mastered.

Thirty-three years ago when the Democratic Party sought a replacement for retiring Sheriff Foust, officials dismissed out of hand the young strapping man whose campaign was limited to a few homemade roadside posters. But at the time, Harris worked at Bradberry Funeral Home where for three years he made a point of being visible at visiting hour. He shook hands with each and every bereaved soul, always placing his full name before and after his comments on what a fine person the deceased was. More often than not, Harris never knew the person that had passed on, but when survivors and friends went to the primary to vote, they remembered Harris, connecting him to that time of great loss when he proved such a considerate young man. At twenty-four years old Harris won the primary overwhelmingly, becoming the youngest man ever to be elected sheriff in the state. Harris then undertook a strategy of ingratiating himself with party chieftains, using his department not as law enforcers but as tireless campaigners who saw to it that every Democratic candidate's war chest was full. Within a decade he changed the who's who of the party. He was no longer known as Sheriff Harris but as The Sheriff.

His redoubtable size and polished demeanor enhanced his office. Not many looked as physically powerful, and no one was as politically powerful. Harris left an impression with the solidity of aged black walnut. His head was a whittled block; only the jutting jaw saved it from appearing square. His profile brought to mind those of heroes and statesmen stamped on coins. He wore well-tailored suits, always a shade of gray. Even after a heart attack suffered five years ago and the twenty-odd pounds he gained after he quit smoking, his attire retained its crisp cut. The heart attack changed only one feature: his long face was now forever fierce and flushed.

Tinnin rapped lightly on the doorjamb.

The sheriff continued to write without looking up. "Come in and close the door."

The deputy centered himself in front of the polished desk, his hands clasped over his butt, his fingers wicking away sweat.

A minute or two later, Harris finished writing and capped the pen. Without ever looking at Tinnin, he asked, "What's that crap all over your uniform?"

"Uh … sir … uh …," he said as he inspected his brown shirt and found gray shades where onions must have landed from a cheeseburger. "Uh … an apparent oversight, sir."

"An apparent—Tinnin, you ever heard of a napkin?"

"Sir, yes, sir."

"In the future use one."

"Yes, sir."

"So …" he said, pausing to rub one corner of his bright eyes. "So everything going to suit you, Carson?"

"Real fine, sheriff. It's real fine."

"Good. Glad to hear it." With only the slightest hesitation, he added, "So what in the hell were you doing at the vice squad office last night? Who authorized you to go over there?"

A third chin swelled under the other two. "Uh, had some information I—"

"I said, who told—who gave you permission to go over there?"

"That would be no one, Sheriff. See, I didn't think I needed permission bein' on account as how I was on official business."

"You didn't think—" He drummed the black pen against the leather edge of the desk blotter. "You keep your fat ass out of there. Understand?"

"Yes, sir. Never—"

"And how'd you come by this information?"

Tinnin cleared his throat. "Believe it's called a confidential, reliable source."

"I don't give a damn what it's called. Who told you?"

Tinnin's gaze passed over the sheriff's neat gray hair in an effort to avoid meeting Harris's eyes. They were reputed to be better than a polygraph. "The truth is … well, the truth is, it's hard tellin'."

"Try," drawled Harris.

Tinnin filled his cheeks with air, which he held for a moment and then swallowed. "Well, sir, in the course of my investigation I—"

"Whoa … what investigation?"

"Into the murders." He appealed to the hard eyes. "You know, Billy Blake and the—"

"Who told you to do any investigating?"

"Ain't that what we's s'posta do?"

"You ain't supposed to do nothin' unless someone tells you. Now, how'd you come by this information?"

The deputy looked at the wall behind Harris, blinking dumbfoundedly. "I never did get the name."

"What name?"

"The name of the confident—"

"Tinnin!"

"Sir?"

"Who the hell told you?"

"That's what I'm trying to tell you. See, I didn't get a name, so I used confidential—"

"Was it a girl?"

"Believe it was, though what with all this long hair—"

"A M.J. Henson?" asked the sheriff, reading from the dispatcher's log. "She the one?"

"Weren't her. Alls she wanted was her stuff … some of the stuff in the trailer they impounded."

"You know her?"

"I've never set eyes on her."

"Then why'd she talk to you?"

"Hard to know, sheriff."

"Tinnin …"

"Sir?"

"Tinnin, you're either the sorriest liar I've ever met or the dumbest individual I've ever run across."

"Sheriff, I might be dumb, but I'm no—"

"Get out of my sight. And stay out. Or else I'll have your fat ass in a two-man at the French Quarter."

That evening Tinnin followed his usual routine but not daring to visit the men at The Store, much less risk a trip to town for a Whopper. As his shift passed through nightfall, he continued to feel like the sheriff was watching. So he stayed in the patrol car, crisscrossing his territory. His watch was quiet. There was very little traffic on the radio—at least until 10 p.m.

The shift commander ordered three units to the Rock. At the same time, the dispatcher requested an ambulance to the jail, code three. Still feeling as if under surveillance, Tinnin called in to see if further assistance was needed.

The dispatcher said, "Stand down, thirty-four. Just a prisoner burned with acid. Throwed right in his face."

"Which one?"

"The one down your way, D. Trollinger."

"Where'd he get the acid?"

"In the face."

"Then who threw it?"

"Unknown, thirty-four."

# CHAPTER THIRTEEN

Oversized nose or not, Boggs was unable to detect the smell of formaldehyde or any scent for that matter, not so much as a whiff of perfume emanating from the spinster nurse escorting him down the stark hallway. At ten-step intervals they passed numbered doors, each with a rack on the wall beside it. Examination rooms, he surmised, and all empty.

The door to the last room stood open, but without invitation. Layers of cigarette smoke wafted over and through an afternoon sunbeam slanting dagger-like through the venetian blinds. Boggs hesitated at the threshold, believing no one was inside, but then the nurse, arms folded, tsked and said, "Doctor?" Boggs's perfunctory smile fell when the padded leather chair swung around and Dr. Lesley Allen failed to acknowledge him.

Allen possessed an old face that had suddenly gotten older and wasn't accustomed to it; key expressions had been lost to him, some as simple as a smile. His long, liver-spotted hands crossed perpendicularly under his pleated chin. His thinning hair was brown except for the gray streaks over the elongated ears. The watery eyes behind bifocal glasses were too steady to see anything at all.

"Doctor?" said the nurse petulantly.

"Hmm?" He glanced toward the door without seeing. A second later his eyes jumped toward the big man in the doorway. "Oh, it's—it's—you're Mr. Boggs?"

Boggs fumbled with the doctor's extended but limp hand, barely managing to shake it. He sat in the closer of a pair of red leather chairs with stiff backs. He was uneasy with the surroundings, with his proximity to a doctor, to the accursed profession that six years ago had to insert three screws in his right ankle to correct mistakes in setting the bone. It was this very profession that had declared lunatic Rufus Grover insane and thus innocent of murdering his partner.

Allen reached for a pack of Kool cigarettes beside an astray littered with crushed butts. As he lit one, he said, "Started back."

Boggs shook his head at the offer of a smoke.

Exhaling loudly, Allen asked, "Well, where do we begin? I don't care what your fee is. I want you to investigate my daughter's death, no quarter asked nor given."

"Why me?" Since leaving the DA's office six years ago, Boggs's stock-in-trade had been alienation of affection suits, missing persons, or witness interviews for defense lawyers.

"You were the only one in the phone book."

"Well, whaddya know." He smirked because he had always doubted the value of his yellow-page ad.

The remark passed over the doctor without notice. "So what do you need from me?"

A remnant of that buzzing from the shotgun blast plugged Boggs's ear. He lumped air in the back of his throat and swallowed. The sound didn't disappear but softened. "There are at least three detectives on this full time, and I don't know how many deputies. I don't believe there's a whole lot more I could do." He added, "But what has the sheriff's department been telling you?"

Allen watched the exhaled smoke before answering. "Nothing. Nothing that has substance. They say they can't discuss too much because it's under investigation." Almost to himself he barked, "Under investigation? Of course, it's under investigation."

The outburst startled Boggs. He held back, unsure if another outburst of some sort was to follow. When none did, he said, "Well, unlike the sheriff's boys, my investigations cost money, but I'll sure as hell tell you something, even if it's bad news. I mean, it only makes good horse sense."

"Results," said Allen, stringing the last "s" out into a hiss. "That's what I want, Mr. Boggs. I want results. I want to see this man. I want to kill this man. I want you to find him and bring him to me. I will kill him. But I can't see this man. Do you understand me, Mr. Boggs? I can't see him. I don't know who killed my daughter. Or why. I don't know why. This man, this killer, is like a shadow. He's empty. Not given to thought. He's nothing. Not a man, not a beast. A nothing that breathes, that walks, that talks. A nothing you can't see until it sees you, and then it's too late. Am I getting through, Mr. Boggs? Do you understand what I'm saying?"

"No, and I don't believe you do either."

Allen cut his eyes at Boggs. Sweat broke out in the channels across his brow. He threw himself back into the plush chair. "She was only twenty-one. If she hadn't changed her major so often, she would have graduated by now and started on a career or a family. But she didn't. She didn't know what she wanted to do … not that she was mixed up or anything. She took the spring semester off to travel. She and a friend toured Asia."

He paused and laughed. "What a lark! They met this man in Singapore, and on a whim, all three took off for Mexico to see the Yucatan. I believe she was in love with this man, this Simon … Simon Sasser. If she wasn't in love, she wasn't far from it. I know she was serious about him. Maybe she needed to be serious."

Again he paused, all humor gone. "She was always serious about her running, though. She was training for a marathon the day … you know, Mr. Boggs, I can't see this man. I can't picture him. I have no … no reference. He can't be human."

Boggs reached for the double frame on the desk.

"The one on the right is Wendy. The other's her sister, Sally. She's eighteen … eighteen going on eighty-eight."

At a glance, only the hairstyles distinguished one from the other. Wendy had long honey-blonde hair. Her sister's was dark, cut short in a pixie style. Both had prominent cheekbones, clean complexions, and deep-blue eyes. Wendy smiled as if laughing. Sally tucked her smirk to the right corner of her mouth.

"They're both very attractive." Boggs set the photo back. "They look a lot alike. Ever think it might coulda been Sally they—"

"You don't …" Allen was unable to finish.

"No, no. The way I hear it, it coulda been anyone." He added, "Tell me what happened. What did she do the day she disappeared?"

The doctor's voice lacked any emotional register. He spoke at a slow, methodical clip, telling Boggs that Wendy's traveling companion, Gail Etheridge, and his daughters went to Greensburg Country Club Sunday morning. After an active day of tennis and swimming, the girls drove Wendy to the southern end of the county so that she could run the eighteen miles back to town. That was about six-something in the evening. Everyone expected Wendy to be back just before dark. He said she wore those florescent whatsits just in case.

He went on to explain that about half past nine, his wife became anxious. An hour later, they called the highway patrol to see if there had been any accidents. When they got no answer, not even a recording, they called the sheriff's department. The next day, detectives concluded that Wendy had been kidnapped, but there never was a ransom attempt. Her body was found three days later in a cornfield off McKenney Road.

"That would have put it … that was the tenth, right?"

"No, it was July 11th."

"The day after Billy Blake was killed."

"Is there a connection?"

"None that I can see." He paused reflectively. "So tell me about your enemies."

"My what?" The silver rims of his glasses glinted when he screwed up his face. "I … I imagine there are some folks who don't particularly like me. But I know of no one capable of carrying a grudge this far."

"She take drugs? Does Sally?"

"Drugs?" The sound of his swallowing was audible. "I believe we're getting a little far afield here."

"Just answer the question."

"No. Absolutely not. Wendy was a runner. She was in training."

"What about her friends? They do drugs?"

"Uh, she … well, there's Joyce Eaddy from her high school days. Once she started at UVA, she didn't see Joyce very much. Most of her friends were from college, like Gail Etheridge."

"Boyfriends?"

"No one that I know of—around here, that is. She seemed very much smitten by this man she met in Singapore. She'd write him almost every day. Sometimes twice a day. I know because Gentry, our maid, complained about having to make so many trips to the post office."

"What's his address?"

"Well … well, quite frankly I never asked. I don't know. Singapore, that's all."

Boggs told him to find the address. "He American?"

"Why I … I suppose so. But why all the questions about him? I told all this to the sheriff's man. They didn't seem very interested. After all, how could someone on the other side of the world kill her?"

# CHAPTER FOURTEEN

In taking on the Allen case, Boggs felt he had no choice but to observe a basic premise in a plunging economy: cut your losses, meaning drop the Blake investigation. Although one case was as unpromising as the other, the doctor's money was the decisive factor. The decision bothered Boggs, but only for a moment. What it came down to was not a question of ethics, even assuming there was such a thing in his line of work, but of shaping his future. Because he was middle aged, he had to heed one code: get to the golden years with the gold. And besides, he had no leads now that Trollinger was in jail, and after he heard an assailant had thrown sulfuric acid in Trollinger's face, Boggs seriously doubted whether the boy would ever talk again—about anything. The trouble at the jailhouse probably sealed off any approach to Mary Jane Henson as well; if she was mistrustful before, she was a mute now. With those two out of reach, Boggs didn't know where to look.

In the Allen case, he didn't know where to begin, much less where to look. Too concerned with the Trollinger stakeout to be bothered with the details of another murder, he actually knew very little about the killing other than the girl was abducted, raped, and thrown alongside the road. And because the murder was now weeks old, he figured that he had as much chance of uncovering new evidence as molasses had of running uphill. Even so, eight hundred dollars a week plus expenses brought the doctor hope. Money really could buy such things.

To avoid any ill will, Boggs decided to return the two-hundred-dollar advance from the Blakes and place the exact sum under expenses for Dr. Allen. It was damn generous of him, particularly in light of the fact that Will almost killed him a week ago. The episode at Trollinger's trailer was reason enough to bail out. Folks who shot once were liable to shoot again and again until they hit the target, and a bull's-eye was no guarantee that the shooting would stop, because there was always another target. The lunatic Rufus Grover proved as much. Boggs had heard that the man was still firing at the enemy, still persuaded he was a guerrilla commander on the verge of overthrowing the government and marching triumphantly into Washington—not D.C. but down Washington Street.

The hate that Grover conjured gut-clenched Boggs as he swung his Malibu onto Blake's dirt road. Approaching the screen door in the back, he noticed a small clear-plastic bag of water tacked beside it. He had heard of this remedy for keeping flies away, but he had never seen it in use. The sounds of quarreling stopped him. He coughed to announce his presence. The shouting ended abruptly. He knocked. After a moment, Will's frame filled the screen. He was silent until he realized he had to undo the latch, then he cussed his wife.

"Whaddya want?" said Will. Not waiting for a reply, he returned to his seat and tea.

"To settle up," said Boggs. He tossed two hundred-dollar bills on the white-and-yellow-checkered tablecloth.

Had Will torches for eyes, the money would have been ashes. "What's this for?"

"Givin' you back your money."

"Ain't no one asked for it."

"I couldn't find the man that killed your boy, so there it is."

Will looked up when Agnes came in through the hall. She braced her tiny figure against the doorframe. Will said, "Says he quittin'. Can't find who done it."

"I heard," said Agnes. There was no trace of the argument on her face, yet she distanced herself by folding her arms.

"S'pect now you can get a new TV," said Will and looked to Boggs. "She done kicked the stuffin' out of it."

Boggs, his back to the counter, slid away from the small fan humming on the windowsill over the sink. "Look, I did the best I could. I don't know what else to do, to be honest about it."

Will said, "Carson Tinnin's still tryin'. He was down here the other day."

"Doing what?"

"We gone through the trailer piece by piece."

"Find anything?"

"Don't know for sure. Never knowed what we was looking for to begin with. Carson said hair, but I don't know. Anyways, we didn't find any hair or anything else."

Agnes said, "Seen where David Trollinger got his."

"Mrs. Blake, he didn't kill your boy."

"Then who did?" Her thin voice cracked.

Will put in, "He was a right good shot with a pistol."

"You don't have to be a good shot to kill someone close up."

"Yeah," said Will. "And that's just how they done that girl too."

"Wendy Allen?"

"The doctor's daughter."

"She was shot close up?"

"Like if she was a horse you'd put out of its misery." He added, "Only gut shot."

Boggs glanced away, his eyes resting but not looking at the small photograph on the sill or at the tiny straw asters in a miniature milk can in front of the picture. He asked, "What kind of gun?"

Will laughed without mirth. "You really done some first-class detective work. A .38."

"No," said Boggs. "In the Allen killing, what kinda gun?"

"Listens worse than a suck-egg dog," Will said to Agnes. "I told ya, a .38."

Agnes said, "Leastways that's what it said in the paper."

"Don't reckon you read—"

"And no one's put it together?"

Will laughed. "Folks round here did. It's kinda simple, like two and two is four. You can do it on your hand."

"They do a ballistic test?"

Agnes answered, "Never did say."

"Give me back that money. The TV can wait. Your boy know Wendy Allen?"

"Her and the pope."

Will's laugh brought a smile to Agnes.

"He's better than Jerry Clower," said Will.

"He is that."

# CHAPTER FIFTEEN

To expect the best or the worst from a man was foolhardy. Most did enough to get by and called it a job well done. Getting by—it was all that life really asked.

No one Boggs knew ever consciously obeyed the law; everyone got by it. Those veering too far off sometimes were caught, but the penalties were seldom severe enough to coerce a man back. Boggs appreciated those who got by on the fringe, and if possible or profitable, he helped them when they took the fall.

The type he instinctively reacted against was the achiever, the one who did more than just get by, the loner driven beyond redemption to get within reach of the dark idol of his goal and then strike so quickly as to be almost unobserved. By far, most criminals weren't achievers. Ninety-nine out of every hundred that passed through the courts paid not so much for their crimes as their stupidity. They were stupid enough to allow themselves to be blinded by passion, deluded by drink, or in thrall to the thrill coursing through their blood.

The only link between the horde and the achiever was the criminal act itself; the former acting out of thoughtless desperation and the latter calculating within the shadow of the idol—the long-desired goal—and the obstacle that stood before it. The swift and sure dispatch of Billy Blake had the hallmarks of an achiever, one so determined he left nothing but ashes. There was no evidence of, and it was pointless even to look for, signs of an impassioned quarrel or something as ordinary as a grudge. No, the murder wasn't the work of an outraged person but a bent businessman. The fire suggested just how profitable the business was.

Blake was a liability that had to be removed. But what fire Wendy Allen set in the mind of the killer, possibly just her killer, eluded Boggs. As a result, Boggs fell in with everyone else, concluding solely on the basis of the swift and sure way the killer plucked her and then dropped her spent carcass that he—the anonymous he, the killer—came out of nowhere and thence returned. As imposing as the silence protecting the mystery of the Allen slaying was, it scarcely compared to the insufferable silence coming from another quarter: the sheriff's department. Boggs realized that a certain prejudice was at work here. His last two years at Greensburg Police Department were spent in the detective division. The rivalry between the city squad and the county's was such that when Boggs joined the DA's staff as an investigator, his inclination was to work against the sheriff's men. They were not so much inexperienced as inept. Yet their laziness and clumsiness weren't what disturbed Boggs now.

Through the years, Boggs came to realize that the most concise and cogent statement a man could make was a fart; words utterly failed men. In the field and in the courtroom, time and again, he watched helplessly while well-meaning people so distorted the truth that it became irrevocably lost. So for Boggs, the safest course was to pay close attention to what a person didn't say. And the sheriff's department failure to say anything about a possible connection between murder weapons was deafening.

Standing woodenly before the barbwire-rimmed fence surrounding the jail, Boggs wondered if what he *saw* could deafen him. He plugged a finger in his ear and concluded what he heard was only the remnant of the shotgun ringing. He resumed his examination of the four-foot slice in the links. It was a neat vertical cut, already mended with thicker, darker wire. Absently, he touched one of the tips of the new wire and watched a thin crease of blood surface. As he sucked the blood, he scanned the compound, passing over the trustee mowing burnt grass and over Trollinger's Plymouth and trailer, and alighting on the walls of the jail, a structure that brought the Alamo to mind. Everyone was safely inside those walls, numbered and stored in rows and niches, from the orange-clad trustee to the half-naked inmates hanging on darkened windows. Everyone was safe but Trollinger.

The screech of tires diverted Boggs's attention toward the back of the jail. A gray cruiser rocked after hitting the curb and coming to a stop. Tinnin pulled himself out from behind the wheel. Boggs called to him.

Tinnin's big smile looked pinned. The pinch of snuff under his lower lip seemed responsible. His stride reminded Boggs of a dog irrepressibly shaking with excitement. For this, Boggs granted his best smile to Tinnin. "How you gettin' along, Tinnin?"

"The hurrier I go, the behinder I get." The deputy's walkie-talkie squawked. He spoke into the receiver saying he was 10-7, the code for out of service, and holstered the radio.

"Hear you was down at Blake's trailer. Find anything interesting?"

"Can't rightly say." He spit juice and added, "Noways for sure."

"Can't stir you boys with a stick." Grinning, Boggs shook his head reprovingly. "S'pose you can't say what happened here either?" He pointed to the slice in the fence.

"Was one 10-55 coming to fetch another, but you might could say the boy sorta missed his turn."

"Naturally it happened after Trollinger got his?"

"Yep, third shift. They was gettin' it all night, way I hear it."

"And where's this drunk driver now?" Boggs nodded toward the Alamo jail.

"Fled, I heard." He spit.

"Fled?" Boggs jingled the coins in his pocket. "Seems like a man can't get in jail easy as he once could. I mean, the boy all but drove up to the jail door."

Tinnin shrugged. "There's them that get away." Tinnin told himself to leave, to avoid being seen talking to Boggs, a man who was once recognized for his police work and then banished for letting his partner die, and who then became an outcast by deliberately thwarting the sheriff's department when he was an DA investigator. Later, he was labeled a pariah for his less-than-honest work with defense lawyers. He further dishonored himself with his philandering, causing marriages to split and separations to become permanent. Why Tinnin didn't walk off puzzled him.

"Yeah, and sometimes with murder."

Tinnin smiled. "Ya know, why just the other day I come over here—'fore they done the mendin'—and I'll be damned if there weren't no paint on the fence, no glass, no nothing on the ground, not even a buckle in the fence. Sure seemed like that DUI sorta blessed the fence 'stead of crashin' into it."

"If you want my theory, I'd say this drunk driver of yours slipped right through here and went up to Trollinger's window."

Tinnin spit. "Me, I don't know nothing about theories."

Boggs asked if the deputy was aware Trollinger had been taken to Central Prison in James City for safekeeping.

"Heard they was fixin' to. Judge Hardy sign the order?"

"Shouldn't he?" asked Boggs.

"Just seems like he's taken what you might could call a real special interest in the boy's case."

"Why's that?"

Tinnin said, "Oh, I was there for his first appearance. Cleared the courtroom and everything. Wasn't like your usual not-guilty hearing."

The silence that intervened was broken when Boggs jingled his coins. "Say, they ever—I'm sure they did. But I never did hear no one say what was the results of the ballistics they run on Blake and Allen."

"You on her case too?"

"Strictly charity work."

"Thought when they threw out the lifeline, you was the one drifting away."

"What about the ballistics?"

"Can't say as I heard." Without prodding, Tinnin explained that unlike other major investigations, there was very little talk about the Allen murder. "No jokes or nothing. But there's a good reason for it. Like the old men down my way say, if you can't protect your women, ain't no hope of protectin' the children."

"Seems like you boys woulda done it first thing, seeing as how it was a .38 in both."

"Everybody's got hisself a .38."

"Almost every cop does," said Boggs.

"Yep, that or a .357 or a Glock 22 or a 9 mil or a .45 … I could go on." Tinnin wanted to say more but hesitated. He wiped a trickle of juice from the corner of his mouth. He studied Boggs, wondering how far he could go. Where men were concerned, there were no guarantees, not anymore, and certainly not from the likes of Boggs. Guarantees or no, the five days since Trollinger's court appearance defied any standard of caution. Time lost track of itself, forgot how to count, so the days were interminable and the nights infinite. The nickel-plated .38 special he now carried at all times wasn't much of a companion. Still, while he knew he wasn't safe with it, he felt threatened without it—without it and the AGT .22 rifle with the long clip. With or without the weapons, he distrusted everything he saw, heard, and imagined. He distrusted himself most of all.

His deliberations took him a step further—maybe by telling Boggs what he knew, the heavy hand on his conscience would lighten with the sharing.

"Boggs, I'm gonna tell ya something on account—know why?—on account there ain't no one that likes you. Hear them that do like you can't say why for sure. So I'm gonna tell ya something."

Tinnin had scarcely started when Boggs broke in, "What's 'sense'?"

"What they call marijuana buds. S'posta be real strong, kinda like grape brandy only you smoke it."

Boggs never stopped jingling the coins. So voluble as to surprise even himself, Tinnin told him how the franchise worked; how he learned about it; how Mary Jane knew Trollinger wasn't safe in jail; how Shorter, Wynne, and the sheriff were more interested in the informant than the information; and how he found the butt of a Kool cigarette at Trollinger's trailer.

"So what? Know how many people smoke Kools?"

"Yeah, but Shorter smokes 'em. Go see for yourself. Yeah, go on over there tonight and see if he still's got all that dope—bags of it, just lying around on his desk. Said Wynne seized it, but he ain't made no arrest or nothin' to show for it. I checked. So it ain't like it's evidence. He told me he was fixin' to burn it. The onliest thing is I ain't never heard of anyone burning dope or anything else for that matter. Ya know, how's they're s'posta burn confiscated weapons every so often? Never heard of one burning."

"So why you tellin' me all this?"

Tinnin's stomach cinched. "Cuz everyone hates you, and won't no one believe you if you go repeatin' it."

# CHAPTER SIXTEEN

The dried underarm stains reappeared within minutes of Boggs leaving his air-conditioned office. The crescents were wet again and growing larger. The forecast was for cooling temperatures, down in the eighties, a feat the steamy night showed no signs of performing. The stagnant air resembled a membrane, one pliable sheet after another.

Boggs hooked his suit coat over his shoulder and loosened his tie further. He rolled a flat toothpick over the tops of his lower teeth and swept his gaze across the law enforcement quad. Bats, too quick to count, dove through the streetlights lining the walkways. Boggs crossed to the police department side of Davis. From a block away, he heard the profane merriment coming from a dingy bar called Gipper's. The place was a veritable pharmacy, bootlegging all sorts of highs. Times harder than the loneliest night found Boggs there, slowly sinking with all the others toward dawn and greater desperation. Those times allowed for others when information was what he needed. Boggs turned away from Gipper's and toward the river, cutting down Bragg. He had a blind date with a calculated risk.

Boggs had plans for some of what Tinnin told him. A great deal of the information was unserviceable, even if it was true, and Boggs believed it was. Even so, he laughed with mirth and malice at the neatly wrapped way Tinnin implicated Shorter simply because the sergeant smoked Kool cigarettes—one single cigarette, one of hundreds of thousands made each year, and Tinnin or any other deputy or detective over there concluded the case closed. Tinnin was likeable enough; in fact, it was impossible to dislike the man. No, the problem with the deputy was the outfit he worked for.

The sheriff's department did nothing so much as sink to new, as-yet-unexplored or even unimagined depths of incompetence. Its deputies made the common criminal seem a mastermind, and pitted against the Blake killer, the entire bumbling bunch was drowning in the hadal depths of its own ignorance. In the Allen case, without a clue, without so much as a scene of the crime, deputies roared up and down the county in great officious haste, so determined and persistent but only persisting in their incompetent ways so that any chance of examining what they already had or finding anything new was lost, trampled, and buried under their own rushing tread. Yet even as they worked against themselves, a few seemed to be working for themselves.

Of all the prominent figures in the department, the cocksure captain of vice was one who deserved to be brought down. Wynne didn't so much fit the description of an achiever as redefine the limits: decorated special forces officer with three tours in Vietnam, a meteoric rise through the ranks at Greensburg PD, and the well-publicized promotion to captain and chief of the then newly created vice squad, an elite unit under the sheriff's command that was to rid the city and county of all its sins—all this despite the continuing controversy surrounding the man and his methods, despite this blatantly illegal use of criminals on probation and prostitutes to catch would-be felons.

Many of Wynne's busts never got past the preliminary hearing due to that stickler of a concept called probable cause. Those cases that did pass muster were generally plea bargained because Wynne had this embarrassing knack of explaining an individual's rights with a blackjack. Miranda could have been an illegal Mexican for all he cared. The thing of it was that Wynne knew better, better than anyone else. He was the only cop ever to attend the FBI Academy, an accomplishment even Boggs respected. Yet all his training paled against that troubled kind of liberty exercised by an achiever. In wedding himself to the community, Wynne took it not for better or worse, but for richer, period. In many ways Wynne was very rich indeed. More than that, he was proof you could take your riches with you. For whenever he fell, he landed firmly on his feet, ready, more than willing, and extremely able.

Having associated with Wynne while a DA investigator, Boggs knew that the man met everyone head-on, as if he or she were an obstacle, something to be overcome or overpowered, preferably crushed and removed. Such a personality seemed tailored to the Blake killing. But to assume that Wynne was involved in selling drugs wasn't merely an assumption but a fantastic leap.

The man dedicated his life to law enforcement, certainly not for the money or the hours, probably not even out of respect for the law, but for the job itself, a job that allowed him to flex his powerful personality. A man had to have a place in which to fit. Finding it was as important a force as sex, and once he found it, instinct would prevent him from jeopardizing it. Wynne's niche was that of a cop, albeit a rogue cop. It was his place where time became his. To think he would endanger his one and only place in life was no less absurd than to think an extinguished cigarette was enough proof to arrest a man. Wynne's only known connection to drugs was to stamp out its illegal trade. And while drugs doubtless played a role in Blake's death, since he was a dealer and stupid, two of the surest ways to get killed, there was no evidence, not even a hint, of drugs in the Allen case. If Wendy Allen wanted to slum it and buy "sense," she could surely afford to meet any price. But by all accounts, she wasn't interested in drugs. She was an athlete, a competitive runner.

Overwhelming as the reasons were to dismiss any link between Wynne and the murders, Boggs saw no reason why he shouldn't pursue the possibility, if for no other reason than to run the cigarette theory up Wynne's flagpole and watch it flap. And besides, he was available tonight since his latest sugar was home at mother's and his wife was probably in bed, holding out no hope of her husband joining her.

Boggs walked down the drive of the brick house, headed for the yellow light over the side door. When the light went out, he hurried to meet whoever was leaving. His stride faltered when no one came out. Just then, the dark windows brightened. He hastened to the door, giving it a solid rap. No one answered. To his disbelief, he thought he heard sounds inside. He knocked again.

"Get in here!"

Boggs wrapped the paw he had for a hand around the knob but hesitated, then cautiously turned it. The door was locked. He jiggled the knob.

"Kick it in!" came a yell.

Rearing back, Boggs hoisted his beefy left leg and then stopped. He smiled. He removed a thin blade with a wooden handle from his inner coat pocket and picked the lock. The grin he toted in split. A man the size of a pony was stretched out on the floor. Dressed as usual in his country club casual, Wynne ordered Boggs to call rescue.

Wynne continued to administer CPR. Boggs stood beside the black phone on the secretary's desk but didn't dial. Something was wrong—or at least very peculiar. He studied Wynne, but not until the captain rose to take in a heavy load of air did Boggs see what it was. He was wearing sunglasses, dark sunglasses at night.

"Call 'em, dammit!" Wynne shouted, then dropped to deliver the next payload of air.

Boggs picked up the receiver but again didn't place the call. He stared at the fallen man's rumpled pant leg, fascinated by the stark contrast between the black sock and the white skin. He thought only glossy paint could be that white. The lifeless face was losing color, awash in a bluish gray, a shade many times lighter than that of the man's disheveled suit. The clay-like texture of the man's skin was so malleable that Wynne's thumb sunk deep under the chin. Boggs broke away, and when he pushed the first of the three digits, it suddenly occurred to him who the prostate man was. The flushed face! That was why he failed to recognize him. In all the years Boggs had known the man, he never once saw the sheriff so quiet, so white, so composed.

He completed the call. In the second it took for an answer, he looked at the sheriff and Wynne, the two locked in a dedicated regime with a sense of hope almost tactile. Just as he was about to speak, Boggs burst into laughter. He clenched his teeth to stifle the sound.

"Just what in the hell was so funny?" asked Wynne after an ambulance had carted off the sheriff.

"I wasn't laughing," said Boggs as he watched the deputies who had gathered disperse. He looked at Wynne and fought back the curl of a smile. The captain still wore the sunglasses. "What happened?"

"I don't know." Wynne rested his butt on the rail. "We were leaving. Just about at the door when all of a sudden he fell, keeled right over. He said something about retiring and just fell over." He snapped his fingers to illustrate how quickly it happened.

Boggs said, "The way it happens sometimes." He added, "But the EMT's think he'll be all right." He settled into a pause. "Probably be as good as new."

"You sound disappointed."

"Oh, me and Harris go way back. Use to let him cheat at cards so long as the pot wasn't too rich. After all, he provided the liquor, the good stuff too."

"So what're you doing here anyway? And where were you when I was outside with the ambulance?"

"Snoopin' around." Boggs had found no trace of the marijuana Tinnin mentioned. "Got a smoke?"

"Find what you were looking for?" Wynne flicked up a pack of Marlboro cigarettes. Boggs pinched one. Wynne took one himself and lit his first, then the one Boggs pressed to his lips.

Watching the flame dance toward him, Boggs said, "Don't reckon I did." He puffed and exhaled in squirts, fighting back the urge to cough. "Ya know, I never knew you were an arson specialist. Where'd you—"

"Stick to your cheating wives, Boggs."

Boggs admired the smoke, rolling the filter. "S'pose with that kind of training, you'd know how to start one with just—"

"I said, stick to your cheating wives."

"Hey, they told me you smoked menthols. What's with the cowboy smokes?"

Wynne drove his fist into the big man's jaw.

# CHAPTER SEVENTEEN

The silence rang out. All day long, masons worked on installing the seventy-four-foot obelisk in the center of the new law enforcement quad. Why they needed jackhammers confounded Boggs. They were, after all, only relocating the Confederate monument, not tearing it down. Yet in the quiet aftermath, without any immediate annoyances to complain about, Boggs couldn't stay still.

His office felt confining, too cluttered with baleful reminders. One was the tape recorder that contained the ludicrous tale of Gail Etheridge, the girl who accompanied Wendy Allen through Asia and Mexico. Reached by phone in Charlottesville, Etheridge gave a glowing account of their trip, saying that whatever problems they encountered were not too difficult for their friend, Simon Sasser, to handle. Wendy met him jogging one day, and he befriended the pair, at once taking charge of their affairs. They saw him every day while in Singapore, Hong Kong, and Macao. In Mexico, he proved to be a knowledgeable tour guide, fluent in Spanish as well as Portuguese, Mandarin, and Cantonese. Altogether, they were with him for twenty-seven days. Despite all the time they spent together, Etheridge knew very little about the man; she wasn't even sure where he lived. She thought his home base was Singapore. She knew he was in shipping, but in what capacity, she was uncertain. Likewise, she was at a loss as to how to contact him. What she was sure of was that he was the handsomest man she had ever seen, and why he chose Wendy over her was a decision that barred the admission of rationality.

Boggs stopped pacing. At the door, he switched off the overhead light. The room huddled around the desk lamp. He resumed his walk, feeling the claims the walls and framed displays made on him with their certificates, licenses, an associate degree, an honorable discharge, and an expertly rendered architectural drawing he used in a murder case some years back; they all worked for and against him. He stopped at his desk, sneering at the heap of scribbled notes, none of which amounted to anything. He went to the window and let the rattling breeze from the air conditioner roll down the slope of his belly. He looked out at the night. All was at a standstill; no traffic, no noise. He cussed and went back to his desk. He stared into the dark and forced himself to go down the dead end of maybes once again.

Maybe there was an address for this Simon Sasser hidden in Wendy's room; if there was, the doctor couldn't find it. But there had to be one somewhere; after all, she wrote to him every day. Maybe this man thousands of miles away could have killed her, or ordered her death, and the executioner took it upon himself to rape her, to beat and bludgeon her; after all, there was no prescribed way to murder.

Maybe Sasser and Wynne knew each other, having met in Asia when Wynne was in the army or when they both were in the army. Maybe it took more than ten years to establish a supply line from Asia. Maybe Wynne wasn't involved at first, but once he discovered the line, he took charge and became the sole distributor, the so-called franchiser who had all the kids spooked, this McDonald's of the underworld. Maybe Wendy and Gail, so smitten by the man-who-lived-everywhere, never took a good look, never knew or suspected enough to look behind his so-called shipping concern. Maybe the incorrigible captain took more than his share, so Sasser hired someone to perform the brutal rites and leave a trail back to Wynne, so some unsuspecting character such as Carson Tinnin would have no other choice than to believe, doubt but at the same time believe, that Wynne was the killer. Maybe it wasn't happenstance that Tinnin fell into this role. Maybe Sasser's man or men ran a check on Tinnin and knew at what point the deputy would be forced, through personal conviction, to sever ties with the department and betray a fellow officer. Maybe Sasser's operatives knew more about Dinwoodie County than Boggs himself.

And then again, maybe not. Maybe Tinnin was a confused paranoid, acting out of some desperate remorse for a deed committed on the night of the Blake murder when he should have been on patrol. Maybe he suspected Wynne out of a newfound dislike because the legendary Wynne, maybe even a hero to Tinnin, couldn't catch the killer. Maybe Tinnin wasn't striking out at Wynne but at the department for turning its back on Blake and concentrating, if such an activity could be attributed to the department, on the Allen case. And maybe Wynne could punch like a contender, but he wasn't big-time; after all, this was backwater U.S. of A., a town not unlike any other and just as capable of killing as any big city. And maybe they were selling "sense," but if it was homegrown, the need to import from Asia or Mexico disappeared. And maybe Sasser was nothing more than Wendy's paramour. And maybe Wynne was what he represented himself to be: a cop, underpaid and overworked. And maybe Tinnin was just plain dumb, so reckless that before long he would accuse the sheriff himself of a crime perpetrated while flat on his back in the coronary unit. And maybe …

"Maybe I ought to get a drink." Boggs left for Gipper's.

In the midst of the usual crowd of kids outside sitting on cars, drinking beer, and smoking whatever, was Sally Allen. Although he wore loafers, Boggs bent down and pretended to tie his shoes. His surveillance told him that she was no debutant. Her wardrobe was the same as the others'—tank tops and jean skirts—but her speech was fouler than the others'. She was downright common: swilling beer, smoking, spitting, and letting any arm reach around her shoulder.

Rather than bypass the group as he usually did, Boggs waded through it. He received the greeting of a regular. While he joked about underage drinking, he steadied his sights on Allen. "Buy you a beer?"

"Sure, why not?" She examined her tall-neck bottle and drained it.

At this time of the night, the scales at Gipper's tilted toward the pool tables. That end, overcast with smoke, smelled like sourdough starter, but the young and old, either playing or perched on the elevated benches, didn't seem to notice. Boggs steered Sally toward the far end of the bar where they could talk without interruption. He ordered two beers, drinking his before the bartender had a chance to pour a shooter from a plastic pitcher. He threw back the bourbon and held out the glass for another. Once he finished the second shot, the bartender quickly removed the glass, concealing it under the bar. Another beer in hand, Boggs asked the girl, "Need something else?"

"Like what?"

"You tell me."

She shrugged and took a pull on her bottle.

Boggs said, "Ya know I work for your father?"

She cut her eyes at him. Through pressed lips she said, "That—what, he got you following me?"

Smiling, Boggs explained who he was and how he had been hired to investigate Wendy's death.

"So what's that got to do with me?"

"Nothing. Just—"

"Good. See—"

"Don't run off."

She squared herself in front of him. "You're a fucking creep; you know that?"

"Yeah, and your sister was raped and murdered. Ever think it was you they were after?"

"No," she replied defensively. "Why should I? Wendy wasn't the—she wasn't the all-American girl they make her out to be. She got around."

"Around here?"

"Oh, no. She was too good for that. It was always Charlottesville. Everything was always better at UVA."

"Even the dope?"

Sally sneered. "Her? Dope? You must be kidding. She's one of those fitness freaks. Going around all the time saying how a joint was the same as a pack of cigarettes."

Boggs drank. "You didn't like her?"

"No, I like her enough," she said, her voice fading as she cast her eyes down. "Just that she's always—well, I'm always compared to her."

"That day you dropped her off for the run, you see anything unusual?"

"Like what?"

"Oh, I don't know." After a moment, he told her to forget the question and showed her a newspaper photo of Wynne. "Ever see this guy?"

"No, who is he?"

"A narc." Boggs drank. "How many times a week she run?"

"Every day, just about."

"Where?"

"Just about anywhere, depending on where she was. She liked running down around Random because there was very little traffic."

"What, she just slip into her outfit like Superman?"

"No, she's always brought her stuff along with her. You know, shoes, socks …"

"You know the Blake boy that got killed?"

She shook her head. "I know where it was. Used to take Wendy down there."

"She ran down there, huh?"

"All the time."

"She ever have any … any, let's say, uh … encounters?"

"Like what?"

"I don't know. Anyone ever harass her?"

"If anyone did, she never said."

Boggs turned to the bartender.

"Well, there was that one time."

He swung back. "Say what?"

"A truck … it almost hit her. Came out of a dirt road. She said it never stopped, swerved out onto the paved road, leaving rubber. She had to dive into in a ditch."

"What kinda truck?"

"All she said was red, a red pickup truck."

"You tell the sheriff's people about this?"

"Nope," she shrugged. "They never asked." She paused, "Besides, it happened before the murder."

"When, a week before …?"

"As best as I can recall, the day before." After a moment, she added, "Or maybe … no …"

"Damn. All she could say was it was a red truck?"

"She was too busy pulling her ass out of the ditch." Sally paused and said, "No, wait. We went to the club on Friday or—"

"The club?"

"Greensburg Country Club."

"Oh, right. The club."

"Whenever we went to the club, we took Wendy down by Random. It's closer, ya know? So we went Friday … or was it Saturday? And then Sunday because Gail came to town. So the truck had to knock her into a ditch on Friday or Saturday." She taped the bottle rim against her lip as she considered the sequence. Nodding, she said, "Yep, that's it. Friday or Saturday. And she went missing on Sunday." She added, "Or was it Monday?" After a moment she said, "Oh, hell …"

"Well, it was a month ago," said Boggs to ease the painful twist of her mouth. "You keep a diary or anything like that?"

She laughed, "Yeah, sure."

"No, the reason I ask is if you do, you'd have a reference to consult. Got anything? Maybe a calendar you jot notes on?"

She drew in a light breath, stopped to exhale and then said, "I remember we went down there—what, a week after they found Wendy? Wanted to see the field where they found her and check out what the fire looked like." Without waiting to explain why, she added, "There's not a whole lot going on around here in case you hadn't noticed. So we went down there to take a look. We never could find the field, but we did the trailer. And I remember thinking, I wonder if the ditch along that road there wasn't the one Wendy fell in?"

"I'd bet my next drink it was." Boggs signaled to the bartender for another shot. He snatched the shooter, downed it quickly, and followed it up with a slug of beer. He pointed to the second beer, telling Sally, "This is ready when you are."

The girl nodded, her eyes distant. "So you think Wendy's murder had something to do with that killing in Random?"

"Ya know what I think, young lady? I think that if you can put two and two together, why can't the sheriff's department?"

"Ask them." She switched out her empty for the sweaty bottle.

"I will. Trust me, I will." He paused. "I wonder … you say the truck left rubber, huh?"

"That's what Wendy said."

# CHAPTER EIGHTEEN

Saturday marked the fourth week since the first slaying. The morning started hot with guarantees it would get hotter. Boggs, as clear-headed as he would ever be, tried to recall when it rained last. To the best of his recollection, two or three afternoon thunderstorms blew through last week. But that didn't discount the prospects of finding tire tracks; Boggs had seen a deluge on one side of the street, while the other side was dry as a dripping faucet when stared at. He phoned the Blakes, presuming a farmer would surely know. Getting past the pleasantries took less than ten seconds.

"Rain?" said Agnes. "Can't say. Last week sometime. Didn't amount to much. 'Member looking at the gauge. Less than nothing, as I recall."

He asked her to put Will on because he had an assignment for him.

"He ain't up yet."

Boggs inspected his watch. It was 7:40 a.m., a fact that erased the longstanding impression he had that farmers rose before dawn and worked late into the night. "Y'all're in the eastern time zone, right?"

"Do what now?"

"Can you get him up?" When she agreed, he added, "I'll call back in about ten minutes."

At 8:15 Boggs reached Will, telling him that they might have overlooked some evidence. He explained about the tire tracks and asked him to see if they were still there.

Will telephoned back in less than half an hour. "There's something there. Ain't real ... real ..."

"Defined?"

"Oh, it's tire tracks sure enough."

"I'll be down in a little while. Don't let it rain till I get—"

"Why? We need the rain."

"Never mind."

When Boggs arrived, Will and Agnes were ready to walk him down. They shared little conversation apart from a brief discussion of the heat wave. The track impressions disappointed Boggs. The rib-cuts were too smeared for a positive identification, and the widths measured less than five inches. Nevertheless, Boggs took pictures with a Polaroid camera, using a wooden ruler to give them scale.

"What ya think, Rockford?"

Boggs ignored Agnes and asked Will, "You think this is the same size tire we found on that path down yonder?"

"Might could. If not, damn close to it."

Agnes asked, "So what's that mean?"

"Means that truck that sent Wendy Allen into the ditch was probably the same vehicle that used that old wagon path."

They were silent as Boggs looked down the road.

"And?" asked Agnes.

"And I don't know what. I'll take this photo to Henry's Tire and see if he can ID it." He added, swabbing his neck with a handkerchief, "And even if he can, I believe it's too much of a smudge to narrow it down."

Agnes asked, "Why didn't the sheriff's people do this when they was like ants that you just stirred with a stick?"

"My question exactly," said Boggs. "The more investigating I do, the less I find that they did. But it's par for the course with those boys. A bigger bunch of idiots you'll never find."

"Amen," said Will.

"Even a blind hog finds an acorn once in a while," said Agnes.

"Ma'am, no disrespect, but these boys wouldn't know to look under an oak tree."

Back in his office late that afternoon, Boggs poured himself a drink. The news about the tire tracks was less than breathtaking: Goodyear … possibly? *Bourbon and bear it*, he told himself as he stared out the window with the view of the quad. He swallowed with a neck-stretching gulp. His veined eyes fell back on the amber whiskey, and he licked his lips.

"Wendy Allen," he hummed. She was the other side of the Sally coin, the tails to her sister's head. Wendy was innocent, innocent until proven dead. Her father was wrong to believe that the man who executed her acted without conscience. There was a very legitimate reason for shedding the firstborn's blood; Wendy must have crossed paths with the person who killed Blake, probably while running on Stiff Branch Road. She must have seen an argument or possibly a fistfight or even something as mundane as two men talking. Whatever she saw, it was enough to incriminate the killer.

After making a fiery spectacle of Blake, the assassin must have realized such an attack would generate headlines. He also must have realized that Wendy would either hear about or read those headlines. The fear that she would make a connection must have made the manhunt all the more urgent. Yet if Wendy was aware of a connection, however remote, she never let on, never expressed any trepidation. She acted as carefree as ever, taking no precautions. In fact, she went back to run on Stiff Branch Road the day after she took a header into the ditch.

Boggs refilled his glass and stared blankly at the depleted bottle. He blinked when it occurred to him that the way to test his theory was to find out the results of the ballistics test. He doubted the sheriff's department failed to conduct such a test. For investigators to ignore something so basic went beyond any known estimate of stupidity. Lame and laggard as the sheriff's men were, they had to have the results by now.

The first theory Boggs constructed on the possibility of the same weapon was that Wynne was not the killer. Although the vice captain ran off the reservation now and again, he had more sense than to use the same gun twice and give detectives one path to follow instead of two. If the results showed there were two guns, then there were probably two gunmen, each with his own designs. But then Wendy's abductor, whatever raging precedent set him in motion, might have read about the .38 and used the same caliber as subterfuge.

Boggs took a seat, took a drink, and accepted the start of a smile, for the challenge was just beginning. He now had to devise a way to get the results. Approaching the department directly promised rebuff. Boggs was a permanent persona non grata. Calling on the DA's office was also out of the question. He doubted whether the DA even remembered him—the wethead so advanced by now that he failed to recognize himself in the mirror. As for the prosecutors with whom he worked, they had long since departed for more professional settings.

Getting a dog soldier like Tinnin to assist was probably too great a risk. If he made any inquiries, it would only create suspicion, and then if questioned, he would doubtless unveil his cigarette theory and traduce Wynne in front of many opened jaws. Boggs also needed Tinnin to remain in the rear guard; he was the only working channel Boggs had into the department.

Taking a drink, the PI cast about for another source, a person on the outside but with access, someone who knew the deputies well enough to probe but with impunity. His glass stopped on the downswing. He considered the answer for a moment and then rooted through the desk debris for the phonebook.

To his surprise, his call went directly to the city desk. It happened so quickly that he swallowed hard, causing his request to sputter forth between burning gasps.

The newspaperman said, "Yeah, I'm Lee Barnes."

"Yeah, you the one what done the articles on the murders?"

There was a moment of silence. "Why?"

"You sound mighty young. You know what it's all about?" Before Barnes could answer, he went on, "Heck, s'pect you do. Leastways y'all talk like you know it all. But look here—well, it's been nagging me worse than a woman. See I read where the boy down my way was kilt with a .38 and then, come to find, so was the girl, ya know, the doctor's daughter. And it might could be I missed it somewheres, but I don't recollect y'all saying if it was the same gun."

Boggs waited, unable to detect even the sound of breathing. "Hello? Any—"

"Yeah, I'm here." The reporter paused, almost indefinitely. "Uh, no, we haven't said."

"Well, damn! Why not? They do one of them, what they call—"

"Ballistics test?"

"'At's it. They do one of them? Y'all think to ask about it?"

"Uh … I don't believe I got your name."

"The name's Harlan." He scanned the names below *The Herald Chronicle*. "Harlan Herlocker. Live out here off Garner Road."

"Well, uh, well, what's your interest in this, Mr. Herlocker?"

Boggs shouted, "Boy, you got to be reminded there's a madman on the loose. A mad-dog Negro more than likely, and our women—well, I don't aim to get all riled up. But y'all's investigators, ain't ya? Cuz we can't get nothing out of the sheriff's men. Shoot, they're as worthless as tits on a boar hog. Now don't get me wrong, I like that Carson Tinnin boy well 'nough, but if I had a nickel for every time he says, 'I don't know,' well, I'd be the high sheriff. And besides, ain't we got a right to know? Guaranteed in the U.S. Constitution and all, us White—"

"Okay, Mr., uh, Mr. Herlocker. I'll—all I can tell you is that, yes, they have done a ballistics test."

"And what'd it show? It was some sort of mad dog, wasn't it?"

"Uh, the test—" Barnes cleared his throat. "The test wouldn't show—wouldn't determine the identity of the shooter."

"Okay, and …?"

"Well, we were asked in the interest of the investigation not to release the results. Least not for a while."

"Do what now?" snapped Boggs. "You mean to tell me folks—ain't we the ones getting killed? Ain't we got a right to know what's going on? You don't hear about no deputy being kilt, now do you?"

"Well, their thinking is—"

"Whose thinkin's that now?"

"The sheriff's department. They, uh, asked us not to release the results because they don't want the murderer to know what they know."

"Run that by me one more time, son?"

"They asked us not to print the findings because they don't want to jeopardize the case. He—"

"Case?" cried Boggs. "What case is that? They don't got no case if what y'all put in the paper's right." He heard the sound of flaring nostrils.

"As I was saying, the sheriff—"

"Hold on there, partner. Just back her up a minute. If I heard right, they told you not to print it. Didn't say nothin' about telling one of your paying subscribers, did they?"

Barnes replied immediately, "What's the difference?"

"The difference?" Boggs dialed down a holler. "The difference, young man, is I got me a damn fool wife goin' 'round carryin' a loaded pistol that she ain't got no business carryin'. Gonna kill herself sure enough."

The reporter sighed audibly. "For your peace of mind then—"

"Ain't my mind. I know a coon what done it. It's that crazy wife of mine. She ain't got no mind to have no peace with. Why she had the damn thing slung inside her—"

"OKAY!" There was a long pause. "The results were inconclusive."

"Mean to tell me they don't know what everyone else knows: a colored done it?"

"That's not what I'm saying. The test—well, they couldn't perform a test because one of the bullets was too fragmented."

"Well, ain't it just like 'em to go and use inferior bullets." Having to take the questioning one step further, he asked, "Who done this test? The NAACP?"

"The SBI."

"The what now?"

"The state bureau of investigation. In James City."

"Them, huh?" He added, "It them that told you or the sheriff's men?"

"No, I called James City."

"Well, damn. You ain't no help. S'pect that fool wife of mine'll still be in an all-fire hurry to shoot herself." Boggs slammed down the receiver.

# CHAPTER NINETEEN

The jackhammer began promptly at 8 a.m. To Boggs, it sounded right outside his office window. The noise prevented him from going through the motions of a Monday morning. His gnawed no. 2 pencil flipped up through the vibrating air and plopped down on the papers scattered across his desk. He sat back, growing increasingly anxious.

The racket triggered the memory of a quiet day, one so uneventful that Boggs and his partner, A.D., had nothing better to do than count banana stalks outside the stores on Hinton Street, the main drag in the Halifax ghetto. There were seven stalks, three more than the last time they counted, meaning three more bootleggers in operation and three more minutes before the real story began, a story that pressed itself against his heart so that its beat sped his own. The recurring tale of certified lunatic Rufus Grover had a life of its own in Boggs's mind, sucking life from him like a parasite. Boggs didn't need to think of the event; the memory unfolded on its own accord.

At first the call seemed routine enough: assist a uniform patrol in apprehending a man accused of assault and public indecency. They kept within the speed limit for the three-block drive and never even considered using the strobe lights mounted in the grill. After conferring with the uniforms, Boggs and A.D. agreed to cover the rear.

No sooner had they gotten in place than Rufus Grover, his feeble mind frightened beyond belief by the police presence in front of his ramshackle house, burst out the back door. Boggs and A.D. stepped out from behind the two trees used to hang a clothesline. Only Boggs pointed a gun, his snub-nosed .38.

Boggs never managed to finish his order for the man to stop and get down on his knees. The burly man barreled into him. The two tumbled. A.D. flung himself into the fray.

Grover possessed the legendary strength of many men. The three became a furious ball tumbling over and over on itself for what seemed like a lifetime, although the official inquiry concluded that the struggle lasted only two minutes. Boggs never realized he had lost control of his revolver until he heard the shots. His choke hold wrung the madman's thick neck, even after the discharge, even after the man went limp. Boggs had to be pulled away before he strangled the unconscious Grover. There the story ended: A.D.'s life for the apprehension of a man who fornicated with an abandoned couch on a nearby curb and then beat up the three women and two men who tried to stop him.

But that wasn't the whole story. There was a point beyond which memory and words couldn't—or wouldn't—go, where the telling stopped dead. Boggs never wished that he had been the one to take the bullet. He wished for only one thing: that something else in his life would have more meaning than death, the death of his partner.

As Boggs emerged from his memories, he jerked back. A man stood before him. The unannounced visitor wasn't so much bony or what country folk called "spindly" as trim. He had a neat, well-designed figure packed with a compelling presence, a seldom-seen level of self-assurance that demanded focus and became the center of whatever space it occupied. Everything about the man spoke of cool confidence: his dress, a well-tailored khaki suit that said almost as much about him as about the so-called well-dressed lawyers in town, and not only those who scraped together a living from court appointments but also the ostensibly prosperous ones. The color of the man's horn-rimmed glasses was an even match for the corkscrew curls of his hair. His face was lean with a distinguished cut running from cheek to jaw. There was something else about the face. It looked as though it had never known trouble, never had to reel at the sight of itself, and never seen how ugly such a handsome face as his could actually be. His expression was too alert and too serious around his almond-shaped eyes. He appeared too cocksure to know that no matter how cautious and calculated his plans, an act as simple as crossing the street could part the curtains and show him for what he was—a man like any other, capable of the despicable, the heinous, the ignoble. Yet the smile parting his clean, white, perfectly aligned teeth said he believed himself capable of none of this, that as victor of himself he was entitled to be amused by others, so he could smile as if he invented the smile.

"I knocked, but there was no answer." The man extended a manicured hand. "I'm Simon Sasser. If you have a minute, I'd like to talk to you."

"Well, I'll be. Wendy's beau in the flesh." Smiling a crooked smile, Boggs stood to shake his hand. Sasser continued to squeeze after Boggs let up. "Ya know, I sorta been expectin' you. Sit down. What can I do for you? Been in town long?"

Sasser dusted off the client chair before sitting. "I've only just arrived," he said without a trace of an accent. He propped a burnished brown loafer over his left knee. He was about to speak but turned toward the upsurge of racket outside.

"Ya get used to it," said Boggs. "It's what we call progress—puttin' up a marble monument to our Confederate dead."

"How can—" He raised his voice. "How can you get anything done?"

"Do something; that's progress. Now what brings you here, Mister Sasser?"

"I've just come from Dr. Allen's office—"

"Feelin' a might irregular, were you?"

Sasser's smooth brow wrinkled slightly. "I don't follow. What do you mean?"

"Ain't come down with somethin', have you?"

"No, I was there—"

"So how's Doc Allen? Still smoking better than a pack?"

The man nodded tentatively. "Yes, he was smoking. He seemed very preoccupied, very—"

"What about?"

"Why, naturally, the death—"

"Death? Looks to me like that's what a doctor's s'posta think about. Ain't like we're possum. No such thing as playin' dead." He added, "Or is there?"

Boggs's self-satisfied smirk further confused the visitor. "Mr. Boggs, what exactly are you trying to say?"

"You mean about doctors? Now, I can sure tell you about them. That's one helluva protection racket they've got going. Only they don't know a whole lot when it comes down to the protectin'. I believe they have 'em study business 'stead of medicine. Just think about it now. You ever seen a doctor who didn't know how to spend his money? Now, what we got there is one pennywise bunch, and our poor bodies is the pound foolish. I'll tell you what, I ain't never seen a poor one. But a sorry-ass one, oh, hell yeah."

"I don't doubt that you have." The visitor cleared his throat. "Let me ask you—you are the private detective the doctor hired, aren't you? I haven't—"

"Yeah, that be me. Why?"

"Well, the reason I've come—"

"Yeah, what is the reason? Ya know, we're kinda in the middle of nowhere. We ain't even halfway to somewheres else." Boggs pressed the broad smile against his teeth.

Raising his voice, Sasser said, "Let me finish, and I'll tell—"

"Heck, yeah. Go right ahead and finish. Don't mean to be butting in all the time. It's just the way us folks round here is. Don't mean no disrespect or nothin'. Just being friendly the best we know how."

Sasser delivered a steady look that silenced the room, even the outside. "I've come to offer my assistance, Mr. Boggs. In my meeting with Dr. Allen, we came up with the idea of offering my assistance to you. I want to help. Now, I understand—"

"Well, I'll be damned. Is that what you're here for?" His mouth opened as if he were braying. "Tell you what, Mr. Sasser, I got a way with me sometimes. Seems like I just come right out and say what's on my mind." He crowded the desk. "And the only thing I gotta say is shit. Here you come all the way from the slope side of the Earth just to offer your assistance. Well, I wouldn't buy that if it were gold. Why don't you just back on up and tell me why you come in the first place? How'd you know she was dead?"

The question sparked laughter, which the resumption of the jackhammer ended. His voice raised, he explained that he and Wendy had arranged this visit in the latter part of June. He had written that he would be in Norfolk on business and how he had a week before he had to return to Asia. Wendy had replied that he should come to Greensburg as soon as possible, even if it were just for a few days. "We were in love, Mr. Boggs. I was going to ask her to marry me."

No sooner had Sasser finished than Boggs asked, "You American?"

Smiling, he replied, "Born, but not bred. I grew up in Singapore. But I came back to matriculate at Cal Poly."

Boggs gave his weighty chin a massage and then rolled his coated tongue over his front teeth, punctuating the move with a smack. "Got a driver's license?"

"An international one, yes."

"Boy, they pull you and see some fancy paper, they're gonna haul your ass off to jail. The police here have what you might call a vendetta against cars. They just love to pull 'em. Fancier they are, the quicker they get pulled. And when they get a holt of that international thingamajig of yours, they're gonna think it's a restricted license for DUI in Singapore or wherever. Man, I can see 'em now, just a-conferring."

Still smiling, Sasser said, "Then why don't you chauffeur me around town? You are for hire, aren't you?"

"You got a business card?"

Complying without any sign of annoyance, Sasser removed a thin but long brown leather wallet from an inner coat pocket. He withdrew a heavily starched white card and passed it. Boggs held it lightly with his thumbs and index fingers as he examined it. The card read: Trimet Ex-Im Ltd. It listed addresses in Singapore and Hong Kong, in addition to telephone numbers, telex numbers, and cable letters.

"Exactly what is it y'all import, export, Mr. Sasser?"

"Basically soft goods: textiles, fabric, synthetics."

"Hmm, they do some of that round here."

Sasser recrossed his long legs. He folded his hands on his lap. He waited a moment and said, "Now assuming my credentials are in order, I'd like once again to offer my assistance. From what Dr. Allen tells me, you've made a connection between Wendy's murder and one that preceded it by a few weeks."

"By days or a day." Boggs stared at the visitor who didn't avoid the scrutiny. "You know this neck of the woods?"

"This is my first visit."

"You don't know it, you best leave it." He added, "Ever in the service, the United States Armed Forces?"

"No." A sigh flared through his thin nose. "And let's hope this is your last question." He paused. "I was 4-F or H or whatever they call it. I injured a knee playing intramural football."

Boggs sat back and folded his arms. "You'd be about Vietnam age, I s'pect."

Sasser ignored the remark. "About this connection you've made. The Blake boy—"

"Y'all say 'boy' in Singapore?"

"The Blake man then. From what the doctor told me, he was involved in drugs. I know Wendy wasn't. So what connection could there be?"

"She seen who killed the boy." Boggs waited for a reaction. There was none. "But she never knew what she seen. She was running and come up on Blake and the killer. This was before Blake caught his."

Sasser broke a brief silence. "You have any suspects?"

"Nary a one." He shrugged. "'Cept maybe you. It just don't seem a coincidence you bein' here." After a moment he added, "You a gamblin' man, Mister Sasser?"

"I have in the past, yes."

Boggs opened the desk drawer and removed a pack of cards, held together with a rubber band. "I've got … I believe I've got forty-seven here. Let's play poker. Game I call Cowboys. Queens or better to open."

"What are the stakes?"

"Ya leave town if ya lose. I tell ya what I know if I lose."

With hesitation, Sasser said, "Deal."

The first five hands went by the wayside. Boggs reshuffled each time. On the sixth, Sasser closed him down with three queens. "I suppose that means—"

The jackhammer stopped.

He lowered his voice. "Means I'm your partner."

Boggs laughed in derision.

# CHAPTER TWENTY

As he walked beside the nurse, Boggs once again tried to detect the smell of formaldehyde; why he couldn't puzzled him since he always associated the suffocating odor with medicine. Perhaps Dr. Allen practiced another brand of medicine, one that truly abided by the pledge to do no harm.

Any attempt at conversation with his escort, the spinster nurse, was a simultaneously humbling and vexing exercise. More often than not, she wouldn't even reply to such probing queries as, "It's a nice day, isn't it?"

As was the case on his first visit, all the examination rooms were empty, and the door to the last room on the left was open. With a brusque wave of her unfurling hand, the nurse ushered him into the office.

"Hey, doc, how's tricks?" asked Boggs, entering. The thick smoke assaulted him immediately. He coughed and took the same chair as before, making no effort to shake the doctor's hand. He didn't see a pack of cigarettes on the desk, but the ashtray overflowed with ashes and butts.

Dr. Allen wore a white lab coat whose blandness made the red of his silk tie and the blue of his starched shirt all the more colorful. With his liver-spotted hands folded on the desk pad, he stared at Boggs for a moment and said, "Detective Boggs, good to see you." He unfastened his hands, placing them on the armrest of his large chair, which squeaked when he sat back. "So how're you coming with the case?"

"Movin' faster than a herd of turtles."

"I'm sorry, did you say a herd of turtles?"

"It was a joke, doc. Just somethin' to lighten the mood."

He steepled his hands and then entwined his finger. He looked at Boggs, expressionless.

Before the silence became too burdensome, Boggs said, "Well, here's what we got. They killed your daughter because she saw who killed Billy Blake. You remember the Blake killin' down in Random?"

The doctor's watery eyes performed a peculiar task: remaining steady even as he nodded in response to Boggs's question.

"Well, that killin' had to do with drugs. No question about it. Now, I know Wendy never did any, but she had the misfortune of runnin' down that way. We think that she might coulda seen Blake and the killer or killers. Maybe they were arguin' over a drug deal or somethin'. And she apparently witnessed it. She didn't know she saw it. She was focused on her runnin', right? But even so, she became a liability, a huge liability. She could identify the killers. They had to get rid of her."

Although slow to respond, Allen asked, "So why not just kill her? Why do all those abominable things that they did?"

Boggs frowned, shaking his head. "Don't know. I'm sorry to say, but I just don't know. But it sorta gives you some insight into what kind of people the killers are."

Allen arranged his bifocals to better see the detective. He spoke in a slow monotone. "That's what I want, Mr. Boggs. I want to know who these people are. I want to know what kind of animal could do what they did to my little girl. I have to know. Do I make myself clear?"

"Yes, sir." Boggs leaned forward a bit. "Doctor Allen, we'll get these guys. Believe me—I will get these guys. We're makin' progress."

"Would that you could."

"Sir?"

"Get these bastards."

"Right." Boggs paused. "Which sorta brings me to why I'm here. It's about this guy, Simon Sasser. What can you tell me about 'im? He showed up at my office yesterday, said he had spoken with you."

"Simon Sasser?" Allen said the name as if he had never heard it until now. He mused for a long moment. "Yes, the boyfriend. I suppose he's a little too old to be calling him the boyfriend. Wendy's admirer, let's say. A nice fellow from the looks of him. Very proper and decent. Showed me a love letter he'd received from Wendy inviting him down for a few days. When I read it, it was like hearing her voice all over again." He stared off to the side.

After a moment Boggs asked, "Well, what do you know about this guy?"

"Very little, I'm afraid." He added, "Only what he's told me. But he seems very keen on helping you with this case. How will—"

"That's another can of worms."

"I don't understand."

"I don't trust the man. I don't trust coincidences, and here he comes right smack in the middle of a big coincidence. Boyfriend arrives to avenge death of his sweetheart." He groused. "I just don't know. It all fits too ..." He let the thought trail off.

"Well, they were corresponding. That must stand for something, don't you think?"

"I don't know, doc. The guy's slick as whale sperm."

"And how slick is that?" said a voice in the doorway.

The doctor's eyes rose over Boggs, who turned his head. There stood Simon Sasser.

The spinster nurse squeezed past Sasser, her high cheeks flushed. Arms akimbo, she said, "Dr. Allen, I told this gentleman you were in a meetin' with Mr. Boggs, and he barged right on down here anyway. Said somethin' about a ten o'clock appointment."

The doctor displayed a supportive smile. "That's all right, Miss Marsh. I'll take it from here."

The nurse narrowed her eyes as she glared at Sasser. She departed with a less-than-dignified grunt.

Allen apologized to Sasser for having forgotten the appointment and said, "I believe you've met Mr. Boggs."

Boggs straightened not so much because of the introduction but in surprise at how the doctor's behavior had changed. All of a sudden, he seemed more alert, more of a presence amid the office surroundings.

"Yes, yesterday," said Sasser, whose navy blue poplin suit conveyed the semblance of a solicitor about to make his closing arguments to the jury.

Allen extended his hand, gesturing for Sasser to have the empty seat beside Boggs.

Once settled, Sasser said, "So, detective, just how slick is whale sperm?"

"Slicker than even owl shit."

"First whales, now owls. What will you think of next, partner?"

Dr. Allen said, "Detective Boggs was just briefing me on his findings. Seems my daughter witnessed a crime, which persuaded the criminal to kill my Wendy lest she identify him." He added in a distant voice, "One crime begets another."

"If that's the case, it seems to me we have to solve the first crime before we can solve the second," said Sasser.

Boggs leaned on the armrest and cast a baleful look at Sasser. "Tell me, Mr. Sasser, what really—what's your interest in all this?"

Without hesitation, Sasser professed his love for Wendy Allen. "Dr. Allen, your daughter was unlike anyone I have ever met. I was deeply in love with her. I've never been so charmed by a woman. I felt transcendent when I was with her. In fact, this business in Norfolk was arranged solely so I could see her again. And I can't express the sorrow I feel at having lost her. I'll do everything in my power to see her murderer brought to justice."

Boggs said, "Nice speech. So tell us: what is in your power to do?"

"My mission is your mission is Dr. Allen's mission. There's nothing that the doctor and I wouldn't do to help you catch the killer. In fact, we're going down to the sheriff's office this morning. We want answers. Isn't that right, Dr. Allen?"

The doctor response was to smile benignly.

Boggs squared his shoulders to face Sasser. "Mr. Sasser, bein' as how you ain't from around here, I'll give you the Sunday school version—don't be pissin' on my leg and tellin' me it's rainin'."

Sasser smiled and said, "What're you trying to say?"

"Gentlemen, please," said the doctor. "Don't we have enough to concern us than to have some petty squabble?"

"My apologies, doc."

Allen opened his desk drawer and took out a pack of Kool cigarettes. After offering a cigarette to his visitors, he lit one with a plastic lighter. He inhaled deeply and shot the smoke off to his right. Stifling a cough, he said, "So, detective, what's our next move?"

Boggs said to Sasser, "You got the letter you showed to the doc yesterday?"

"Not with me, no."

"Damn, that's convenient. You suppose you could drop it off at my office later to—"

Boggs stopped himself. He had an appointment with Sally Allen later on, and for reasons he couldn't explain, he didn't want to tell the doctor about it. "No, I'll tell you what. Can you drop it off tomorrow mornin'?"

"Why's the letter so important?"

"Oh … let's just call it a piece of the puzzle."

"The puzzle?"

Even the doctor suspended his smoking in anticipation of the answer.

"Yeah, the puzzle … just who are you."

Sasser looked to Allen for help. He visibly slumped in his chair when Allen said, "Well, who are you?"

# CHAPTER TWENTY-ONE

Sally Allen was indeed common, but she possessed an uncommon talent. Boggs couldn't remember the exact sequence after she came into the office. They had arranged to meet at 4:15 p.m. when she finished work at Mayberry, an ice cream parlor. He sipped bourbon in the stillness preceding an afternoon storm. Twenty minutes late, Sally arrived like a rock through a window. Her eyes refracted the candy stripes on her skirt and bib. Because of a deep tan, her white blouse appeared in the foreground, leaving room between her clothes and body for his imagination to prey. The tan along with the uniform put on such a production that Boggs was willing to bet she sold a lot of ice cream.

Within minutes of her arrival, the sky loosed the rain and thunder. Quickly knocking back his drink, he suggested they both have one and wait out the storm. To be on the safe side, he put the desk between them. She relaxed and crossed her legs the way a man would. To avoid the temptation of peeking, he pushed his chair back against the wall.

Sometime, somewhere between then and now, she revealed her fantasy about doing it with a private eye: to be hidden under the desk and feel the musky air drawing her deeper into the crevice of his legs. "That from some movie?" he recalled asking but couldn't remember her response. Although Sally directed him to look officious with pen in hand, Boggs could only think of the thunder and lightning happening in two places at once.

"Didn't take as long as I thought," said Sally, standing and smoothing her outfit. "I mean, for someone your age."

Smiling, Boggs placed his hands on her waist.

"No," she said, outraged and shocked. "Don't do that."

Any contact he initiated would sully her, he thought. He pulled up his pants and walked to the window. His back to her, he arranged his clothes. Her talent was legitimate even if she led an illegitimate life. He wondered how she behaved at home, at the dinner table with mom and dad—probably prim and proper, a return to that other life of devoted daughter.

While the last of the tempest passed, he poured another drink. She finished what she had, relaxed as ever, as if nothing had just happened. Boggs felt uneasy. She had taken control of him, and she could do it again. He knew it even as he tried to deny it. He knew too that she was well aware of what she was doing. The question he couldn't answer was why. Still, pleasure was pleasure, so why ask why.

At his insistence, they left. Her smile broke, and her mouth acquired a peevish set. Still, despite the sudden rush, she remained quiet, closing the office door without knowing or caring whether it was locked. Boggs wanted her to show him all the locations in the Random area where she had dropped Wendy.

Besides Stiff Branch Road, there were McKenney, Boydton Plank, and Cherry Hill, all side roads that paralleled Highway 1 or intersected with it. Sally said her sister avoided the highway because of traffic. For convenience, Boggs headed south on the main road. Just south of the community of Dewitt, he turned onto Stiff Branch.

Thunderclaps rumbled behind them. Ozone imbued the air. The renewed splurge of life after the storm buoyed Boggs. The countryside thrilled with movement: red clay rills whipping like snakes alongside the road, ribbons of mist rising from their imprisonment in the pavement and ponds, trees and cornfields swaying as one after a sun-beaten day of torpidity. Boggs breathed deeply, feeling he was moving with it all. Enlivened, he glanced at Sally. She crowded the passenger door, looking out the open window with her hands tucked between her legs. In the silence, Boggs sensed a change, a change so in keeping with the faint angel-hair whorls trimming her ears and upper lip. She seemed a child, surrendered like a child as though she knew Boggs would get her safely to where they were going. He would handle any problem, from negotiating the rain-slick curves to swerving around fallen limbs.

At the intersection with Boydton Plank, he turned east. He went as far as the Hico store, one of the many shaky, clapboard filling stations dotting the county roads. Boggs surveyed the roadside, noting the three community dumpsters across the way. He asked Sally if she had ever seen Trollinger's old

Plymouth or the red pickup over there. He showed her photographs of Blake, Trollinger, and Wynne. He explained that Blake had let his hair grow since the high school graduation picture and that Wynne's attire might have been a little less social. Sally shook her head almost before she looked. She asked for money to buy a drink. With an edge to his voice, he insisted she examine the photos. She splayed them as if a poker hand and shrugged. He gave her fifty cents and said he wanted the change.

While she was inside, he went across the street. The tall rusty containers overflowed with garbage. A sour stench hovered over the littered area to the delight of yellow jackets and sweat bees. Giving the dumpsters a wide berth, he went around back, swatting at gnats. Strewn from far back into the woods to where he stood were torn plastic bags with their guts disgorged, castaway tires, broken furniture, papers of all description, cans, bottles, and plastic. *A scientist ought to study this*, he thought.

"Find anything?" asked Sally when he returned. She sat on the hood, her dress hiked high. She handed him the change with a staged smile.

"Let's go."

Heading south on McKenney to Garner Road, he leaned toward the window to let the air dislodge the lingering scent of fermented garbage. At the intersection, he swung the Malibu to the side. As he got out, a pickup passed, its bill-capped driver raising his index finger from the wheel to acknowledge him. Boggs nodded to return the greeting. He walked to the front of the car on the lookout for something other than woods and fields tall with tasseled corn. The only landmark was a dilapidated tobacco barn that briars and honeysuckle were ready to swallow whole. "See any—" He swung around. Sally was still in the car. "Get out here and look around."

She pushed the door open with her foot. She stood, looked this way and that, and announced, "Nope, nothing."

"You sure?"

"I only drove her down here," she whined. "I never looked."

"Well, try looking now." It seemed impossible that she was the same person who had taken control of him. He folded his arms and waited, watching her so intently that he scarcely noticed the three cars that passed in the westbound lane.

After a moment, she said, "I don't know what it is I'm supposed to see."

"Something that's not here now that was then." He stared at her in bewilderment. "C'mon, get in."

On the way to Stiff Branch, Sally tossed the empty soda bottle.

"Hey, wasn't there a deposit on that?"

"I dunno."

"There was a nickel deposit on that."

"I want to go home."

"Suits me."

Boggs accelerated down a steep hill. The car gained speed even after he let up on the gas. The needle bumped against the sixty mark when an explosion sent the Malibu hurdling out of control. It happened so fast that the car teetered over the shoulder before Boggs ever attempted to brake. The front end popped up, and the car plunged down an embankment. Boggs looked at Sally, saw her open mouth, and then heard her scream. In an instant, he was falling headlong toward her, into the scream.

The Malibu overturned before broadsiding a tall pine.

When Boggs came to, he was on his back in the grass, feeling as if the embankment was pulling him by the feet. Something black encroached against his right eye. He blinked. The black was still there, throbbing. Then a second point above the eye announced its presence; it ate its way down, delivering lightning cracks deep into his skull. He strained to lift his right arm but stopped when he became aware of someone caterwauling, "I wanna go home!" A raised voice rose up against the wail. With a grunt dying in his dry constricted throat, Boggs rolled on his side. All he could make out was a vague image of one, maybe two, very short people. His right eye flashed shut when a stream of blood swept over it. He damned the flow with the palm of his hand. Through a painful squint he saw Sally. She was a blur of red, her face red, her blouse redder still. A kneeling man held her against his white shirt. He too was red, his hands red, his hair … Sasser! It was Simon Sasser.

# CHAPTER TWENTY-TWO

"How is she?" asked Boggs.

A dark suit gave Sasser a funereal appearance. He said that Dr. Allen feared the nineteen stitches around Sally's mouth might leave scars. A greater, far more unreasonable fear prompted the doctor to send his daughter to the coastal town of New Bern to stay with relatives. Sasser was quiet for a moment. "I trust you feel better than you look?"

A white short-sleeve shirt and wide diamond-patterned tie were only minor elements in Boggs's distinguished appearance. He had a two-inch stitched gash under his right eye and a larger one above it. The eye itself, cast in a reddish purple, was swollen shut. The codeine painkillers made it possible to dispense with the sling for his right shoulder. Even so, what use he had of his arm was restricted; it moved as one crooked, recalcitrant piece. Worse than the injuries was the news that his Malibu was beyond repair. As a temporary, very temporary, replacement, he stuffed himself into a rusty red Falcon station wagon with a Save the Whales bumper sticker. The engine sounded like loose change, and the vehicle itself gave the impression it would go as far as loose change. For the thrill of driving from zero to sixty miles per hour in twenty minutes, he paid five hundred dollars. After his insurance agent asked if he wanted collision, he decided to charge the totaled car and the wagon to Dr. Allen.

"I'll be fine when Allen pays up." He fidgeted in his high-back office desk chair, unable to find a comfortable position. He finally settled on the right armrest with a slight grimace. "Costin' him a sight more than he bargained for."

"The cost will go higher." Sasser leaned back in the client chair.

Boggs turned his good eye on him.

His hands folded, Sasser said, "It wasn't an accident."

"The trooper ought to know a blowout." He paused reflectively. "But now that you mention it, he didn't say what caused the blowout." He paused again, "Hell, it's these damn drugs they give me. I should've asked."

Without a trace of repentance or an explanation as to why, Sasser said he had followed Boggs and Sally Tuesday afternoon. He indicated that he had kept a quarter of a mile between them, at least until Boggs suddenly accelerated. When Sasser topped the steep hill, he heard what sounded like the report of a rifle, coming from a hedgerow on the right. In the second it took to look over and back, the Malibu was out of control.

With a grimace, Boggs shifted his weight onto the left arm pad. "Why didn't you tell the trooper?"

"I don't need their help."

"Saw where the newspaper said you was from Washington."

"Arlington," Sasser corrected.

"Amounts to the same thing."

"Not quite."

"Well, just where is it you're from, Mr. Sasser?"

"For the moment, Arlington will do."

"Plan on stayin' long? You do have the import-export business to tend to."

"Oh, that reminds me. I have that letter Wendy wrote. Care to see it?"

Boggs gave a tired wave, saying, "I was just yankin' your chain ... but—" He paused. "On second thought, yeah, let me see it."

Sasser removed a folded pink sheet from an inside coat pocket and passed it. Boggs unfolded the letter creating six creased boxes. The writing was neat and large. Boggs read the ten sentences in a matter of a minute and then considered the smile on Sasser's face, trying to interpret it. Was the man gloating about what was clearly a woman in love?

"And you let Dr. Allen see this?" he said, handing back the letter.

"I have nothing to hide. I meant what I said about Wendy the other day."

"S'pose so." A moment passed before he asked to see the letter again. He turned up the top half of the pink sheet. "This is dated the sixth. Where are the ones for the seventh, eighth, and ninth?"

"I never received any letters after that one."

Boggs gave him a sideways glance. "The doc says she wrote you every day."

"Not on those days, she didn't." He paused and then added, "Look, what's with all these questions about the letter? She wrote. I wrote. We talked. For God's sake, we were in love."

Squinting, Boggs pressed his fingertips against his right temple. "Yeah, all right. I get it. You're in love." He winced, shutting his good eye. "So, uh … so what happened when you and Allen went to see the sheriff's boys?"

After a grunt of disgust, Sasser said, "They said they couldn't discuss as it was under investigation."

"Not even with the victim's father?" Boggs tried to muzzle a laugh.

"Apparently least of all with him."

"Those boys have a certain way of doing things, don't they?"

"I was absolutely speechless."

In an effort to get comfortable, Boggs wiggled in his chair and then suddenly flinched, his back shooting straight up as if under the influence of an electric current. It took a moment for him to settle back in his chair. He said, "Okay, so let's get back to business. What I want to know is, where is it you're from? Washington? Arlington? Singapore? Maybe plain old Greensburg?"

Sasser stiffened but kept his voice level. "Boggs, we can either work together, or I can go it alone. With your help, though, I should be out of here sooner than later. Perhaps within a week. But a week or two or a month—I don't care. I'm going to find out who killed them."

"Them?"

"Yes, them. You know as well as I that if you find Blake's murderer, you'll find Wendy's." With a less-than-ingenuous smile, he raised a finger to make another point. "But then again, perhaps we shouldn't work together. Whoever shot at you will doubtless try again. And I'd rather be behind you than beside you."

All along, Boggs felt that he had locked himself into some desperate agreement with the killer or killers, an agreement that resembled a wager, but a wager in a singular game of chance that, once begun, could not stop. Boggs had known the stakes would rise, but until now, he never thought that he would be a chip tossed on the table. To assess the threat, he had to know who sat across from him at the table. The more he considered Wynne, the less likely a candidate the vice captain was. The murder of Wendy Allen didn't point to a resourceful cop who would kidnap, rape, and kill a girl just because she happened to be jogging past him on a country road and might have seen him talking to a young man. So with Wynne only a remote possibility, Boggs felt he need look no further than in front of him at the man in the expensive suit who exuded self-confidence instead of sweat, who was so self-assured sitting there with an almost mocking smile, probably thinking that he was dealing with some rube who didn't know any better than to accept each and every story: the concoction about the prearranged visit with Wendy, and then the forged love letter, and now this one about a sniper. Yes, it could very well be this man, so certain of himself that he dared to surface after the killing for the thrill of watching a hayseed private eye blunder into and entangle himself in the intricacies he wove.

"Know how to use a gun?" asked Boggs.

"I'm an experienced hunter." When Boggs arched his brow over his good eye, Sasser added, "Africa, Alaska, the Rockies. Shall I go on?"

"Tell me about this sniper."

"I went back there yesterday." Sasser rose and moved a linen handkerchief from his pant pocket. He unfolded it very carefully. Bedded in the center was a spent shell. He set it on the desk as if it were fragile. When Boggs reached for it, Sasser held up his hand. "Fingerprints."

"You want to testify in court you found it?"

Sasser sat back down and gestured to Boggs to take it.

"Didn't think so." Using the handkerchief, he picked up the brass casing. He cocked his head to examine its markings: .30–06. While Boggs folded the handkerchief back up, Sasser said that he found it at the edge of the hedgerow and that there was a field road that went back about a mile to an abandoned farmhouse. "The sniper went back there after the shooting."

"Anything lead out from there?"

"Two narrow—well, you could call them paths. I didn't find any tracks, so I didn't bother following them. But I did find some very good impressions on the field road. It is my guess that it was something large, like a Jeep or a truck with an unusual tread, almost—"

"Like knobs?"

"Yes, how'd you know?"

"I reckon you want me to keep this?" Without waiting for an answer, Boggs placed the shell in the desk drawer. He rolled his chair back. "The way I see it, this Jeep or truck passed you and me on Garner Road. The guy pulls off onto the homestead road and sets up shop. Soon as he shot the tire out, he hightailed it back behind the house. That how you're figurin' it?"

"Yes. The shooter couldn't have known where you were going. He had to be following you, but once he saw where you were going, he jumped out ahead of you and set up in the brushes."

"But you were followin' me. Was he behind you or between you and me?"

"There were cars between us. I didn't see anyone pass … that is, when you were moving. When you stopped there on … what was it? McKenney? When you stopped alongside the road, I didn't count how many passed you. Maybe—what?—less than a half dozen passed you."

"You recall seeing a red pickup?"

Sasser didn't answer at first. He looked down for a moment and then up. "No, why? Is that our vehicle?"

"Our?"

"The shooter's?"

Boggs said, "Had to be one helluva shot. I was doin' better than sixty when the tire blew. You really gotta lead somethin' movin' that fast. Think you coulda hit me?"

Sasser nodded calmly. "But then I wouldn't have come down from my position to pull you out."

"If ya had—just theorizin' now—but if you had, no one woulda suspected you for the shooting."

"You already have."

Boggs waited a moment. "Think whoever done it is drivin' around with muddy tires from that homestead road?"

"I doubt it."

"Me too. Folks clean their tires before they even think to wash their cars. But ya know, this shooter had to know Garner Road pretty good. You can't even see a lot of the old roads until you're up on 'em. How'd he know that road was there?" He paused and cringed as he adjusted his position. "Maybe it's these pills I'm taking but—but I don't recollect you sayin' where you was from?"

"Arlington, remember?"

"And, uh … I don't recollect you saying why you were following me?"

Sasser smiled. "To see where you were going. What else?"

"Winning a little hand of Cowboys don't entitle you to tail me."

"Well, trouble sure seems to follow you—"

The door opened, interrupting Sasser. He stiffened. The change in his demeanor brought a wry smile to Boggs's face. It was the first time Sasser appeared to lose control; it was a good sign. With a nod, Boggs told Deputy Tinnin to come in; he was welcome.

Once Boggs laid eyes on Tinnin's loose-fitting bib overalls and dirty T-shirt, he shot at glance at Sasser in the hopes this buttoned-up, squared-away visitor would display some kind of gesture to indicate he disliked and disapproved a bumpkin in his presence. Boggs was sure the tobacco juice seeping out the corner of a ridiculous simper would extract a reaction. But it didn't, not so much as a trace of a grimace.

Instead of testing a sore knee, Boggs remained seated and made introductions. He refrained from telling Tinnin that Sasser was Wendy's alleged beau, saying only that he and Sasser were just discussing the Allen case. Neither Tinnin nor Sasser attempted to shake hands.

"You a lawyer?" asked Tinnin, who closed the door and approached the desk, carrying an empty McDonald's coffee cup.

"No, he come out of Christian charity to help in the investigation."

Tinnin came up behind the second client chair. "A friend of the doctor's then?"

"Something like that."

"Tell you what, Boggs, you ain't lookin' so good."

"The eye's worse than a pee hole in a snow bank."

"S'pect so. But look here, got some news for you." Tinnin cut his eyes to Sasser.

"He's all right. Ain't ya, Mr. Sasser?"

The deputy nodded and spit in his cup. After wiping his mouth with the back of his hand, he said, "Don't reckon you heard. They done got Trollinger. Died last night at Central. Said it was a drug overdose."

Boggs looked at Sasser when he said, "Didn't give that boy much of a chance of gettin' to trial." He paused. "That makes three, 'less the sheriff has a mind to depart from this world."

"He's in—" With his fingertips Tinnin caught a bit of dark drool. "He's—they've taken him out of the coronary unit. Restin' easy, they say."

"Mr. Sasser here believes I might could be number four."

Sasser asked, "Who's Trollinger?"

Boggs half smiled. "Hmm, thought you'd know. He's—was Blake's drug partner. But tell the deputy your theory."

Sasser let his eyes run up and down the standing figure. "Simply put, I don't think Boggs's accident was an accident."

"Hear that? No 'mister' or nothing, just 'Boggs.'" He glanced back at Sasser. "We've come to be good friends in the short time we've known each other, haven't we?"

"Weren't no accident, what was it?" asked Tinnin.

"Say," Boggs said to Sasser.

Sasser's posture was now formal, shoes planted on the floor, forearms atop but not resting on the chair arms. "From what—I found a spent shell casing out there. I went back yesterday and found a shell, a rifle shell. I think someone shot the tire out."

"You reckon he knows Wynne?" asked Boggs.

Before Tinnin could answer, Sasser asked who Wynne was.

Boggs ignored him and continued to look at Tinnin. The deputy shoved his chew to the far side and shook his head ever so slightly.

"Damn it, who's Wynne?"

Although Boggs was uncertain if Sasser pretended not to know the vice captain, he figured he had little to lose if the deputy divulged the purported mystery of the franchiser and the role of Billy, Trollinger, and Mary Jane Henson. He said to Tinnin, "Give 'im an earful. And don't leave out the part about the cigarette butt."

To Boggs's surprise, Sasser never gave any indication that he found the cigarette theory preposterous and asked only one question at the conclusion of Tinnin's tale. "So the only one alive now is this Mary Jane Henson?"

"Bet her young little butt has long since gone from this little burg," said Boggs.

Tinnin fitted his hands inside the bib. "You'da thought, but nope. Heard she was snappin' open beers down at the French Quarter."

"Oh, now there's a good spot for her," said Boggs. "Probably hook up with another dealer."

# CHAPTER TWENTY-THREE

Turning onto the dirt and gravel road leading to the Blake residence, Tinnin slowed the gray cruiser to a purring crawl. Lightning bugs spotted the start of twilight with their short circuits, almost saying look here ... and here ... over here ... look over here at how the homestead has deteriorated. Will had let a dozen head of Angus chew through the cornfield on the far side of the north pond; he would pay dearly for hay if he didn't sell the stock before winter. The grass between the south pond and the white house was tall enough to invite snakes. Will would have to use a bush-hog or burn it back. Beyond the line of forty-year-old cedars, from the far end of which came the infernal call of bobwhites, Tinnin saw that the lugs of the tobacco plants had been pulled. But if Will kept on with drinking the way everyone said he was, the deputy wondered if the cured crop would ever get to auction.

When Tinnin swung behind the house, he stopped the car before he intended to, boggled by the sight of the two buzzards hanging upside down from a water oak. Neither lore nor logic applied. The deputy didn't know what to make of it. Finally, he eased the car closer to the house, parked, and pushed himself out. A fetid smell pinched his nose. He didn't have to look to know it came from the chicken house.

Stooping with a grunt, he reached back inside for his clipboard and walkie-talkie. Since Will had called the office, Tinnin had to fill out a formal complaint. Blake was the fourth victim of what the lieutenant called "The Eggheads," probably just a bunch of kids cutting up one last time before school started. They first belted the post office with eggs, then The Store, and then Shine Walker's Quonset hut.

A specter-thin silhouette settled behind the screen door. Tinnin called out, "Evenin'." Agnes unfastened the latch and held the door open. She seemed shorter and thinner than the deputy remembered. The only curve in her sleeveless blouse and jeans was the sway of her back. Her clothes weren't nearly as worn as her face, which in the kitchen light shone with a sweaty film.

The room was as hot as a depot stove. A large blue pot sat atop the pale blue flame of the gas range. Mason jars stood as parade soldiers on the adjoining counter. Tinnin asked, "What're you fixin' to put up?"

"Beans."

*The last of the beans*, Tinnin thought. Beans black with bug holes—no amount of Sevin dust was capable of preventing the blemishes. Time, not insecticide, settled the perennial dispute between bug and bean, and the bug won out, causing the last picking to be both the easiest and the hardest because the spots had to be carved out with a paring knife.

Agnes motioned to a chair at the kitchen table. She took the seat opposite him. "You here about the eggs?"

"Yes, ma'am," he replied, almost apologetically.

"Well, there ain't nothin' to it. Will only done it to complain. He halfway expected y'all not to respond."

"Where is he?" The deputy eyed Will's yellowish upper dentures on the checkered tablecloth.

"Yonder on the porch. Passed out cold from the grape brandy Shine give 'im."

Tinnin flicked the edge of the white complaint form on his clipboard.

"Misriz Blake, you been knowin' me—your family been knowin' mine a right good while now, and you know yourself my daddy's got a place like this. But, ma'am, this place of yours is getting plum' run down. Now I don't mean no disrespect. Only a place like this can sure enough go to the dogs. You and Will, you just can't be taking it like this, this long."

"Carson, you ain't tellin' me nothing what I don't already know." She pressed her knotty hands together, pressed so hard the praying hands trembled. Tinnin saw just how thin-skinned her hands were, an unpleasant sight in that it reminded him of his deceased mother whose skim-milk-blue coloring seemed to expose veins and bones.

Agnes drew air with a faint wheeze. "Billy was our last. Like a last chance. And forgettin' takes as much doin' as chores, from the time you get up to the time you go to bed. Even try doin' it in your sleep. And for Will it's harder. Last words he had with Billy were in anger. Billy come up wanting to borrow five hundred dollars."

Agnes shook her head in disgust. "Like we carry that kinda money around." She stopped to reflect. "But anyways, he promised to pay us back a thousand. Can you imagine? A thousand dollars paid back in a day? Now where was he going to get that kinda money? The way Billy asked, like it was nothing … Well, it got a way with Will. I swannee, if he didn't light into the boy. Said he was damn fool and he ought to be working 'stead of playing cards. And Billy, he wouldn't hear none of it. They was fixing to fight. Will said he'd kill the boy … And he meant it. And that was the last he seen Billy. The last thing he said, how he was gonna kill him, and then come to find Billy killed. It liked to tear Will up.

"But I s'pect he'll find his way through it. Like he done when An—when my other boy, when they told us he was missing in Vietnam. Him—Andy— Him and Will was all the time stayin' mad at each other. And Andy didn't help matters none when he told us he was leaving. Said he was going to better hisself, like we—like the life we have here wasn't good enough for him. We all knew he wouldn't be going too far on account of the draft getting him. But that didn't change nothing 'tween them. The day Andy left Will still wouldn't have nothing to do with him." She looked down as if she could see how her lips twitched, making the surrounding wrinkles even deeper.

In a hushed tone, almost as if she were speaking to herself, she said, "Always believed their fighting held Andy back. Like maybe he woulda gone to college but wouldn't just to spite his father. He was bright enough to go. But …" Her voice faded as if what she expressed was a beaten path she had gone down too many times to see any reason to finish the thought.

After a moment she said, "About twenty months after the army took 'im we heard he was missing. Will took it worse than when his momma died. But he come around after a while. Though sometimes I wonder if Billy ever did. Those two boys were real close to be so far apart in age. Billy was all the time tryin' to act like his big brother. He couldn't rightly understand what happened to Andy, the army saying he was missing and all. He was just a boy. But maybe he blamed it on Will cuz he seen the last fight they had. I swannee … if Will ever hit Andy, Billy sure enough woulda jumped all over his daddy."

She paused and examined her uneven fingernails as if they were shiny gems meant to fascinate her. She looked up at Tinnin. "Now with Andy, there's—there's nothing we can do. But if only Will had made up with Billy, 'stead of fussing like they done. I believe they woulda swung at each other hadn't I been there to stop them. They both was hot, and both got a temper what come straight from hell itself …. If only they made up. Will'd be all right now. But he's living with it. He sees it, he hears it, he feels it all day long. Can't fault him much for drinking like he does. It's a burden won't let itself down."

The deputy was quiet, thinking to himself of separate slaughters: of an enraged father gunning down his son and, in the horror of what he had done, burning the trailer; and of a faceless man, an angry man reeking of liquor, who stole Wendy Allen as if she were an empty bottle. These were discrete murders kindred only in so far as they were the reek that sired the bugs. It made no sense. It also made Tinnin feel uneasy; why, he couldn't say.

Agnes ran her watery eyes past the deputy to the sink, to the window behind it. A blink brought her back. "Them buzzards. It's like I know why, but don't know to say it."

A silence blessed them.

At length Tinnin asked, "You see in the paper where Trollinger was killed?"

Once again her gaze froze. "Said died … The boy just couldn't lay off a them drugs. It was the death of both of them."

"Misriz Blake, don't go repeating this, but Trollinger was killed. He didn't overdose like they said."

"Whoever done it is—" Tears welled.

"Can't say for sure who done it, but there's a chance we might catch 'em. Boggs thinks that whoever done it tried to kill him the other day."

Her mouth and eyes closed as if in concentration. "That car accident in the paper?"

"Weren't no accident. Someone shot his tire out."

"And that poor girl with him …" After a moment she dried her tears with a white knuckle. "Tea, Carson?"

"Please." That she offered told him that maybe he wasn't the community outcast that he thought he was. He heard the sound of ice rattling in its tray. He hitched an arm over the wooden chair and watched her take a plastic pitcher from the refrigerator and pour. For some reason he turned to the window. His eyes dropped to the sill, to the small photograph in a golden frame; he was too far away to see anything more than a shape. "That picture there your other boy, Andy?"

"Will got all upset when he read about the accident." Agnes ignored the question and set the plastic glass in front of him. It was already sweating. "He don't think Boggs is worth a hoot. Not no two hundred dollars' worth."

Tinnin sipped his tea to test it for sweetness and then took a big swallow. "Boggs is … well, I reckon if anyone's gonna find out who's been doin' all this, it won't be no one else but Boggs. He ain't much of a detective, but he's doin' the only thing he can—lettin' whoever it is think he knows more than he does." He took another swallow. "That kinda thinkin', though, is bound to get somebody killed. And Boggs won't carry a gun. Says he don't believe in 'em no more."

"Will's a good shot." She folded her hands in an attitude of an attentive student. "Half-drunk the other day, he shot a buzzard plum' out of the sky. With his thirty-aught too." She stopped and then added, "Will ought to help Boggs. Do 'em both a favor."

The deputy jingled the ice cubes, took the last swig, and set the glass in its own sweat ring. "Don't know about that now. Boggs, he don't like to be around guns. I was over his office yesterday, and after this fellow come volunteerin' to help on account of 'im being a friend of Dr. Allen's—after he leaves, Boggs blessed me out like he was the sheriff himself. Mad as fire for me carryin' a gun into his office. Just a little baby Browning, no bigger than your hand. And me, a deputy what's s'posta carry a gun." After a moment, he added, "Don't know how he knew I even had it."

"Maybe that's why he don't come around here none. On account of Will all the time carryin' a rifle. But you're right. He can't be much of a detective with no gun, no Rockford no ways."

After drinking what little melted ice there was, he said, "Yeah, ya gotta wonder if he's gonna be alive long, what with everybody gettin' killed and shot at."

# CHAPTER TWENTY-FOUR

Boggs stood before the air conditioner with his hands parting back his fly to cool down an often-overheated body part. To get the full force of the chill, he pushed his heels up and out of his loafers. Every so often, he eased up higher, mindful of but unconcerned about the stiffness in his hobbled knee. The bourbon to which his right hand strayed saw to whatever pain announced itself. He grasped the dingy glass atop the clanking machine and sipped casually. He let his good eye slip shut and stared out the office window with the injured eye.

Hours ago, a sliding red sun had stilled the east in gray. The unassuming approach of night had almost mirrored that of dawn's, a shroud of gray that Boggs had witnessed while on his way home from his valentine's apartment. The morning sun had risen red and without beams on which to build its heat; it had shone no brighter than the remnant of a camera flash. Yet come noon, the heat was such that it singed the nostrils. For Boggs, the day began without rest, and the night promised no reprieve. To count the hours he had been awake was to tally the score against him. He took a deep drink, set the glass back, and spread his fly.

When the telephone rang, Boggs turned toward it with the indifference of a cat. The answering machine clicked on with the fourth ring. "Hello, this is Boggs. I'm out, but leave a message after the beep, and I'll get back to you just as soon as I can. Remember now, wait for the beep." The tape rolled up the silence until: "Boggs, Simon Sasser, I think we—at least—" The line went dead.

"Be that way," said Boggs. He took a drink and continued to air himself. Although this was the first contact Sasser had made since learning of the franchiser, Boggs gave it no thought. Drink and the timeless stretch ahead of him and the weary hours behind him set him to thinking. He wished he had started a security guard service. He envisioned himself a natural leader: the commander—no, commandant—with brocades and tassels on his epaulets ... a commandant of a brigade of uniformed guardsmen who would pull long hours and leave him to fret over the retained earnings. It would have been so much easier, but it would have been impossible. That mad bull Rufus Grover did more than kill his partner.

Boggs saw clearly how prevailing (though never quite public) opinion ordained that he was to be left alone, that he was to be stripped, as quickly as Grover stripped him, of any genuine stake in the community. The ayes never rose in his defense, and the eyes no longer beheld him. He was not exiled, but he wasn't given a chance. It happened without notice because—and he came to understand this only years later—there were no more chances. In taking on Rufus Grover, he had taken all his chances at once; he bet the future and lost. He saw too how unimpeachable yet unapproachable civility worked, how the sidewalk decency, the feigned friendliness removed any hope of his learning exactly what it was that folks held against him, held as closely as a poker hands.

Boggs took a drink but didn't taste it. He saw that no form of address, neither word nor deed, could bring forth or provoke or beguile townsfolk into saying what was on their minds. The reasons were to remain unspoken, maybe even unspeakable. Boggs saw himself clearly; he was on the outside and looking in at himself so intently and balefully that he didn't hear the steps in the stairwell. Not until the knob turned did he realize someone was at the door, someone who had no intention of knocking, at least until the door proved to be unlocked. Then the intruder knocked. Boggs's response was to suck in his gut and zip his fly. He leaned against the wall and let the rap go unanswered. The brass knob turned again. The door pushed back. Simon Sasser crossed the threshold as if entering his own office. He neither stopped nor appeared startled to find Boggs.

He said, "I thought you'd be here. I've been trying to reach you." He checked his forward progress at the desk. He trained his eyes on Boggs.

Boggs prolonged the silence by casually uncrossing his arms and legs. He reached for his drink. "What about?" He pushed himself away from the wall and walked slowly to his side of the desk, looking at the dredges in his glass. He swished the last of the bourbon and drank, shutting his eyes.

Sasser took the client's chair, spreading expansively. "Well, what have you been doing? Turn up anything?"

"What? You gone to clown school?"

"What are you—"

"The clothes, man," said Boggs, referring to Sasser's blue parachute pants and orange T-shirt, a getup Sasser had purchased that morning and wore earlier to try and blend in with the French Quarter crowd. "Auditioning for the big top?"

Sasser smiled good-naturedly. "Oh, this." He spread out his hands as if to bring his attire into full view. "I thought I'd try to look like I was in the swing of things." He refrained from telling the detective how he had gone to the French Quarter to talk to Mary Jane Henson but succeeded only in quickly dispatching the bouncer who claimed there was a dress code.

"Oh, you're in the swing of things, all right." Boggs's laughed, a genuine expression of mirth.

"So what's up? Have we learned anything new?"

Boggs let the "we" remark pass. He edged back into his chair. "Mean today? This afternoon? In the heat?"

"This afternoon, yesterday. What's going on? What have you been doing?" He crossed his legs and inspected Boggs's bad eye with a slight trace of a wince.

"Only just got in. Kinda got at cross purposes at this place, I know," he lied, adding, "Why?"

"Well, I called this afternoon. I wanted—"

"Yeah, done heard it on the tape. You'da left a message I would have called." He laced his fingers over his belly. "About what time was it you called?"

"Not too long ago. An hour, two at the most." He tried to stare down his opponent's skepticism. "What I—"

"You said you was tryin' to get me all afternoon, but there was only the one thing on the machine." Boggs rolled the chair up to the desk and opened a side drawer.

"The point is—"

"I'll tell you what. Folks 'round here hide their pleasures." He removed a depleted bottle of Ancient Age. "Honest to God, they keep their *Playboys* and *Penthouse*s hid, their bottles under the sink or out back somewhere, so come Sunday when the preacher's up there denouncin' porn and whiskey, they got a clear conscience. I believe from now on I'll just set my bottle out. Like every good Baptist, I takes me a drink. Only I ain't fearful of tellin' it." He poured liberally and set the bottle within Sasser's reach. "You take a pull if you have a mind to." Boggs drank, looking over the glass as Sasser waved off the offer. He sat back. "So what's this point you been itchin' to make all day?"

Sasser took a short but audible breath. "I've been thinking about what that deputy—whatever his name was—what he—"

"Tinnin. Deputy Carson Tinnin. Damn near one of the shrewdest men I've ever run across."

"Tinnin then. In thinking about what he said, it occurred to me—"

"Say, you always try the door and then knock?"

Without fluster or frustration Sasser said, "The light was on. I knew you were here but thought better of barging in."

"That so?" His ham of a hand slapped the desktop. He leaned toward Sasser. "I ain't one what won't say somethin' to a man's face. Won't say it 'less it's to his ugly face. And, boy, I'll tell you what. I don't believe you for a minute. Don't trust you if your sweaty hand was flat on ten Bibles high." He sat back, took a sip, and added, "But then that don't mean a whole lot. I don't trust nobody 'cept maybe my wife, and only her on account of she's long since quit trustin' me. But, hellfire, you had a point to make, just dyin' to make it all day."

Sasser crossed his legs. "It makes no difference to me how you feel. None whatsoever. What matters—what's important—well, you know why I'm here, and you might do well to listen to me because you're here for the very same thing."

"I'm all ears."

Sasser's glare never broke, even as he said, "Apparently, you've overlooked one terribly obvious point. This—"

"Now ya know, I might not be hittin' on a whole lot, but it just don't make sense. I mean, you bird-doggin' me all day like you done just to tell me I've overlooked somethin'." Boggs carefully set his glass down and folded his arms. He pressed his lips tight and then massaged their edges. "Nope. Ain't a whole lot of sense to it. Now I s'pect you got a ready-made list of twenty, thirty answers, but mind debriefin' me on just what in the hell it is you and me are here for?"

"To catch the killer." He recrossed his legs and added, "Or killers. After listening to you and Deputy Tinnin I'm convinced this can't be the work of one man, especially not a cop. When you think about it, this drug business can't be a one-man operation, this so-called franchiser. There has to be someone else. Perhaps more than a dozen at the street level and two or three at the top of the pyramid and probably a layer in between. And let's not forget that drugs aren't cheap. To be operating on the scale you described, the leadership must have financing. A cop doesn't make that kind of money. Even if there were a group of—"

Boggs, grinning foolishly, interrupted. "Damn, if it ain't them simple things that are all the time confoundin' me. Here me and Tinnin was laboring under the notion that Captain Wynne was our man. I mean, who else but Jesus Christ himself could make ten pounds of dope become two and then take the eight and resell it? It's the loaves and fishes, my son. The loaves and fishes. But then here you come along and quick as a whip show us the big picture. But the truth to tell, Mr. Sasser, I don't believe Wynne ever done it. Tinnin does. I don't."

"Then how do you see it?"

"I believe you done it."

"Oh. I see." Sasser paused. "So what you're saying is that I single-handedly stole from either a drug pusher or the authorities themselves more than eight pounds of marijuana and then brazenly turned around and sold it on the streets of a town I don't really know?"

Boggs shrugged.

"And just how did I get … get this … how did I steal these drugs from the authorities? Oh, I know." He snapped his fingers. "I simply teleported myself inside their offices, located the marijuana, and then whisked my ethereal body safely away … like magic?"

"Possibly."

The earnest cast of Sasser's face broke. He lifted his almond eyes to meet, penetrate, sear the obstacle on the other side of the desk. "Boggs, forget your imbecilic, provincial prejudices for a minute and try and listen to reason. Wynne—he couldn't be the only one involved. He's only a cop. If there's a drug conspiracy, it has to be bigger than him. He's a pawn being moved by someone behind the scenes. And you, better than anyone else, probably know who's directing—who's calling the shots."

"You reckon it might could be the sheriff himself?"

"Perhaps. Perhaps it is. I don't know. The idea occurred to me. But I don't know the man. I tried—" Sasser stopped himself.

"What?"

Sasser watched Boggs drink. "I tried to see him."

"You went to the Icebox?"

"The what?"

"What folks call the hospital because it looks like an icebox."

"Yes, I was there, but they wouldn't let me in to see him."

"Who didn't? His men or the nurses?"

"Deputies, but—"

"But why see him if you believe he might have done it?"

"To gauge him, to see what kind of a man he is, to determine if he's capable of killing. Or at least ordering his stooges like Wynne to do his bidding."

Boggs smiled wryly. "Sasser, if you ain't somethin' else. Sure he's capable. Ain't no one been sheriff longer, even now when we got free elections. But the man ain't capable of doing what they done to Blake and the Allen girl. I know him. Used to be that I knew him good. We used—there was a bunch of us used to play cards right regular. There was me, the sheriff, Judge Hardy, Doc Hargrove—he's dead now, some six years or better—and then two or three others to fill out the table. Never Wynne though. I used to beat the bejesus out of Harris … and Hardy too. It was that game you and me played that time, Cowboys … but … come to think of it, why not cowgirls since you need queens or better to open?" He paused reflectively.

"Anyway, if Harris had two boys, you could sure enough bet I had the other two, and they was riding aces. It liked to tickle me the way he'd get all red. Losing the way he done made him drink hard, drink till come the next day, he couldn't stand the sight, much less the smell, of it for a week or longer. Make him puke something awful. But the man never did show hisself, never said nothin' or done nothin' 'cept drink that much more. And the man could drink. That's for sure. A fifth or more."

Boggs smiled to himself and took a drink. The grin turned dour. "Least that's the way it used to be. I run up on some trouble, and they suspended me. I was reinstated and all, but it was like none of 'em took to me winnin' anymore. And then one night, me and the cowboys was riding home a whole lot richer, and damned if I didn't get pulled. A city patrolman pulled me—me—his superior. But I never once believed it was Harris who called it. I figure it had to be the judge. Parting with so much as a thin dime chaps that man's ass. And he don't mind if he shows his ass and don't give a flip who he shows it to."

Sasser asked, "Judge Hardy is the judge you're talking about?"

"Yeah, the judge … the chief judge." After a moment he added, "I reckon … reckon it's on account of him having nothing to achieve. He's been judge so long ain't nobody figured there could be anyone else. Like a building. Ya just don't tear it down. You come to expect it to be there. You come to expect Hardy to be there, and he expects to be there. So what's left for him to do? He's got everything he ever wanted. Well, 'cept one thing. Riches."

Sasser asked, "I take it these two men are tight?"

"Like ticks on a dog." Boggs stifled a laugh behind a closed yawn. He stared off at nothing in particular. "I went—it was a joke—but I went to Harris's office the day after I was pulled. I'd filled a vodka bottle with water. He wasn't lookin' none too good, rough as rocks around the edges. And here I come with my bottle and tell him how I got pulled and damn near arrested for drivin' under the influence. He didn't laugh or nothin', just looked sicker than a dog. So I set the bottle down and said, 'J.B., so you don't think I'm accusing you, let's have a drink together.' He reeled back and waved his hands like he was washing a window. And in a real hurry about it too. So I undone the cap and drank the water down. Didn't really need to drink it all. Let it sit there on his desk a little longer, and he woulda been off and runnin' anyways." Boggs's conclusion to the story seemed more of an interruption. He looked into his glass. "But then that was a long time ago."

"There—you said it yourself," exclaimed Sasser. "It was a long time ago. The man has probably changed. You can't be certain. You really don't know."

Boggs shook his head. "Sasser, it's you what ain't listenin'. I said the man didn't laugh or nothin'. Had he done it, he woulda laughed. Because he woulda tried to say it was a joke, nothin' more. No, it was that weasel Hardy what done it. He made the call."

Sasser rested his chin on a loose fist. After a weighted moment, he said, "Let's consider Hardy then?"

"Naw, he ain't got the stones. Or the sense. And if he's the one, how's he keep it from his door? And for all this time? No, it ain't him. He's not an overachiever. An achiever, yes, but not an overachiever. He's already done his achievin'." Boggs cut himself short. After a time, he added, "But then if Wynne's just a cop, it's for damn sure he's one smart cop. Only theorizing now, but to crack a drug ring, don't you have to know how it works? And maybe he believes he can outsmart everybody, and then he comes to find he can't, so … so he buys 'em off. Maybe Wynne's smarter than I ever gave him credit for." He paused in thought. "You only just arrived in Greensburg. Not so long ago, the feds popped a bunch of congressmen for takin' bribes. And I heard the evening paper asked—Hardy told the evening paper that everyone's got his price, including him. Imagine him a judge and sayin' some dumbass thing as that."

Boggs gazed at the dark windows. He looked back at Sasser after a time. "Now that should give you somethin' to ponder." He stood and finished his drink. "When you get it all figured out, let me know."

Sasser remained seated. "Where you going?"

"Can't remember her name," he replied on his way to the door. "Lock up when you leave."

Boggs emphasized every step on his way down the stairs. The glass door closed without a sound. Night pressed itself on him. He felt sticky. He walked slowly past two storefronts and turned down the alley leading to the parking lot. Once inside the cramped confines of his car, he was unsure where to go. As envisioned earlier, his plans called for posting himself across from the vice office to wait for Wynne to make his rounds: the sniper attack made even a doubtful suspect a possibility that had to be either confirmed or eliminated. But now having talked so long with Sasser, he might have missed the vice captain. It was probably for the best. The reminiscence, the speculation, the confusion over who had the stomach, the nerve, the sense, left him tired, sober, and lonesome. All he really wanted to do was drink. But so as not to feel too derelict, he decided to swing past Wynne's office.

A maroon Dodge Diplomat was in the driveway. The vehicle had no official markings, nothing in its design or shape to suggest it belonged to the city or county. Boggs knew at once to whom it belonged. He didn't have to look to see no lights were shining in the vice squad office. He cruised thirty yards to the traffic light, coasted under a yellow signal, deciding and then undeciding and then redeciding what to do. His foot off the pedal, he let the Falcon decide. It stopped at the curb. He shut down the engine and killed the lights.

Wynne's departure ten minutes later suggested to Boggs that the deputies used black curtains to darken the windows; why, he couldn't say. Maybe to give the old house some mystique. Or maybe the boys were smoking so much of the confiscated product that they were paranoid?

Wynne backed the unmarked car out and turned in Boggs's direction. As soon as Wynne passed, Boggs switched on the ignition. The engine heaved a little, hacked a lot, shook, shimmied, and died. Slapping the wheel, he pumped more gas. He flicked the key. The engine heaved a little, hacked, shook, shimmied, and died. Boggs stamped down on the pedal, roaring with undelivered oaths. He twisted the key. The engine heaved, hacked, shook, and finally caught.

Boggs didn't wait for the whine to stop or the exhaust cloud to settle. He made a U-turn and saw the Diplomat waiting to make a left at the red light on Davis Street. He listened to the transmission groan and pop from second to third. He watched the speedometer so closely that he nearly rear-ended the Diplomat.

Wynne crossed the Appomattox on Jeff Davis Highway and drove through Colonial Heights. He kept within the speed limit until he reached the outskirts of town. There, the signs allowed for fifty-five miles per hour. Wynne steadied his speed at sixty. Because the highway was straight for the next fifteen miles, Boggs was able to keep Wynne in sight. The captain appeared to be headed to James City, the state capitol. *Why* was the question waiting to be answered.

He turned east on Ruffin Mill Road to access the interstate, heading to the capitol. He exited onto Broad Street and then onto south Fifth Street. He parked in the lot in front of the Southside Police precinct.

Minutes behind, Boggs eased into the parking lot across the street, home of Bert's and the best fried baloney sandwich in town. By the time Boggs extricated himself from the wagon, there was no sign of Wynne, only the unmarked car. Boggs leaned against the closed door and folded his arms. The shouts of two kids riding their bikes in circles caught his attention. He whistled and waved for them to come over. They made one last loop and pedaled to him. He proposed a deal: five bucks now and five bucks after they poked a hole in the Diplomat's taillight, just a chip so that one light would burn white. The kids made quick work of the assignment and returned for the final payment. In addition to the ten dollars, Boggs offered to buy them sodas if they brought him one as well.

When the kids returned, Boggs ignored them at first. He studied the Chevy Camaro Z28 that had just pulled into a visitor's space at the police station. Sasser, unmistakable in his clown outfit, climbed from the car and went into the precinct, pulling the door back as if familiar with its weight. Without looking, Boggs took hold of his drink and told the kids to keep the change.

"So that's how you teleport your smart ass into their offices," he said to himself, unable to deny a sneer.

About ten minutes later, Sasser and Wynne exited the building, both smiling. They stopped at the bottom of the steps. Wynne pointed west. Turning his head in that direction, Sasser nodded. The two talked for another minute and then shook hands. Wynne went back inside, while Sasser drove off in his Z28.

Boggs stood like a stone. Eventually, he unwound a smile. He resisted the temptation to follow Sasser and waited on Wynne, believing the captain would lead him back to Sasser before the night was over.

When Wynne left forty minutes later, the white beacon worked admirably. Now, it didn't matter how far Boggs fell behind. He could spot the car from a distance. His efforts, though, were for naught. Wynne drove directly to Greensburg. There was no further sign of Sasser.

# CHAPTER TWENTY-FIVE

The night was so muggy that Boggs felt as if a barefisted pro had worked him over. Taking stock of old and new wounds was unnecessary; they surfaced with an avenging sentience. Pain breaking quicker than any promise burst above his right ankle, zapped his right shoulder, and stung the swollen eye. All the while, a chorus of wadi-dry cells in his brain howled for more bourbon. To humor himself as much as to kill dead time, he hummed the "Dem Bones" tune.

His surveillance of the vice office was now in its second hour. Before parking at the intersection of Tabb and Franklin about 8 p.m., he called the vice squad office. That Wynne answered disappointed him; he loathed stakeouts. What made this one especially detestable was the station wagon, which not only cramped his style but also all 236 pounds of him. For lack of leg room, his thighs crunched against the wheel, and his knees butted underneath the dash. His feet were crammed behind the pedals like knotted socks. His shoulder complained that the passenger seat was too close, and his head felt the roof a threat. The seat of his pants had an incriminating stain, and sweat likewise adhered his shirt to his back and the seat.

Worse still was the maddening desperation to know who the overlord was. Was Sasser a mere accomplice or the overachiever? Boggs had to be certain. Throughout his career he always depended on certainties, even though his conclusions seldom proved true in the end. Unless he was sure, he couldn't act decisively; he couldn't be sure of himself. He had been sure that his service revolver would stop Rufus Grover on that long-ago June day. Now he was sure he had no need of guns. Knowing this gave him a tremendous edge because, more often than not, an armed man would point the gun but not pull the trigger.

As he had done last night, Boggs planned to tail Wynne but this time in the hopes the vice captain would rendezvous with Sasser. At 10:23 p.m. the yellow light over the door brightened. Wynne literally skipped down the steps and climbed into the Diplomat. Boggs prayed that the broken taillight hadn't been discovered. He crossed his fingers so tightly that he nearly tore the index out of joint. What began as a snort became a snicker when Wynne cranked the engine and turned on the car lights. Boggs repeatedly pumped the pedal. All four cylinders fired, discharging a cloud of gray toxins. Wynne stopped at the same light as he had last night and made the same turn. Boggs waited until the Diplomat cleared out before following.

Wynne rolled onto Highway 1 South.

Assuming he was headed toward Random, Boggs didn't panic when his wagon struggled to keep up with Wynne; after all, there were only so many places the captain could go.

He was a quarter mile back when Wynne suddenly, almost recklessly, wheeled onto Harry Jenrette Road and sped up. His tires screeching, Boggs swung wide at the turn and nearly lost his rear end in a ditch. The white light had jumped at least a mile ahead.

Wynne barreled past a stop sign and struck south onto McKenney. Boggs likewise ignored the red sign, his forehead nearly pressed against the windshield. He questioned whether Wynne knew he was being followed or whether he had just received an emergency dispatch. Boggs assumed it was an emergency by the way the Diplomat fishtailed onto Boydton Plank Road. To make the turn, Boggs had to slow down, but once on the flats, the wagon raced west under the pressure of Boggs's size thirteen triple-wide shoe.

At the intersection with Stiff Branch Road, Wynne swung south. Again Boggs had to decelerate. But he gained speed as he neared the Blake farm and then decelerated. Parked diagonally in the road was the Diplomat, the blue lights in the rear window blinking. Boggs coasted up to Wynne. He rolled down his window.

Armed with a flashlight in one hand and a pistol in the other, Wynne approached. He blinded Boggs with the light. "Boggs!"

"You doin' all right, captain?"

"Get out of the car."

Boggs killed the engine. He braced one hand on the top of the open door and curled the other over the roof. He hoisted himself out with a grunt. His feet under him, he turned in time to see Wynne holster the weapon.

"You don't learn, do you? Thought we had an understanding."

Boggs stepped into his space. "Ain't nothing says I can't drive this road."

"You're following me. Why?"

Boggs shrugged. "To see where the action is."

"Well, you found it."

"Well, it don't look like a whole lot of nothin' to me."

"What're you doing, Boggs?"

"Tailin' you. What's it look like?"

"You've been drinking. Get against the car."

Wynne pushed him, the meat of his hand landing squarely on Boggs's right shoulder. Boggs winced as he faced the wagon. Wynne patted him down.

"You're under arrest. Driving under the influence and possession of a scheduled—"

"Possession of what?"

Wynne held up a thin joint and grinned.

"You—"

A gunshot spilled them onto the pavement. A second bullet slammed through the back of the Falcon. Boggs scurried on hands and knees to the other side of the wagon. Wynne fired three times in the direction of the sniper and clambered around to safety. A third shot struck one of the two blue lights in Wynne's car. The captain popped up over the hood and returned fire. He crawled over to his car, opened the driver's door, and reached in for his radio. "Two to Rock, two to Rock, 10-33 at—"

The door window shattered. He scrambled into the vehicle. "Repeat: a 10-33 on Stiff Branch Road near—"

The windshield shattered. "Near Boydton Plank Road. Over." Wynne dropped the radio and slid out of the car and onto the ground. He wormed his way to the front, now protected by the full length of the Diplomat. He sprang up and loosed a wild shot to draw fire. He had to keep the sniper occupied until help arrived. He waited a moment, then jumped and fired. The answer from the woods was silence. Soon, the crickets and frogs reemerged. Wynne hunkered down and called to Boggs. He said, "He's either circling or running. You have something to cover me?"

"How about your flashlight?" Boggs replied. As Boggs laughed, Wynne raced across the street and threw himself in a ditch. In the distance came the sound of a car engine starting. Wynne sprang to his feet and sprinted down the road.

From the opposite direction came a cruiser, its siren wailing, lights spinning. It skidded to a stop at the station wagon. Grinning, Boggs came around his car, his hands in the air.

"You?" hollered Tinnin. "What in the hell?"

Boggs dropped his arms but not his laughter. "Your boy's gone after 'im." He pointed south toward the Blake residence. "Might need your assistance."

Tinnin ran back to his car, jammed the stick into reverse and then drive. He left rubber as he passed the two vehicles.

Boggs's laughter suddenly stopped. He scrambled back to his car and drove to the Blake homestead. A light was on in the kitchen. He pulled in back. The sight of the two buzzards stilled him. He sat in the car, staring, until Agnes stepped outside.

"Heard sirens," said Agnes as she pattered up to the wagon.

It took more work than he ever imagined to yank himself out of the car. "Yeah, sniper fire up the road. Tinnin and the vice captain went after him."

Before Agnes made any sort of a comment, he asked, "So where's Will?"

"Where he can't be drinking."

"Where's that?"

"In the bed."

"You sure?"

"Mean can an old man too drunk to walk get his rifle, run up the road, and fire upon the law?"

"Something like that."

"Well, you can look for yourself or listen real close and maybe hear him snorin' from here."

# CHAPTER TWENTY-SIX

Through the windshield, Tinnin saw the midnight sky as a stovepipe. He didn't see stars. Instead, he saw bullet holes, the black pipe riddled and the piercing light only a faint suggestion of some mysterious and immemorial holocaust sunk deep in eternity and only now coming forward to confess.

Tinnin suspected the sniper was like that fire, burning without regard to the law of consumption. The sniper was also like the holes, a .30-06 slug slamming through a windshield, the brass casings that were so telling and yet revealed nothing, neither who nor why. Before the sniper, there was no true mystery, only the effluvium of fear resulting from ruthless, brutal murders committed for one all-consuming reason. The sniper dashed the hope of uncovering that reason any time soon, for the attempt of Wynne's life removed him as a suspect.

*The Herald Chronicle* emblazoned the banner: "Sniper Stalks Vice Captain." The front-page story quoted Wynne as saying his investigation pointed to the man who killed Billy Blake. A television crew, so Tinnin heard, even went to the hospital to talk to the convalescing sheriff. Harris said he was relieved to hear no one was injured and vowed to return as soon as possible to add his years of experience to the manhunt.

Yesterday's shooting brought all attention to bear on Wynne and the unknown assailant, reducing the unsolved slayings of Blake and Allen to less than an honorable mention. The urgency comforted Tinnin. He no longer had to carry his suspicions and the attendant fear of what Wynne might do, not necessarily to him but to the law. At the same time, it frightened Tinnin to think a man, a civilian, would try to take out a cop. He could understand a fit of passion, but the calculation of a sniper outraged him.

The brazen assault on his own turf and on one of his own infuriated him to the point that his concerns for his outlander image in the community took a back seat. He rejoined the rank and file of the sheriff's department, no longer feeling like a stranger among his peers.

Tinnin now cringed for ever having confided in Boggs. Everyone held Boggs in disrepute and dislike, and now Tinnin had reason to do likewise. He encouraged Boggs to think he was close to the killer, when all along it was Wynne who was making progress. Unbeknownst to anyone, Wynne had been conducting his own investigation, but not for money. Wynne was closing in on the killer. Why else would someone try to take him out? Why else would the sniper aim only at the captain? The so-called attempt on Boggs's life was an accident, but if a sniper had in fact been involved, he'd meant to eliminate Sally Allen. She was probably in the same predicament as her sister, unaware she had seen the killer. But who was the killer? Tinnin resisted the notion of the hatchet-faced Will Blake and considered the stranger, Simon Sasser. After all, it was Sasser who produced the .30-06 casing.

In retrospect, it was a grave mistake to tell Sasser about the franchise, about Wynne. Confiding in someone you found odious was one thing, but trusting a stranger was perilous. For all Tinnin knew, Sasser could be the franchiser, and if he was, Tinnin's name was right below Wynne's on the hit list. Still, a man simply couldn't write a shopping list and then execute each person one by one. A man might get away with one murder, maybe two, but three or four was unthinkable. If Sasser's target was Wynne, the assassin would never take him from close range, and from a distance, he demonstrated he wasn't much of a marksman, unless he meant to take out windows.

Tinnin eased off the gas in anticipation of the first of three speed bumps on the quarter-mile drive leading to the Moose Lodge. Only incoming traffic had the benefit of thin yellow lines to indicate the obstacles. Once past the first two, set on either side of a sharp curve, the woods fell back, and the grounds opened. The third bump awaited below a knoll beyond which was the parking lot.

Tinnin found the parking lot nearly empty, in keeping with a Sunday night. Even though his shift was on call in case of renewed sniper attacks, he had the day off. And since his Atari was on the blink, the idea of tossing back a beer or two appealed to him. The Moose also offered a viable video alternative: an El Grande – 5 Card Draw arcade machine and, if he lost too much there, a Playboy pinball machine.

Under the portico lights, he searched his wallet for his membership card. Finding it, he wiped his canvas sneakers on the green, all-weather carpet and stepped inside. He inserted his plastic card in the appropriate slot. The lock clicked, and a buzzer sounded, the signal to open. He walked into a thirty-table dining room, which was dimly lit and nearly empty.

A long horseshoe-shaped bar commanded the far side. The members, fully aware that the bar was the center of attention, strung its prized possessions along the walls: paintings of its orphanage, Mooseheart; retirement community, Moosehaven; and a neon American flag with a clock set among the stars. A moose head was mounted under the bar television. Tinnin couldn't remember a time when the TV hadn't been silently glowing.

A boisterous gathering at the center table drew Tinnin's attention. Three brown wine bottles, thick as store-bought logs, rose above the crushed cans, dead drinks, crumpled napkins, and dirty plates. Tuned to the laughter, he thought that more than bottles and cans were empty. Judge John Hardy sat like a totem at the head of the table, his contentious voice pitched, his pontifical speech slurred.

Tinnin plunked a ten down and asked Wiley, the bartender, for change of five dollars in quarters. In addition, he ordered a draft and chips. The corn chips came first and were the first to go.

"See the judge's here."

Wiley finished counting quarters before he spoke. "Holdin' court as usual. You his escort tonight?"

Tinnin stopped the mug on its upswing. "It's a damn sorry sight for the chief district court judge to be drunk like that."

"Ain't no one to arrest him."

"I reckon." The deputy left for the back rooms.

A pool table and bottle lockers filled the first room. To get past the next closed door—where a no-limit poker game was always going—required more money than Tinnin was willing to part with. He ambled into the doorless room to his right to play El Grande.

His concentration was loose, too loose to win. His mind was elsewhere, at times on the Honorable John Hardy, at others on the drive home the judge was unprepared to make. Let any other man be caught driving in the same condition, and the judge—the one sitting out there lording over the dissipated remains—would leave him as poor as Job's turkey: license revoked, fine imposed plus court costs, and insurance company notified.

After losing his eighth quarter, Tinnin finished his beer and went back for a refill. The sight of the pay phone in the first room stopped him. He smiled until he remembered he now had to deposit a quarter instead of a dime. He tried to do the math on what percentage of an increase the price hike represented. His answer was 300 percent but he wasn't sure. Why isn't the sheriff giving me a 300 percent raise, he asked himself. Without bothering to answer, he dialed 911.

"C-COM."

"Yeah, I want to report a DUI."

"Where?"

"Well, he hasn't gotten in his car yet."

"Then—"

Tinnin hung up upon hearing how ridiculous he sounded. His anger now doubled, half aimed at the judge and two-thirds at himself. He went to the bar.

The judge's party was at the door. When Wiley approached, Tinnin slid his mug across the bar and said he was finished for the night. He cashed in his quarters for bills.

Under the portico, he stuffed the ones into his wallet. He heard what sounded like a quarrel in the parking lot. He smiled; this was much better than video poker. The judge belonged to the enraged voice, his wife to the demure one. She matched his vitriol with sweet reminders of how much he had drunk. Tinnin stifled a laugh.

"Well, damn you to hell. You can walk home," shouted the judge.

A door slammed. A powerful engine started. Tires squealed. A gray Lincoln Continental Mark IV flashed into view. Hardy hit the first speed bump as if it wasn't there. Only the jouncing shock absorbers told of the impact. The taillights disappeared.

Smirking, Tinnin strode into the lot. He listened to the Mark IV motor while looking at the still-life pose of the wife. The grinding of metal and splitting of wood suddenly riveted him. The cacophonic piece ended with a pop and shatter of glass. The wife turned calmly to the clubhouse. Tinnin raced up the knoll.

At the second speed bump, he was so badly out of breath that he had to stop. He bent over and inhaled fitfully. Under the streetlight, he looked down at the swath the Mark IV had cut through the woods. The judge probably never knew he went off the road until the car struck a tree. Tinnin started down the embankment, slipped on the slick grass, and rolled to the bottom. Cussing, he lifted himself and then brushed his clothes off as he stepped to the car. He opened the bent door with a yank and jerked the moaning judge back against the seat. To stop the heavy bleeding along the hairline, he took the handkerchief tucked in the judge's breast pocket. Though it was stained and crusted at the center, he pressed it against the wound. He flinched at the shards of embedded glass and resorted to using the fat of his palm. As he applied an even pressure, he looked out for any indications of fire. The smoke hissing from what he assumed was a broken radiator persuaded him not to take a chance. He dragged the heavy man away by the jacket. The sleeves tore at the shoulders but held as Tinnin struggled up the rise. The judge groaned and mumbled. Tinnin dropped him in order to catch his breath and to wrap the handkerchief around the man's head. The judge jerked his head with surprising strength. "Get us all killed … you'll get us all killed …" He drifted into incoherence.

Unsure what to do, the deputy felt Hardy's pulse. It seemed strong enough.

The judge gasped, "It doesn't make sense … no!"

Tinnin sat back on his heels. He repeated what Hardy had just said and then leaned over, asking, "What don't?"

Hardy muttered a no.

"What don't make any sense?"

"Cowboys … all the time cowboys."

"Cowboys?"

Hardy rambled beyond comprehension. Tinnin was about to slap him when he heard a siren. He stood and looked down at Hardy. "Cowboys and Indians," he sneered and kicked the judge in the shoulder.

# CHAPTER TWENTY-SEVEN

Tinnin's only ambition was not to work on the farm or in a mill. The monotonous way the farm grounded his father's life and the loom foreshortened his mother's outlook decided that much for him. Upon graduating from high school six years ago, he snatched the first opportunity to come along: the sheriff's department. Tinnin never envisioned himself as a deputy, an upholder of the law. That was why his predicament alarmed him. It seemed he wasn't in the employ of the law; he worked for a lie, upheld a lie, a lie that effectively removed any designs he might construct on tomorrow. Ironically, without a tomorrow, there was no end, no end to today, no place for doubt and despair to reform themselves.

*The Herald Chronicle* perpetuated the lie. That afternoon's edition used unnamed department officials to reinforce the lie. The article said that the judge's car had been tampered with and in the next paragraph went on to summarize the sniper attack on Wynne, thus leaving the clear impression the same man was responsible for both deeds. The story had no mention of alcohol, but Tinnin knew the man would have blown at least a 0.20 on the Breathalyzer. The article also said that the judge walked away from the wreck, suffering a mild concussion and needing twelve stitches to close a head wound.

Because Tinnin had fled before the rescue squad arrived, he understood the misinformation about Hardy walking away. Yet other glaring errors left him no choice but to conclude that the reporter had been duped into building a grandstand for Wynne, a platform on which Judge Hardy also stood. To Tinnin's way of thinking, the judge's remark about cowboys was as inane as the headline: "Law Enforcement Under Attack."

Tinnin surprised himself by not hesitating to contact the man he so despised only two days ago: Boggs. The remission was a direct result of the full faith Tinnin placed in the dollar. Boggs worked for money. So did Wynne, but Wynne—and the judge—had a duty to perform. The only obligation Boggs was under was to make money. Tinnin trusted money. Money made Boggs all right.

But Boggs was not all right this evening. In fact, he was half-drunk and peeved that he wasn't more inebriated. He waited for Tinnin at his office, fulminating that the deputy was able to track him to the apartment of a legal secretary. He wasn't worried his wife would find out but rather that the secretary would find out what all of Greensburg already knew. Tinnin's call upset her as well as Boggs's well-laid plans to sip bourbon and branch water between performances.

As soon as Tinnin entered, he fired, "How in the hell did you know where I was?"

To the deputy's astonishment, Boggs looked worse today than he did after the accident six days ago. The disheveled, swollen look Boggs typically found in the morning mirror notwithstanding, the entire left side of his pitted face was jaundice yellow, which was rimmed by a greenish blue. The butterfly stitches under and over the damaged eye were gone, but red skin pursed around jagged purple lines. The eye itself was open but cloudy as rainwater in a ditch.

"Heck, man, that woman you used to mess with in district court done told everyone in town." He added, "Prob'ly told your wife 'fore anyone else."

Boggs settled back in his chair and laughed. He took a sip of bourbon from a coated glass. "Ain't no way in hell anybody can keep a secret in this town."

The deputy told him about the newspaper account, explaining the inaccuracies. "And ya know how in a wreck, how they hollering about the pain like you can do something about it? Well, the judge didn't. It might coulda been he was too drunk, but he didn't say nothin' about pain. He kept on about cowboys, like cowboys and Indians."

"Cowboys?" Boggs cocked his good eye.

"Yeah, cowboys. He said, 'All the time cowboys.' Kinda like cowboys and Indians."

A cruel twist creased Boggs's mouth. "Ya know, Tinnin, one of the first pieces of advice I ever recollect hearin' was 'loose lips sink ships.'" He laughed and took a drink. "So this is what it comes down to: cowboys and Indians." He laughed, looked at the deputy's quizzical face, and laughed harder. A moment later, he told Tinnin about the card games with the sheriff and Judge Hardy. He sat back and rocked in his chair, unable to keep a smile from flourishing.

"So what's it mean?" Although never invited to take a seat, Tinnin plunked down in the client chair.

"It means they done it."

"On account of he said 'cowboys'?"

"No, because he said 'cowboys' because he couldn't forget." He rolled his chair up to the desk to refresh his drink. "Tinnin, you ever think … well, ya know, Wynne couldn't be running this drug business and his men not be in on it. And the sheriff, ain't he the overseer of it all? He's got to know too. Ain't nobody ever accused J.B. of being dumb. Just might could be he had that heart attack because of the stress. The killin' was getting' to him, and he couldn't figure a way to stop it. But now that they got everybody killed that they wanted killed, alls they gotta do is stop folks from tryin' to find out what they done. And seein' as how they can't afford another murder, 'less the whole county panic, they started this snipin' business, but only aimin' to scare me off."

"So it was all planned?"

"Wynne and them got right much publicity out of it. Our newspaper is one very accommodating organization."

Tinnin looked for a place to put his hands. The armrest seemed too stiff. He leaned on an elbow. "Yeah, but how'd Wynne know you were gonna follow him?"

"Maybe he spotted me. Maybe he spotted me the night before. Maybe he spotted me waiting for him to leave the office. That woulda given him time to set the whole thing up." He took a sip. "Get one or two of his boys to set up shop down there in Random and lead me right to it."

"And they used the newspaper with Judge Hardy. It worked once, so why not again. But …"

"What?"

Tinnin leaned forward. "What do you know about this Sasser fellow? It was him what said the sheriff was involved. How'd he know?"

"The boy's wrapped pretty tight, but he did say it stood to reason." Boggs paused. "But reason don't always make a whole lot of sense. So it might be the judge, the sheriff, even Wynne, ain't none of 'em involved in all this, and Sasser's just playin' us against 'em, playin' both sides against the middle."

"But what for? 'Less he's the franchiser."

Boggs bumped a fist against his lower lip. After a minute he lowered it and said, "He ain't got no title, only because he acts like he's got one. Like he's king or something."

"Then what is he?"

"He ain't who he says he is. Wouldn't wonder if he works for the government, the FBI or something."

"The FBI?"

Boggs laughed sardonically. "Now don't go knockin' your balls into your watch pocket. Just theorizin'. He says he comes from Washington. And I don't know when, but I believe he knew the Allen girl. And I know for a fact he's somehow involved in all this. I seen 'im the other night with Wynne, up in James City."

"Doing what?"

"Damned if I know." He repeatedly knocked the loose fist against his lower lip. "Say, what's this about the sheriff coming home? Only been in there ... what? Two weeks?" He added, "That heart of his musta healed pretty damn quick."

"I ain't heard nothin'." Tinnin rose and paced off three steps toward the windows. "This Sasser gives me a ton of trouble." He continued on to the window and turned. "Be glad if the sheriff does come back. Wynne ain't s'posta be in charge, but he's sure enough givin' all the orders. Had the shift called in today, our day off. We didn't do nothin', just sat around like somethin' was gonna happen in broad daylight. Now whoever heard tell of a sniper—well, yeah, I have. But, hell, we didn't do nothin' and don't even get overtime." He went back to the chair to stand behind it.

"Tinnin, sit down. You're making me nervous."

The deputy reluctantly sat on the edge of the chair. Boggs took a drink. "Know what you need?" said Boggs, wagging a finger. "You need a wife, someone to go home to and yell at." He added, "And give it a lick or two if you have a mind to."

"Shut your damn mouth, Boggs."

Boggs held up his hands to signal truce. "All right, all right. No need to get all riled up. Just a friendly suggestion."

"Yeah, well, here's another one." Tinnin stood and paced. "What if I was to say Will Blake done it? He's as good a shot as there is. Tried snipin' at me once. And the snipin' ain't been far from his place. It might could be that him and Billy had an argument and got to fightin', and he killed the boy and then burned the trailer to make it look like the fire done it. And the Allen girl, she was running by when they was fightin'—"

"One thing's wrong." Boggs laced his hands over his gut as he sat back.

"What's that?"

"The girl was raped. Bet Blake can't get it up no more."

"S'pect not." He spewed a sigh. "So what now? What're we gonna do?"

"Sit 'n' sip." He held up his coated glass. "Care to join me?"

"Naw, it's getting on toward suppertime." He shuffled this way and that before heading for the door.

"You on first tomorrow?" When the deputy nodded, he added, "I might be callin' you."

"Not through dispatch, you're not."

"I'll get 'hold of you one way or 'nother."

Boggs tipped back his drink as the deputy's steps resounded in the stairwell. His good eye brightened as he reached for the telephone directory. With an exaggerated flourish, he flicked through the pages until he came to the right one. His finger swooped down the first column and then stopped midway. He repeatedly thrust his finger at the number he wanted. Just as he was about to dial, Sasser entered without knocking, without so much as a hello. Dressed in a dark suit and carrying a leather portfolio whose color matched his shoes, he squared himself in the client's chair, his body at near-perfect ninety-degree angles. "Where have you been? I've—"

"Do what now?"

"I've been trying to reach you all afternoon."

"Let me see if—," he said, interrupting himself for a drink, "—if I understand this ... this ... whatever it is going on here. See, I'm sorta particular. Don't really stand on ceremony, but manners is another matter. Just the way folks is 'round here. So here you come, barging in and want to know what I've been doin'. When—since when do I answer to the likes of you?"

"Boggs, do we really have to cover this ground again and again?"

"What ground is that now?"

"All right. Admittedly I acted hastily. I should have knocked." He flattened his hands on the portfolio with a trace of a smack. "For that I apologize. Sometimes I tend to overreact."

"You best have a drink, son. Hot as it is, you'll die of exhaustion."

"Yes, but let me tell you what I found out?"

"Couldn't stop ya if I wanted, could I?"

Sasser adjusted his glasses with a pronounced shutter of his eyes. "The accident involving Judge Hardy wasn't the work of a sniper or any other type of … of hoodlum. The only thing wrong with the car was the driver. He was drunk."

Boggs held up his glass, twirling its contents in admiration. "Hardy never was much of a drinker. Liked sissy stuff like wine, sweet wine. Sure enough made him walk on a slant." He took a drink.

"But … but doesn't that—"

"Surprise me? Naw. Already knew it. But how'd you come to acquire this knowledge?"

"I went to Woody's Auto Body. Said I was with the insurance company and inspected the car. One of the mechanics all but told me nothing was wrong with it."

"An insurance company man, well I'll be. You're a man of many disguises, Mr. Sasser. But I'll—"

"Please, do me a favor?" He held up his open hands in protest. "Please, let's not go down this road."

Boggs aimed the good eye at him as he refilled his glass.

"Look, I believe we both know who did this. And I think I have an idea how to proof it."

To preempt the sarcastic remark he knew was coming, Sasser expounded on his previously explained theory that the top men in charge of law enforcement in the county were the culprits. The sheriff was the lead, followed by the judge, and then the vice squad, including Wynne.

"The entire crowd, huh? The sheriff, the judge, and then vice?" Boggs inclined his head to the side and nodded with an ever-broadening but thin smile. He sat back, letting his bourbon sit on the desk pad. "So tell me, Mr. Sasser. We've as much as told you all this already, so how you intend to prove it?"

Sasser said, "It's like almost everything else in life. You know what you know, but you can't prove it. Take God. Can you prove he exists?"

Boggs said, "Sure. How do you explain the stars, the Milky Way, the universe?"

"That's not proof. That's a question."

"It's not a question. It's all there, right out there in front of you. Look up at the sky at night. It's all right there. It's what your lawyers call prima facie."

Sasser said, "So is what these guys did. It is all right there in front of us. Only we can't prove it."

"So what're you saying?"

Sasser set the portfolio at his feet and sat back, crossing his legs. "Here, let me map it out. On one hand we know—we're as sure of their guilt as we are of death and taxes. But we don't have one shred of evidence that ties any one of them to the murders."

"We have circumstantial—"

"We don't even have that. What we have is speculation. Conjecture. Guesswork. Suspicions. We have some very well-reasoned opinions, but no one will ever ask us for them. We—"

"I may just know of something we can do."

"No, I have a surefire way—"

"They say 'surefire' in Singapore?"

"Now, listen to me, Boggs, will you? Just this once for God's sake."

Reaching for the bourbon, Boggs said, "I'm all ears."

"Remember those famous Agatha Christie mysteries with the detective Hercule Poirot?"

Seeing that Boggs was about to say no, Sasser pressed on, "Well, what he did, this Hercule Poirot, what he did was round up all the suspects. He'd get them all in one room and then through deft questioning and keen logic, he'd identify the killer. Or the killer, seeing his situation of hopelessness, would confess."

"And …?"

"And what?"

"That's it? You've gotta be kiddin'."

Sasser protested vehemently, indicating it was the only chance they had. The lone drawback he saw was how to get everyone together, what pretext to use.

Boggs arched his good eyebrow and held up his index finger. "Let me just show you how it's done, Mr. Sasser." He referred back to the telephone directory, found the number, and dialed. He cleared his throat, saying "Let's just see if this dog will hunt." He smiled in Sasser's direction.

"Judge Hardy residence," answered a woman.

"Evenin'. This is the sheriff. The judge in?"

"Sheriff, he in the bed. Got—"

"Get 'im," he ordered.

While Boggs waited, he swished his dry mouth with bourbon.

The judge answered with a hoarse, "All right?"

"Sound a touch off tonight, John."

"Who is this?"

"This is the man you was thinkin' about when you went down that ditch."

"I said, who is this?"

"So tell me, John, why were you so preoccupied about me, about what I know? Think I'm gonna put you out of business?"

"I said, who is this?" The voice packed such force Boggs had to hold the receiver away from his ear.

# CHAPTER TWENTY-EIGHT

"Done what now?" cried Tinnin in disbelief. Boggs had told him about last night's call to the judge. "Man, now they'll know it was me what told."

Boggs sat calmly on the worn bench outside The Store. He gestured to him to lower his voice. The caged way Tinnin paced disturbed him. "He didn't know it was me. I hung up. Besides, he don't remember what he said. The man was delirious. And I never said cowboys or nothing. So how's he to know?"

Tinnin turned to face him. "But just saying about the Moose … you've gone and done it now. They're probably watchin' me right this very minute."

"They're doin' no such thing." Even so, he looked up and down the road. "They don't know nothin' now that they didn't already know." He added, "Pitchin' a fit to beat… Here." He offered a pull on the bottle he had in a paper bag.

"Are you puredee crazy? I'm on duty." He stopped pacing. "And what in hell were you thinkin' lettin' Sasser in on the conversation?"

"It's called testin' the waters."

"And how was that?"

"Tepid, a little too tepid for my taste." Boggs shrugged and drank with a pronounced gulp. "Look, the thing you're forgettin' is that they're afraid. And they got good reason to be." He took a drink. "And I got me one surefire idea, all on account of that call." He added, "The 'surefire' was Sasser's word, but damn, that was fun."

As outlined by Boggs, the plan purported to be the only way to bring the judge and company out into the open. It called for blackmail: telling the vice captain that the state bureau of investigation would knock on his door if he didn't pay a small stipend, say weekly.

"You can't blackmail the law."

"There ain't no law, not with them breakin' it."

Tinnin hesitated and saw without seeing Shufflin' Sam, who looked back at him from inside the store. "Ya know, it sure seems that way. But the high sheriff? And the chief judge? What's that if it ain't the law?"

"Listen, all I have to do is call Wynne. Tell him I know what's goin' on and I can prove it. Tell him I want to change the terms of this understandin' of ours, whatever that was to begin with. Change it by, say, fifty thousand—"

"A week?" shouted Tinnin.

"Hang on there, big fella." He took a drink and cast a crooked look at the deputy. "Geez. Pull yourself together."

"Well, fifty—"

"I'll be like your personal banker. We'll work out some easy payment terms." He paused reflectively. "Naw, I'll give them a day or so to come up with the whole lot. Whaddya think? Friday sound good?"

"Nothin' about this sounds good."

"Good, Friday it is. I'll tell them I'll call back on Friday with arrangements for the delivery."

Tinnin called out the private detective's name as if to entreat him, but at the same time he marched toward his cruiser as if bent not on an appeal to reason but on making a quick exit. He stopped abruptly. "We don't know for sure none of them are—"

Boggs interrupted with a smile. "No better time to find out."

"And what stops them from killing you between now and Friday?"

"I'll think of somethin'."

"Like what? Another drink?"

"I'll tell 'em I've mapped out the whole story to a lawyer friend in James City, so if something should happen to me, well ..."

Pleased with the stratagem, he leaned back and pushed out his legs. "Yeah, I'd say this will work just fine."

Tinnin let his mouth drop into a third chin. "If this isn't a damned fool idea—they know you don't have any proof. If ya had ... well, what kind of proof could you have? Anybody that knowed anything is dead."

"Wynne's nobody's fool. He knows that someone else knows. He just doesn't know who. Might could be that I talked with this person, got a sworn affidavit." He paused and then snapped his fingers. "Got a better idea. The sheriff's still in the hospital, isn't he?"

"Yeah, I s'pose. He ain't back at work."

"Good. I'll tell Wynne we want the sheriff there too, and if he leaves the hospital between now and then, then we know for sure."

"Shoot," said Tinnin with bluster. "Even if he was to leave don't mean he done it. And you ain't even got a gun, let alone carry one. What're you gonna do between now and then?"

Boggs tapped his fingers on his belly. There was a thumping sound inside. "Got me a foolproof hideaway. I'll stay home with the wife—last place they'd think to look."

"You're right about that." Tinnin nodded with demonstrative uh-huh. "It'll be the last place cuz it will be the first." He stopped pacing. "This ain't never gonna work. Not ever—"

"Never is now, my friend."

"Well … well, s'pose Wynne turns around and arrests you for blackmail?"

Boggs trotted out a big smile. "You believe Wynne, the sheriff, they're gonna let the DA's office prosecute me? He knows they'd lose. Besides, they can't afford to have this story come out. Everyone'd believe they done somethin' to be blackmailed for."

While Tinnin strode back and forth, he worked his jaw as if chewing a small piece of gum. He stopped when he caught Shufflin' Sam peering through the window. "What're you looking at?" he screamed. Sam turned away. The deputy resumed his trek and, after a while, came to a halt. "So they play along and make like they've got the money, only one—let's say Wynne's wired. And then, of course, he has the most creditable witness in the county, the sheriff himself. And they could arrest you then and tell everyone they caught the murderer. Not even the DA could lose a case like that. Who'd believe you over the sheriff? He's been sheriff for thirty-three years. Ain't no one to oppose him in twenty-nine. The man's reputation is damn near gospel. What kind a reputation you got? Heck, your own clients hate you, what with you diddlin' their wives or daughters."

After a deep breath, Tinnin went on, "DA or no DA, a jury won't waste its time goin' into a jury room. More'n half of 'em'll probably be husbands whose wives you messed with or wives whose husbands found you out."

"A change of venue, ole sod, a change of venue."

"Movin' it somewhere else don't stop Wynne and them from playin' along and gettin' all the evidence they need." He paced and then stopped. "Can't, never could, won't never will blackmail the likes of the sheriff and them."

Boggs coiled from his stretch. He rested his elbows on his knees. "Then it's not the sheriff we go after. It's the judge."

The deputy froze as if someone had jammed a pistol in his back. "The judge?" He spun. "The judge! You gone plum' out of your mind? He's the worse of 'em all! You ain't hittin' on much, Boggs. You ain't hittin' on nothin' at all."

"He frightens easy. Now he don't got as much age on him as the sheriff, but he frightens easy." Boggs hesitated, looking inward. "I've—I'll be a mother's—let's get Simon Sasser in on it too. Let's get 'em all together. Wynne, the sheriff, and Hardy. And we'll probably—yeah! And we'll find out just who in the hell this Sasser is when he comes taggin' along."

"Shoot." Tinnin spit. "If this ain't—what, you just gonna pick up the phone and say something like, 'Hey, let's get together for a beer and discuss how much we should blackmail you for.'"

"That's good, Tinnin. I like the way you think."

"Boggs, by you calling them, you've as much as told them I told you. They'll be after me now. They know I was at the Moose that night. Ain't no one said nothin', but they know. What's to stop them from killin' me and blamin'—"

"Boy, you think you've compacted that gravel down enough? Stop with the pacing or Old Sam here is gonna have to get a new load." When the deputy checked his stride, he continued, "Now Judge Hardy don't know what he said. He coulda said he was the ringleader. He coulda said it to the rescue squad boys. He don't know—"

"But I kicked him."

"So what? He don't know. Hope you kicked him good. He was unconscious. Remember? He was incoherent. He don't know nothin' but that he's in trouble—real, come-knockin'-on-the-front-door trouble. He can't keep his wits about him for fear of losin' all he's got. He's the weak link. I say we go after him."

Tinnin dropped onto the bench. His head fell back, the rolls of flesh under his chin arcing. He closed his eyes and said, "Shoulda never told you nothin'. You're gonna get us all killed." After a moment the fat face lurched forward. "And what'd we do if they confess?"

"Believe we can file this under citizen's justice."

"Justice!" Tinnin's face collapsed into his hands. He motioned as if he were washing it. "Man-o-man, if this isn't the craziest idea I've ever heard of."

"Worked for some guy named Poirot," said Boggs

"What worked?" asked Milt Allison as he entered their midst. His white T-shirt looked too white for his denim overalls.

Tinnin was first to reply. "Craziness ..."

"Used wisely, it works every time," added Boggs.

Milt took a seat beside the deputy.

"There's all manner of crazy," said Milt, leaning forward, elbows on knees. "There's insane, there's ding-dong and loony-tune, there's plum' stupid, there's Coonie Pride nuts, there's mad-dog crazy, there's—"

"I'd say it's kinda like this here liquor. Blended," Boggs said, then took a drink.

"Well, then, don't make it like you're dancin'." He added, "You know, like they say, dance like ain't nobody watchin'."

"Now what in the puredee tar does that mean, Milt?" asked Tinnin.

"Like ya had some sense but didn't give a damn."

Tinnin said, his voice raised, "Sense? Boggs here gonna get us all killed."

"See ya, boys," said Milt and went inside.

# CHAPTER TWENTY-NINE

For the past forty-five minutes, traffic on Garner Road had been sparse. Now it was nearly noon, and people and cars emerged as if in answer to a signal so pitched that only the chosen could hear it. Shine left his Quonset hut, some hundred yards down the road from The Store, and drove his pickup to it, anxious for his can of sardines, pack of crackers, and tea that Sam kept under the counter for preferred customers.

On his way back from the post office, Will Blake stopped upon seeing Boggs and Tinnin. He pulled his pickup beside Shine's and came around the corner. He fingered the bill of his John Deere cap and said, "Carson. Mr. Boggs."

Both men nodded back, saying, "Will" and "Mr. Blake."

"Taking a break from your investigating?" asked Will of Boggs.

"On the case as we speak."

"As we speak, you say?"

"As we speak."

"Better let ya get to it then." Will went inside.

Shine and Will joined Milt and sat on crates beside the cold potbelly stove while Sam tended to customers. Will nibbled on a wedge of hoop cheese and sipped his tea. Shine used the flat of the stove as a table for his sardines, crackers, and drink. Milt sipped his RC Cola. The three watched the confab outside.

Finally Will said, "Done give 'im two hundred dollars and look at 'im. Sittin' out there drinkin' out of a bag without a care in the world."

Boggs was saying, "Get us all killed is right. It's what the judge believes. Said as much at the Moose, didn't he?"

Tinnin saw the community elders staring out at him. Pinching his eyes closed, he shook his head and then looked at Boggs. "Okay, s'pose you do meet with them. S'pose you do. What's to stop 'em from killin' you?"

"You." Boggs broadcast a toothy smile. "You'll be hidin' some—"

"Oh, no, you don't. I want no part of this."

"Carson, you can't fail me now. You're my right-hand man."

"I ain't gettin' myself killed."

"Oh, you'll warm to the idea."

The remark stopped the deputy in his tracks. "Let's see. There'd be Wynne, the sheriff, and Judge Hardy. Probably the three vice agents. And then there's this Sasser guy that we done told everything to. And here we are, don't know the first thing about 'im, and he knows all there is to know about us. Ain't we some sorry-ass fools? And then you've seen 'im with Wynne, so who knows what they're up to. Probably fixin' to kill us for all we know. So let's see. There's seven against two. No, I mean, one. You ain't got a gun."

"They won't know that."

"I reckon you're gonna put your hand in your pocket and make out like you got one?" He took up his march, his steps labored as if his high-gloss shoes were leaden blocks. Boggs didn't respond for a minute, then said, "Naw, it won't work."

"Won't work? Boy, you won't have time to say hello! They'll shoot your ass quicker than a snake and then turn around and tell the newspaper it was the same one what killed Blake and the Allen girl. And that'll be the end of it. Your dead end."

Boggs's smile surfaced slowly.

"Quit grinnin' like some dumbass mule." Tinnin added, "So you believe you can trick them into believin' we're not settin' a trap. Have them believe this jamboree of yours is not some kind of a trick, that it's on the up and up?"

"Man, tricks are everywhere. Half of the time you don't see 'em. The old smoke screen. Take our elections. We put folks in office who are the trickiest scam artists alive. "

"So cuz the sheriff's an elected official, he's a trickster?"

"No, just a crook whose tricks you don't see. His confiscatin' a pound of dope and then calling it a few ounces is the same as pulling a rabbit out of a hat."

"Well, you'd better pull a miracle out of your hat or your ass, one."

"Tinnin, if I've run afoul of as many husbands as everyone seems to believe and I'm still here, don't you think I can get us outta this?"

"Sooner get out of a grave." Tinnin stopped to clasp his hands behind his back, a gesture that caused him to bend at the waist as he resumed his tramp.

"And let's say you do catch 'em. Who's to arrest 'em? Since there's no coroner, there ain't nobody in Dinwoodie County can arrest the sheriff. And I got no idea who can arrest a judge. And don't for a minute believe Wynne's gonna let himself be arrested. Just what'd you think you was gonna do? Kinda walk in, like through the automatic doors at the Piggly Wiggly, and collect the money and get their confessions and then ride away into the sunset? You're a few shy of a load there, Boggs."

"I'll have it all worked out. 'Sides, if they come, it's a confession, isn't it?"

"Might as well hold this get-together of yours on that field General Pickett tried to cross."

"Ya know," he said holding in chin. "It'll be 120 years come next year."

"Next year? That's one thing we won't see. Let me—"

"That's it! We'll have this little powwow at the scene of the crime." He sat back and laughed. "The ole scene of the crime."

"You mean Blake's trailer?"

"What better than the scene of the crime?" He added, "Man-o-man ..."

"Let me ask you this then: what happens when you go to the magistrate, you've got the three most powerful men around, and you say to the magistrate, 'I blackmailed them, and they fell for it, so it means they done it'?" After a cynical snort, he added, "And let's not forget the magistrate's boss man is Judge Hardy. You honestly believe he'd draw up a warrant on his boss man? He'd like to die first. No, Boggs, the onliest thing to come of all this is a quick end to you."

Boggs took a pull on the bottle. "I'll have it all worked out by tomorrow. Make the call late tomorrow night and then call you with the details."

"A gone coon is what we are. A gone coon." At last the thread of their conversation poked through the eye of the needle, for only now did it occur to Tinnin that he was caught up in this life-and-death scheme as much as anyone else, be it Boggs or the sheriff or the judge. Until this moment, the deputy wasn't even sure he was helping, never mind which side. Now he understood that they were not nearer to the truth; they were upon it, all of them. Now all the ideas and doubts, all the speculation and expectation, ceased. Vanished. They reached the end to confront it or run from it.

"The beauty …," Boggs muffled a laugh. "The beauty of it is that it's so dumb I'm ashamed of myself for proposing it. Thank God I didn't think of it; that was Sasser's doin'. But here I am sittin' here plannin' it out. Dumb, man, dumb. But dumb—now never underestimate dumb. See, they're creditin' us with thinkin', and we ain't. But then again, we are, but we ain't thinkin' along the lines they're thinkin'. So when they get wind of what we got in store, they're gonna be thinkin' and thinkin'. And we won't have to do nothin' because we've already done all the thinkin' that's required for such a dumb idea. Now, you tell me: ain't this about the most beautiful idea you ever heard?"

"Gone coons," said the deputy, his mouth slung low. "That's what we are."

"No, we ain't." He paused, "Hey, wonder why Sasser hasn't showed up yet? Seems to know wherever I go. Always only a few minutes behind me. And here we are out in broad daylight." He took a drink. "Ya know, now that I think about it, he never follows me down thisaway 'cept that one time when that sniper shot out my front tire. The trooper said the man couldn't get away fast enough. That strike you as odd?" He took a drink.

"Gone coons."

"Quit saying that, Tinnin. C'mon, take a ride with me over to Blake's trailer."

"I can't leave my car."

"Follow me then."

The station wagon bounced in the ruts on the dirt road leading to the trailer. The shock absorbers squawked and didn't stop until Boggs parked in front of the rubble. The cruiser eased up behind him.

Despite the cramped confines of the car, Boggs jumped out, his hand on his fly. Without regard for Tinnin, he took a leak, exclaiming, "Dear God in heaven, how long have I been holdin' this little pleasure?" He looked over his shoulder at the deputy and said, "Sometimes, somethin' like a good piss is better than a night 'tween the sheets."

Looking skyward, Tinnin said, "Wouldn't know."

Once Boggs finished, they came around to the where the front steps used to be. They squinted under the harsh sun. To ease his discomfort, Boggs held his heavy hand over his eyes for a visor. Tinnin tucked his campaign hat farther down.

"Okay, this is how I see it," said Boggs. "I'll be—"

He stopped himself when he saw buzzards circling. He cursed to himself. Such a clear, clean sky sullied by these harbingers. He continued, "I'll be out here. I'll park the car like I just done. You, my friend," patting Tinnin on the shoulder, "you'll already be here. Let's—" He scanned the area. "Okay, yeah. You'll be hidin' behind the trailer there. That one standin' wall should be good cover. I'll park so you can see and hear everything. Then when they confess, you come out. I'll whistle like—" A two-beat whistle passed over Boggs's puckered lips. "That'll be the signal for you to come out—"

"And get my sorry ass shot."

"Now, Carson, is that any way to be?"

"If stupid was food, we'd have enough to feed the Pharaoh's army."

# CHAPTER THIRTY

They knew.

Tinnin knew they knew.

They knew he was at the Moose when Judge Hardy's accident occurred. They knew he was able to testify to the judge's state of intoxication. They knew he had read the newspaper article that made no mention of alcohol but rather implied a narrow escape. What they didn't know was just how much Tinnin dared to deduce.

Now they knew that they couldn't count on Tinnin's silence. Last night Boggs had initiated the blackmail. Whatever he had said surely led them to one and only one conclusion: that they had been betrayed by one of their own. The conclusion was unavoidable.

Just exactly how Tinnin had gotten into all this eluded him. He couldn't really understand what was happening. To be sure, he was well aware of what had happened: men of official standing had conspired to murder one person and then a second to hide the first slaying. He knew how they had done it. He knew why they had done it. Yet he understood none of it.

Of all that was happening, he was certain of only one thing: that he was alone. The blackmail was indeed dumb, very dumb, for it exposed him. With Boggs in hiding, Tinnin stood wide open. Until something better came along, his lone defense was his visibility.

At roll call this morning, he had acted as if nothing were amiss. He had made a display of yawning and stretching and complained to a few of a hangover. But no matter what he did, they were watching him, watching him as closely as a murderer watched the world.

Not knowing where they were, Tinnin felt they were omnipresent. Wherever he went, they were there. They followed his patrol, monitoring his cruiser's every turn, speed, and destination. Maybe they could even trace his steps outside the car, and if they could do that, then they could listen to every word he said and see him pretending not to look. And they could tell by the way he looked that he was blinded, blinded by the bladed eye of their revenge. For he was the danger, and they were the threatened; he was the offender, and they were the aggrieved.

The deputy caught himself checking the rearview mirror. The morning fog rolled from the high ground he had just covered. He slid the gray cruiser off the road and onto the gravel at Shine's garage. The bay doors stood open and dark. He honked to break the silence and drove inside. In the back, framed by the meager window light, was Shine's scarecrow figure leaning into the hood of an old Chevy Impala. Tinnin climbed out and went directly to the front doors. As he pulled them to, his "mornin'" was lost in the squawk of the door's tracked wheels.

Shine never rose from under the hood.

Tinnin crossed the soft oiled ground. His shoes crushed a carpet of washers and bottle caps, butts and bolts, and veered past half-repaired motors, rusted generators, vestiges of mowers, and bones of tillers. The twenty-foot worktable to his right teemed with dark debris and carbon-coated tools. Because of the dirt, light from the window above the table shone unevenly.

Still busy under the hood, Shine asked, "You see it?"

"See what?" Tinnin looked around him.

"The black snake it's takin' up here."

"Where?"

"It ain't choicy."

"Why don't you put down some sulfur?"

"It ain't bothered no one none." After a moment he added, "'Cept maybe Coonie. He says he can't come down here to settle his account. Says it run him off the other day while I was gone."

"How's he gettin' his—" The deputy stopped himself.

In answer to the unstated question, Shine replied, "He ain't run out yet. Probably still has a jar or two."

Tinnin pushed his hands into his pockets, locking the elbows. He didn't really believe the authorities were listening. Even so, he lowered his voice. "Yeah, well—well, look here. I want ya to help me with somethin'."

"What's that?" Shine rose.

"My car."

Shine glanced over his shoulder at the cruiser. "What's wrong with it?"

"There might could be … well, there might could be something in it what ain't s'posta be there."

"It makin' noise? Running hot or something?"

"No. Leastways not now."

"It was?"

"No."

"Then what?"

"I don't rightly know. Just help me go over it."

"Ain't that what they got the county garage for?"

"Shine, just help me, will ya?"

"How can I help when I don't know what to help for?"

"Okay, okay, look for somethin' that shouldn't be there."

"Mean like a bomb?"

"Mean like a device for tracking or listening or …"

"You in trouble, Carson?"

"Trouble ain't the half of it."

Despite Shine's complaints for details, Tinnin popped the hood and set a mechanic's light. Shine slid underneath on a dolly with another light. Their examination took less than ten minutes. They moved their inspection to the rear of the car.

Before long, Shine rolled the dolly out and swung to the side to sit. "You want to pull the tires?"

Tinnin shook his head, his wet lips pressed against his teeth.

While retrieving the light, Shine said, "If it's trouble, I don't believe it's with this."

Tinnin pushed down on the trunk twice and then had to slam it shut. "I reckon." He mumbled thanks. Just as he was about to get into the car, he turned to ask, "Shine, tell me somethin'. Folks think I'm sorta to blame for all these killins, don't they?"

"Ain't heard no one say nothin' like that." He stroked his bony chin. "Fact is, we're glad you're here."

Tinnin nodded with a noncommittal expression. He went to his cruiser. With some effort he maneuvered himself into the driver's seat. As he cranked the car, Shine approached the window, toweling his indelibly stained hands with a rag. "If it gives you any more trouble, you just come on back. If I can't fix it, somebody down thisaway can."

The deputy nodded and waited while Shine opened the doors.

His stomach felt hollow even though he had eaten two ham biscuits earlier. His vision felt strained as if pushed out of the sides of his sunglasses. He had no clear destination when he pointed the car east on Garner Road. Nothing required his attention; no complaints had been lodged overnight.

Ordinarily, this would have been an ideal day simply riding the roads and stopping occasionally to chat, but Shine's remark exerted its authority. He really didn't know how to accept it—as a compliment or as a dodge because Shine didn't want to hurt his feelings. As much as he wished to believe in the former, the latter was probably nearer the truth. He had no hard and fast evidence that the people of Random found him to be less than competent, less than capable of keeping the peace. But then again, evidence of anything except pain was commonplace nowadays. There was no real evidence the sheriff and his cronies were the franchiser, but some inchoate supposition all but demanded that he believe the hierarchy of crime and justice in Dinwoodie and Greensburg was corrupt. He turned north on McKenney and approached an orange Volkswagen Beetle. While it wasn't the illusive red pickup truck for which he had been searching, he decided to slide in behind it. That the driver watched him through the rearview mirror told him he might be on to something. He backed off, keeping a two-car interval. The driver continued to watch. At Cherry Hill, the VW stopped for the sign. Tinnin pulled up behind it. The VW continued north. The deputy sat at the stop sign for five minutes, then drove north. He saw the VW about a half mile ahead. He accelerated to close the gap. At Boydton Plank, the VW turned east. When the cruiser followed, the driver swung around to look. Tinnin hit his blue lights. The VW obeyed.

Before Tinnin had a chance to roll down his window, the middle-aged driver was there. "What's wrong? What'd I do?"

The deputy looked up at the pallid grimace the man broadcast and then back at the orange car. Finally, he thought of something to say. "Get back in your car."

"But what'd I do? I wasn't speeding."

Tinnin pointed to the VW. "I'll be with you directly."

The man made a slow march to his car. Before getting in, he looked back at the deputy who sat there impassively, gazing ahead, not seeing anything. Finally, Tinnin got out and adjusted his Smokey-the-Bear hat. He hitched his britches and eyeballed the license plate. The driver's face loomed out of the open window.

"Here's my license and registration."

Tinnin made no effort to take them. "It won't be necessary. You can go now."

"But what was wrong?"

"Just go on now." Tinnin went back to the cruiser. He sat and stared. Five minutes later, he realized the VW was gone. He started the engine and made a U-turn. At Highway 1, he turned north. He knew where to go now.

The only chance Tinnin had left was the sheriff. There was no hard, or for that matter circumstantial, evidence to link the sheriff to the killings. Boggs and he worked on the supposition that Sheriff Harris, legend for being where he wasn't wanted and knowing what he wasn't intended to know, had to know about the killings and so had to be involved. But there never was any proof. The times the sniper attacked, Harris was in the hospital.

And the best argument of all was his longevity; Harris had been sheriff long before Tinnin was born. Voters returned him to office term after term because he kept the county quiet, although not necessarily clean. Drugs only became a problem five or six years ago, and murders for profit only happened elsewhere until recently.

Tinnin pushed the cruiser, hoping the sooner he got to the hospital, the less chance of the dispatcher asking for his location. Road traffic was light, and radio traffic even lighter. Even so, he would have to check in on the hour. That left him twenty minutes. It probably wasn't enough time, but once he had spoken to Harris, maybe it wouldn't matter.

At the hospital, he parked in the rear. He scarcely waited for the automatic doors at the entrance to open. At the reception desk, he asked an elderly woman for the sheriff's room. She didn't have to look. "He was released about an hour ago," she said. The clock behind her told him he had five minutes to get back to his car because he hadn't the presence of mind to bring his radio. He didn't run.

As he left the lot, he braked. It took him a moment to be certain. His eyes fell away and then came back to Simon Sasser standing just far enough away for the automatic doors to remain closed. They stared at each other until the hour struck. The patrol cars reported in one by one. His gaze still fixed on Sasser, Tinnin blindly reached for the radio. He said, "Thirty-four, Garner Road."

He drove south until he reached the Hico store. He used the pay phone to report in to Dr. Allen, as Boggs had instructed. He told the doctor about Sasser, a statement without explanation. Upon leaving, he went down to Stiff Branch Road, intent on reconnoitering Blake's trailer for a hiding place.

# CHAPTER THIRTY-ONE

The self-applauding Boggs liked to think of himself as "on ice." For the past thirty-six hours, he had confined himself to room 214 at Memorial Hospital, the four-story structure that resembled a mammoth chest freezer. It was the only public building in Greensburg not built of brick, sandstone, or more recently, blue granite. The architects billed the edifice as an indomitable testament to life. Townsfolk failed to reconcile such an august claim and reduced it to plan English; they dubbed it the Ice Box.

With the help of an unquestioning Dr. Allen, Boggs arrived via ambulance under the name R.T. Tucker. Until the severity of his suspected case of bacterial meningitis was determined, Boggs was placed in isolation, a term that was not quite accurate. He was hooked up to all manner of monitoring devices as well as an IV saline drip. Nurses outside were in constant touch with his vitals.

On the pretext of minimizing the risk of contagion, sDr. Allen left orders that he was the only person permitted to examine the patient. The two scheduled liquid meals were delivered hastily by fully dressed orderlies who, before retreating, had to strip off their gowns, caps, gloves, and masks at the door. A first-shift nurse who deposited soap and water and quickly changed the bed brought the number of visits Boggs had to five.

Isolation had a baleful effect on Boggs. He was helpless not to attend to the noises outside his door. And just when he expected a knock and the knob to turn, the clatter faded. He flung himself back, vowing not to listen, vowing in earnest even as he listened to the renewed commotion outside. At times he thought he heard distant conversations about snipers and faint references to law enforcement. In the end, he was always left waiting for that knock or turn of the knob.

Although what visitors he had were a nuisance, Boggs welcomed Dr. Allen, mainly because the good doctor brought what Boggs construed as a liquid meal: Ancient Age whiskey. Lest Allen think him crude, Boggs sipped from a paper cup rather than take pulls from the bottle. He asked about news, information not found in the newspaper. Allen said that the sheriff had been released and that Tinnin had seen Mr. Sasser at the hospital not long after the sheriff left. Boggs questioned him in a voice weak from the lack of use. The doctor said that a fourteen-day stay wasn't unusual for a coronary patient, although many were released sooner. Coincidence or not, Boggs granted himself the license to think his plan was taking shape.

"So what do you make of Sasser being at the hospital?" Boggs had asked.

"I have neither an opinion nor any idea. I haven't seen the man in … what? A week?"

"Does he strike you as—"

"Mysterious?"

"That will work."

"Yes, he does. But I can tell you without equivocation he is not the man who killed Wendy."

"How so?"

"I'll know the man when I see him."

"I bet you will."

This morning, Allen had appeared early and quietly, his face masked like the others but his dark eyes unmoving unlike the others. He went directly to the bedside to take the patient's blood pressure and listen to the heart. The routine bewildered Boggs, so much so that he had to shake his head a few times after following Allen's raised index finger. The brief examination completed, Allen patted him on the shoulder and went to the window. He stood for a time with his hands clasped behind his back, gazing out on the parking lot. He answered questions with a simple yes or no. The most disappointing piece of news was that Tinnin hadn't reported in. All the same, Boggs told himself, the deputy had his instructions.

Before Allen left, he pulled out the IV but kept the patches so as not to alert the nursing staff. He promised to return about 6 p.m. Boggs begged him to bring some edible food.

Boggs then called his office. That the answering machine worked reassured him. No messages were there. He waited an hour and called back, leaving himself a message: "Don't forget to keep your appointment tonight; we wouldn't want to keep them waiting."

Boggs fell back on the pillow and smiled wearily, flashing back to his call to the judge two days ago. He had anticipated difficulty in getting the judge on the line, but the wife answered and, without comment, turned the phone over to his honor. Boggs spoke in a guttural inflection and kept the receiver at his throat. The measures were unnecessary. Judge Hardy listened in silence, almost as though he had expected the call. It mystified Boggs why Hardy, a man trained to question and probe, made no attempt to ascertain who the caller was and how the caller knew about the franchise. The judge neither flinched nor balked at the $50,000 demand. To ensure against crossed signals, Boggs told him three times that he would call again with further instructions. Then, for the first time, Hardy spoke. He said, "Okay."

It went so smoothly that at first Boggs thought Hardy didn't take him seriously or possibly had been half-asleep, sedated by drug or drink. He dismissed the idea and called Tinnin. For the first time, the deputy didn't try to second-guess him or appeal to moderation. He told Boggs how he had improved on the hiding place by cutting out peep holes. He said, "I reckon we're the law now. All that's left of it anyways."

The deputy's remark told Boggs that his plan was the answer—not the right one or the wrong one, just the answer. The doctor, the judge, the deputy—all did as he bid without question. That they weren't curious or defensive or skeptical frightened Boggs. He sensed the return of defeat.

Defeat had come last night. Having slept most of the afternoon, he had lain awake in the dark trying not to listen to sourceless sounds. His back pressed against the unyielding mattress as the noise rebounded, and then it occurred to him that he approached the end already beaten, beaten by an event that occurred years ago. This end was not of his choosing but of his doing. And he could do nothing now to stop it, to change it, to escape from it. He was lost, even to himself. He felt strangely detached. He was neither inside himself nor outside. He was elsewhere. He was in an ever-recurring place that he knew without knowing, a place without objects, just uneven light. He kept coming back to this place because he was already in it, because he could never leave it, because he was there—there wrestling with Rufus Grover. He was there even after he groped for the light switch. The room burst open. He sprang as if coiled. He was there in the window: an unholy ghost of his reflection watching him. He pulled away and fumbled with the water pitcher. He drank from the spout in gulps. His tongue remained thick. He turned back to the window, his stare blank and unthinking.

About midmorning while working the crossword, he caught the sound of the knob turning. His pencil skidded across the page. He pulled himself and the newspaper under the covers. Through a squint, he watched the door open. A masked face peered around the edge. The intruder stepped inside, gently closed the door, and turned to look at what appeared to be a slumbering figure. The green cap completely covered the head, and the gown was too baggy to tell whether it was a man or woman. The trespasser took one quiet step, passing from the poorly lit entrance into the square of the room. Boggs gritted his teeth upon seeing horn-rimmed glasses. He rolled onto his back, yawned, and locked his hands behind his head. "So what brings you here, Mr. Sasser?"

"Feeling better, Mr. Tucker?"

"Was."

"The doctor tells me you're on the mend. In fact, should be out of here sometime this evening."

"How'd you talk him into lettin' you in?"

"We're of the same mind."

"What … killin'? You hidin' that rifle of yours under there?" With his chin he gestured toward the gown.

"What's going on, Boggs?"

"You and Allen pretty tight, huh?"

"I said, what's going on? What're—"

"Why'd you want to know?"

Sasser stepped close. He yanked down his mask. "I want to know what's going on. What're you doing here?"

For once, Boggs appreciated the man's assertiveness. He could laugh at defeat now. But his laughter sputtered and died before it really started. "The trouble with you is you write checks your ass can't cover. A big game hunter, my ass. You'd been a better shot, and I—"

"What do you mean, a better shot?"

"You were high on the first, wide on the second, and I don't know what you were aiming at on the third."

Silence settled in spite of the noise of the mechanical bed rising.

Sasser curved his hands around the bed rail. "How'd you know?"

"It come to me. Give me a right good whack. See, first I figured they staged it. Like they done with my car. But two snipin's ain't their style. They're too set in their ways, too used to havin' it their way. So then it come to me that you're the only one with a reason, a reason to take out the man you think killed your girlfriend. But what I don't get is—you hadn't known her but what, for a few weeks? A month or better? So ... so she couldn't mean too much. And pussy, now, it'll make you do some crazy-ass things, but it don't make you cross no ocean just to kill the man what killed the piece you was diddlin'."

Silence returned. It nearly approached solidity before Boggs spoke. "But, now, what I can't figure, and I ain't been known for hittin' on a whole lot, but what I can't figure, and you likely got one of the simplest damn answers, but what I can't figure is how'd you know where Wynne would be."

"I called him."

Boggs snorted a laugh. "See there. Didn't I tell you? That's one simple-ass answer." He expelled air and eased back in the pillow. "I'll tell you what, if you ain't a simple Simon. Just getting' on the phone and sayin', 'Here I am. Come get me.'" He paused. "But how'd you know he'd stop where he did?"

"I said to meet me at Blake's drive. He stopped about fifty yards or so away from it. Couldn't miss the blue lights."

"So you ran back up there, in the dark no less, and took your firing position."

"Thanks to you, I had the time."

"What'd you really say to Wynne to get 'im down there? Come and get me?"

Sasser smiled. "Sorry to disappoint you, but that's precisely what I said." He added, "Now tell me. What are you doing here?"

"By the way, what were you doin' at the Southside Precinct in James City?"

"Following you." His smile widened. "I got lost and pulled into the police station to ask for directions."

"Why the police station? Why not a gas station?"

"I didn't know it was a police station until I was in the parking lot."

"Directions? Directions to where?"

"Back to the interstate. I knew I'd lost you, so I figured what was the point. Might as well head back, but I was completely turned around."

"Yeah, I know the feeling." Boggs massaged his lower lip. "I'll tell you what. You gave me a four-drink headache over that one."

"Okay, Boggs, I've been up front with you. Now it's your turn. What are doing here?"

Boggs was no match for Sasser's stare. "Know the trouble with you is, you jumped before you knew the whole story. But then we kinda laid it out for you, only you didn't know how to go about it." He added, "But then you did tell me you were a big game hunter. Now—"

"You're waiting, aren't you? For what?"

"The doc tell you that?"

"I'm putting two and two together." He added, "Waiting for what?"

"Might could say I'm bringin' in the sheaves." He paused. "After all, it was your idea. Just hadn't gotten around to callin' you."

"You're going to meet them tonight?"

"The thing of it is—"

"Where?"

"The thing of it is, you're too damn reckless. If they had caught your ass, they'da hung two murders on you."

"A chance I took."

"All this for Wendy Allen?"

Sasser repeated in staccato, "All this for Wendy Allen." After a moment he added, "Now where?"

"Why not follow me? Seems to be—"

"Where?"

"Just bound and determined." Boggs stopped to enjoy a laugh at the furious stillness taking hold of Sasser. "I'll be damned if I know what you're up to. But it's tonight. Too bad you ain't the shot—"

"I said, where?"

"Now how's this for perfect? Perfect or dumb, one. The trailer."

"Billy's trailer?" A flurry of blinks brought Sasser's stare crashing down. He cut his eyes to the right. The cut was sharp, paring away Boggs and leaving his gaze to lodge on the open wound of blank space. He came back, delivering that fierce stillness. "What do you want me to do?"

"Can't say as I like you behind me, so how about beside me? I believe I'll deputize you. Make you special agent Sasser with the state bureau of investigation. 'Cept you're not carrying a gun. Now go get yourself a badge somewhere, a nice shiny oval one, one you can see in the dark."

"What time?"

"No guns. Even if you learn to shoot 'tween now and then."

"What time?"

"No guns. Understood?"

"No, but—"

"But what?"

"All right. No guns. What time?"

# CHAPTER THIRTY-TWO

Erring on the side of caution, Dr. Allen escorted Boggs through the darkened administrative wing. He held the outside door open without saying goodbye or good luck. Only a small sigh broke his composed but dire silence. Boggs all but jumped out and onto the cement platform. He stretched out his arms as if in pagan salute to the breeze. A rising three-quarter moon stretched its beams to him. He looked back and said, "Smells like fall, don't it?"

Allen didn't answer.

Boggs snapped his fingers. "Oh, almost forgot. The bottle."

From his black bag, Allen removed the pint of Ancient Age.

Boggs uncapped it, held it up as if to toast, and drank. "Damn glad to be gettin' outta this dump. I'll call ya." He strode to Sasser's Z28. Once inside, he took a swig and capped the bottle.

Sasser drove off slowly in keeping with the speed limit in the parking lot. "Any problems?" he asked.

"You kiddin'?" Boggs laughed. "You know what Mr. R.T. Tucker just done? He done the impossible. He went in healthy and came out healthy." He stopped and examined Sasser in his dark blue suit. "Gotta hand it to you, Sasser. In that getup you look like a federal cop or a lawyer, one. When we get out, remind me to frisk you." He instructed the driver to continue on through the light and take the first left. "Gotta pay my respects."

"To what?"

"The ABC store."

Sasser shot a side glance. "You're going to drink? I mean—"

"Damn straight." He held up the bottle. "Been working on this puppy too long now. Time to finish her and get a new one. Maybe a new flavor. This one gave me the willies last night. Heard things that weren't there. Had the sweats … the works."

Sasser replied, "They broke into your office."

Boggs drank.

There was silence.

Boggs said, "Do what now?"

"They ransacked your office."

His elbow braced on the armrest, Boggs butted a fist against his smile. With his left hand, he motioned for Sasser to turn into the ABC store lot. "Wasn't there some general—don't know when—but wasn't there a general what said, 'Now we got 'em where we want 'em'?"

Sasser didn't reply. He passed up several empty spaces, preferring the far end of the lot. He backed the car in so that it pointed to the exit and kept the engine running. Boggs asked to borrow ten dollars. Without comment, Sasser withdrew his money clip. He flicked through the neat stack and removed a bill. Boggs left without closing the door. He returned minutes later, already having broken the bottle's seal.

"Where to?" asked Sasser.

"Destiny, my friend. Destiny." He curled back the sawtooth edge of the paper bag and took a drink.

"The junkyard?"

"That would be the first destination in destiny." Boggs drank. "So what were you doin' in my office?"

Sasser drove out of the lot. "Seemed like a good idea. Seeing what they did convinced me your plan has half a chance. They're desperate."

Minutes later, they headed south on Crater Road.

Boggs asked, "No, in the first place. Why'd you go up there in the first place?"

"To muse."

Boggs sipped, showing no sign of whether the clipped answer satisfied him. He focused on the word "desperate." They were indeed. An inkling of just how desperate surfaced earlier when Tinnin called the hospital in a panic, saying he had been switched to third shift to work a two-man at the French Quarter. That meant the deputy had to report in at 11:30. The rendezvous, meanwhile, was set for 9:30. Two hours provided enough time to conduct business. So against Tinnin's recommendation, Boggs told him not to call in sick.

Near the county line, Boggs had Sasser swing onto the gravel drive leading up to the sign that read Isley Junkyard. Boggs got out to open the twelve-foot-high gate. It was so dark that if not for the headlights, Boggs wouldn't have found the unlocked latch. They drove past the office, a rundown Airstream trailer festooned with hubcaps. They parked farther down, in front of a pile of tires behind which the red Falcon hid.

With flashlights, the pair walked to the car.

"Got gas in it?" asked Boggs.

"Mr. Isley filled it up."

Before Boggs lowered himself inside, he considered frisking Sasser, but he asked himself what he would do if he found a gun. Of all the answers he sorted through, he accepted "add some excitement to the powwow." Besides, he was sure Tinnin would be armed. Stiff from being in the bed so long, he groaned and wriggled his ass this way and that in an attempt to get comfortable. He turned the engine over on the second try.

"You sure you want to take this?" asked Sasser as he dipped down to get in the passenger seat.

Boggs took a drink. "Positive. Cuz if there's shootin', I want this thing killed."

"If there's shooting—" Sasser stopped himself. Feeling as if his knees were under his chin, he asked, "Can we move the seat back?"

"Back as far as it goes."

"They make this for midgets?"

Boggs turned on the radio after returning to the road. The dial was already set on a country and western station. He crooned along to Crystal Gayle's "Half the Way" for a bit and said, "Hot damn! Don't ya just love her? She drives me wild." He took a drink and held out the bottle.

Sasser waved the bottle away and watched Boggs slap his thigh and rock within the cramped quarters. He sang with such fervor that Sasser finally said, "We're not teenagers on our way to pick up our Saturday night dates."

"Might as well be." He hooted and laughed. "Know why I picked tonight? I mean, nighttime. Because in the day, there's not much to hide. Sure, they could be lurkin' in the woods or somethin'. But nighttime is something else.

They won't know how many we are. And besides, they say a snake, no matter you slice it in twos or threes, won't die till sundown."

"And this bit of folklore is what you based your decision on?"

"You ain't nervous, are you? You know you've got to make your peace beforehand. Take me now. I called the wife today. Damn woman didn't even know I've been gone. What? Two days, and she never knew?"

Sasser made no reply. He stared ahead.

Boggs took a drink. "I'll tell you what. At a time like this, the things you remember most are the things you've done."

Still focused on the roadway, Sasser said, "No, it's what you haven't done."

The silence that followed was a tangible presence, despite the radio.

"Say, what's with the suit anyways?" asked Boggs. "You know this ain't no come-to-Jesus meetin'."

Sasser didn't reply.

After a while, Boggs said, "You ever think—maybe when you was musin' up there in my office—you ever think they didn't do the killin'? You know, they just might could be selling drugs and all, but maybe they didn't kill nobody. It might could be someone else."

"If they didn't, who did?"

"Search me." He took a drink. "But, hell, who wants to bust in on a drug ring what ain't had nothing to do with no murder, when it's the murders we're gettin' paid to find out about? That's above and beyond, way I see it."

Sasser was silent.

Minutes passed. Boggs finally said, "Now this weather—"

Sasser reached over and snapped off the radio.

Boggs shrugged and continued, "Now this weather—honest to God, here it is, coming on the end of August, and it sorta feels like fall. But don't be fooled. First week in September, it'll be hot as fire. Burn everything. It'll be like two weeks in September contain all the heat of a July. A whole month in two weeks. You watch. It happens every time."

Sasser was silent for a moment and then asked, "How much of that do you plan on drinking?"

"Oh, hell, I'll leave enough for a few licks on the way back." He took a pull. "S'pect you'll be gettin' on back to Singapore or wherever it is you do your importin' from?"

"I plan to leave as soon as possible."

"You mind tellin' me—now that there's no turnin' back—you mind tellin' just what your interest in all this is?"

He spit out a laugh. "You haven't trusted me from the start, have you?"

"I believed enough to make you a special agent," Boggs's tone suggested injury, which changed when he asked, "Ever seen any experience along those lines?"

"Now what makes you say that?"

"Well, Deputy Tinnin, for one, thinks you're with the CIA."

"Do you really trust him?" He added, "I'm not so sure he can hold up his end."

"Oh, Tinnin's as regular as coffee in the mornin'." Pointing to his right, Boggs went on, "That there's the Blake homeplace."

Sasser continued to look ahead.

In less than a minute, they were on the dusty road Boggs kept referring to as "destiny." The long rectangular field was darker than the sky, leaving the impression that the tree line fenced in a brooding black mass. Every so often, the wind whisked over the pines, producing a moaning melody. The urgent cries of crickets resumed when Boggs killed the engine. They sat very still, letting their eyes and breathing adjust. All the while Boggs repeated, "Mercy, mercy, mud pie."

Sasser said, "We should have brought flashlights."

"What time you got?" Boggs took a last drink before screwing on the cap.

"Nine twenty—twenty-one."

"Reckon we wait."

# CHAPTER THIRTY-THREE

Boggs parked at the far edge of the debris, giving Tinnin a clear view of all that was about to happen. Boggs made no mention of the deputy's whereabouts to Sasser and found it odd that Sasser never asked.

Leaving the high beams on permitted them to maneuver around their immediate surroundings. Sasser seemed too preoccupied with the setting, walking up to the edge of the ruins, craning his neck this way and that as he inspected it. He kicked the ashen rubble with his polished leather shoes, watching as if fascinated by the way it crumbled. He turned to look out over what portion of the field he could see and then back at the rutted road.

"So this is where Billy Blake lived?"

Boggs asked, "What were you expectin'?"

"Don't know. Something more than a single-wide trailer in a fallow field." He grunted as though disgusted.

"Now don't be puttin' down trailers, mister high 'n' mighty. They put many a people around here under a roof."

"Oh, I'm not. It's ... it's just that I thought people would want more than this."

"This is wantin' more."

"Perhaps."

The pair leaned against the station wagon, though neither remained still for very long, constantly shifting, folding their arms, taking a step or two away and then ambling back, neither saying more than a word or two on the pretext of listening for the signal, that burst of tumescent time when the crickets fell silent and hell began to break loose piece by piece.

Sasser shivered at the wind's soughing requiem. He began to tell Boggs how he had found a tick on his ass the night he concealed himself in the woods to snipe at Wynne. Sasser broke the story into small parts, not really listening to what he said, or caring. Boggs waited a moment before telling how one or two people a year died from tick fever. He went on about how he had seen under a microscope a tick's greedy grin, how it was bigger than a Cheshire cat's, how the biting tick lathered worse than a rabid dog.

"How many do you think are coming?" asked Sasser.

"Can't say for sure. But I s'pect there's one or two already here."

"What do you mean?"

"Hiding out there somewheres." Boggs nodded toward the darkness beyond the rim of car light.

A silence made itself felt. Almost breathless, Boggs asked the time. Before Sasser replied, the new silence, the one without the night sounds, intervened. Boggs said, "Never mind."

A rumbling car downshifted, and within seconds, high beams forced their way out onto the field. Boggs recognized the outline of the Diplomat, saying aloud, "Wynne." Both men strained to see how many were aboard. At a less-than-safe speed, the car swung to within fifteen yards of them. The engine died.

Boggs and Sasser stood shoulder to shoulder, off to the side of the high beams but still within its grasp. A searchlight attached to the driver's door combed the area, its sweep thorough and painstaking, coursing over the broomstraw field, inspecting and reinspecting the heap of the incinerated trailer, and then frisking the far tree lines. It finally rested on the two men who stood as if cardboard cutouts.

Wynne's overreaching search prompted Boggs to fold his arm; he was unable to stop flexing his biceps. Sasser maintained a seemingly steadfast pose, so tall and stiff that his blue suit was without wrinkles. This set-in-stone posture was near perfect except for the way he curled and uncurled his fingers or the way he made quick passes of his dry tongue across drier lips. For a finale, he clasped his hands behind his back in a smart parade rest.

"Can ya tell how many?" asked Boggs without moving his lips.

Sasser didn't answer.

Boggs looked over at him, wondering when his alleged partner would show his true colors. He was about to say something to provoke him, but then the driver-side door cranked open with a rusty complaint. He hoped to see how many he was up against, but the interior light failed to shine. "Can you tell—"

A silhouetted figure approached. Until Wynne stepped to the side of the beams, they didn't see he was carrying a paper bag, one not quite as big as a grocery sack.

Wynne wore his best American Dental Association smile. His dress was more appropriate for the first tee at the Greensboro Country Club. Attached to his tooled leather belt was his shiny gold badge. Seeing it, Boggs asked himself if the man actually thought he was on duty. His best answer was "probably." The law, more specifically its enforcers, had slipped over into another dimension a long time ago. Boggs looked for any signs of distress or concern. The one element that seemed out of place was the wavy hair, which wasn't neatly combed. But that, Boggs reasoned, could have been because he drove with the window down.

Boggs meant to comment on the cop's attire, but a more pressing issue prevailed.

"So where's the sheriff and the judge?" He fixed his eyes on the car, anticipating Wynne's agents slipping out like slithering snakes.

The captain advanced, keeping the light on his right side. About halfway between the car and the pair, he stopped and spit. "They'll be along directly."

"And your crew?"

"Out there." He tossed his head back to indicate somewhere in the night. "Protecting the good men and women of this county from the likes of you."

"You mean like they done to the doctor's girl?"

"That was poor judgment on their part."

"So you didn't tell them to do it?"

"Sometimes the boys get a little strung out. Comes with the territory." After a second, he added, "Besides, can't be supervising 24-7. As it is, I spend half my time bailing their sorry asses out of some kind of shit."

Wynne's casual dress and easy tone reminded Boggs of the punch the cop had landed on his jaw, the punch he never saw coming. It was all he could do not to massage the area now. He said, "Got the money?"

"My share." He held up the bag.

"Your share?"

"Harris and Hardy got theirs." He knelt to set the bag at his feet. Standing, he hooked his thumbs in his belt. "Right fair price, sixteen, six. Make that much in a few days' time."

Boggs shook his head, unable to think of a reply. "So who's your silent partner?" asked Wynne, seemingly no more threatened than if among fellow officers.

"Where're my manners?" said Boggs, his voice cracking at first. "Mr. Sasser, meet the renowned Captain—"

"Wait a minute. I've seen you before. Where was it?"

"James City?" suggested Boggs.

"Yeah, that's right. At the Southside Precinct. Gave you directions, didn't I?"

When Sasser didn't speak up, Boggs said, "You probably didn't know it at the time, but Mr. Sasser here is in the same line of work as you."

"Oh? What work is that now?"

"Law enforcement." He fastened a showy smirk to his mouth. "Only he's with the state."

"The state?"

"Bureau of Investigation."

Wynne laughed. "Yeah, right. And my taillight just happened to break. Must've been a rock or something. Man, but you really do come up with some lame-ass stories, Boggs."

Wynne's laugh persisted.

Boggs prepared to whistle for Tinnin until the cop added, "Like the time that dude shot your partner. What was the excuse you—"

"Would it be better if I were in the killing business?" Sasser was unable to subdue a shout. He broke out of the parade-rest stance.

Boggs looked at Sasser with a budding admiration; the man was on his side after all.

Wynne nodded with an almost imperceptible shrug. "Then we'd be in the same business."

Sasser pushed up the bridge of his glasses and rested his weight on his left side. He asked, "Was it you that killed Billy Blake?"

Wynne threw off another casual shrug. "He owed me."

"Not as much as I—"

The "owe you" was drowned out by report of a .45 pistol that Sasser had concealed in the back of his belt. He fired twice, the second missing the falling Wynne. Before he could get off a third shot, Boggs chopped down on his forearm. The weapon flew out of his hand. Sasser stood woodenly, as if transfixed by the thrilling results of his work. Boggs rushed over to Wynne, who had fallen sideways. Boggs saw a 9-millimeter Glock holstered in the back of the captain's belt. He took little notice, pushed the man flat and felt for a pulse. There was one, albeit slight. Boggs rested on his heels, fascinated by the rivulets of blood running out the side of Wynne's gut. He told himself to call an ambulance but never bothered to work out how he proposed to do that. At this point, it was all he could do to break away from the openness of Wynne's eyes. In averting his eyes, Boggs noticed the paper bag. He seized it, looking inside. He saw a white substance wrapped neatly in two plastic baggies. "Sugar! The bastard brought sugar. Sugar to a gunfight. If that don't—"

The abrupt arrival of an unmarked Ford Fairmont interrupted Boggs. He rose slowly and then stepped away from the body. He settled into position beside Sasser. The two seemed to contend for the same space, mesmerized by the gray car's progress and then doubly captivated when an old pickup emerged from the dust clouds the Ford stirred.

Sasser and Boggs made no move to run, to retrieve Sasser's gun, to do anything but gawk at the speeding, twisting vehicles. When they came to a halt, each at a kamikaze angle to the Diplomat, Sasser dove for his pistol. He fired. In seconds, the thunder of the gun battle reached a deafening pitch. A bullet whistled past a dumbstruck Boggs, who screamed without realizing it, without realizing he was scrambling on his hands and knees for the safety of the station wagon. Even before he reached it, the skirmish attained a maddening crescendo.

Boggs crawled under the car without difficulty but quickly discovered he couldn't see what was happening. By then there was no point. A mortal silence reverberated through the field; the night, dark as it was, went darker. Boggs tried to slide back out, but the low chassis held him fast. Exhaustion ended his struggle after a few minutes. He sought to stifle the wheeze in his breathing as searchlights spanned the area. Before long, the strength of the two beams fixed on the wagon.

"Boggs?" a hoarse voice called out. "Boggs, come on out now. Nothing's going to happen that ain't already happened."

Boggs flattened his body and squirmed. He drove his hands into the dirt to establish a prop on which to push. His efforts were for naught; how he had ever gotten under the car in the first place confounded him. He stopped to catch his breath. There was silence. He broke it with, "Don't know as I trust you, J.B."

"Don't see where you got much of a choice."

Judge Hardy stood so close to the sheriff that it left the impression of conjoined twins. He whispered to the sheriff, "You're not going to kill him." It was neither a question nor an order.

Boggs yelled, "Wynne's still alive. You might want to call an ambulance."

"Sorry to hear that." Harris waited. "You coming out?"

Damned if he would come out back-assward into the light and line of fire. Boggs heaved his back against the chassis. It didn't budge. He crumbled with a grunt. He rested for a moment and then sucked in his chest and gut and pressed the side of his head against the ground. He clawed and dug in his heels, inching forward. Stretching, he scratched through the dirt until he grabbed a clump of grass on which to pull himself. At last, his head came free. The rest of him scurried out as if whipped. On his knees, he bent over, feeling nauseous and dizzy. "All right ... all right," he said, barely louder than a whisper. "I'm comin'."

He struggled to his feet and wobbled toward the hood. He stopped, keeping the car between him and the sheriff. He held up his hands, palms out. The effort it took told him just how difficult it was to extricate himself from the car.

The ineffable struggle so manifest in Sasser's fallen pose distracted him from the cautious approach of the three vice agents. No sign of blood nor aura of hope was visible around the stricken body. Sasser looked as if he were climbing a ladder, his face buried from sight, the right arm stretched to its fullest extension, the index finger still looped through the trigger guard, the left arm cocked against his side as if an involuntary reaction to an unsuspecting jab, one leg bent as if to find the next rung on the ladder. Boggs could detect no movement in him. Even the breeze avoided contact.

As the three agents circled the car, a raised voice demanded, "No more killing."

Judge Hardy's remark notwithstanding, Boggs studied the armed men. He called to them, saying he was unarmed.

The sheriff and judge remained behind the light, two shades locked face-to-face in a heated argument. It was loud enough for Boggs to hear, but he wasn't listening. He tended to the black handguns the agents aimed at him. The thin one off to his left had a ponytail and a drooping mustache. He was dressed for the woods: boots, jeans, and flannel shirt. The deputy closest to Boggs—dead ahead—had a witch's hooked nose and a splotchy beard; he wore a Pride in Tobacco cap and three-quarter sleeve baseball undershirt. The hairiest of the three was on the right flank. He had long hair and a longer beard. He was as big as a biker and, in his leather vest and cap, looked like an angry Hells Angel.

Their dispute apparently resolved, Harris came forward into the light; his jaw jutted like the block of walnut it was. A flushed face was the only indication that the sheriff had done anything more strenuous than step out his front door to fetch the newspaper. Though baggy from weight loss, his gray suit held a sharp press. His starched collar was buttoned; his silk tie, blocked. He came at Boggs.

The judge emerged behind the sheriff. His attire was no less striking in that he looked unaccustomed to and uncomfortable in the plaid short-sleeve shirt, blue jeans, and black sneakers. Oversized bandages patched most of his forehead. These combined with his clothes made him forfeit his normally hale mien. The replacement was a chalk-white face and stooped shoulders. His eyes had a milky glaze.

"Answer me this, Boggs. Just what in the Sam Hell did you think you were doing?"

Boggs shrugged. "Lookin' back on it now, can't say as I know. Thought we might point guns at one another. Never thought it would come to this. Men dying on account of what? Your pissant drug deals?"

"We don't see it as drug deals, do we, John?" The sheriff didn't wait for an answer. "No, we like to think of 'em as our own special 401 savings account." He added, "But again I ask you: did you actually believe you could come out of this alive?"

"Outcomes, least the good ones, always seem to elude me, J.B."

"But your smart-ass mouth has never abandoned you."

The sheriff broke stride at Wynne's body. "You've done me a big favor, Boggs." Never once breaking eye contact with Boggs, he pulled the trigger of his 44 Magnum. The bullet made such a splash in Wynne's chest that the flesh and bone seemed to have the consistency of a puddle. He walked forward, saying, "He thought he could do this himself. Do it all by himself. Weren't for him, we would have laughed at you. Just ignored you. Who'd believe a disgraced drunk over us?"

He stepped up to Sasser. "Who's this?"

"Jeez, I thought you'd know."

"How would I know? He's with you, isn't he?"

"Yeah, I suppose he was. But he's dead now, so I won't ever know what his interest in all this was."

"It doesn't matter now anyway."

"No, it doesn't." Boggs lowered his hands.

# CHAPTER THIRTY-FOUR

From his hideout behind the debris some fifteen yards away, Tinnin felt abandoned, severed by his failure to do anything more than listen to the furious argument among guns. His body refused to rise and peep through the hole he bore in the metal, so he became a frightened bystander during this existential dispute called firepower. He bit into the bitter dirt into which he had pushed his face when the first searchlight passed over him. He was no longer in consort with Boggs but immediately alone.

The shooting, coming from all sides at once, was a madhouse of noise and light that stole his breath. But that was fine with him; he didn't feel he had lungs to process air anymore anyway. His eyes worked at random, and that too was okay because he didn't want them to work at all. He prayed that his sense of hearing would shut down instead of reloading mayhem.

The overwhelming weight of his situation placed him in a world apart. He certainly had no place in Boggs's plan. Why had Boggs chosen him to be the man who came in at the end to save the day was beyond his reckoning. He was the wrong man. He needed someone to show him how, someone who would set the example for him to follow, someone operating in a higher gear and not obedient to the law of inertia. What was at rest stayed at rest; what was hunkered down, cowering, stayed hunkered down and cowering.

He curled up in a makeshift fetal position, rocking back and forth and humming tunelessly. He knew that nothing he had done or imagined in his life could have prepared him for this—no training, no prayer, no hope, no imprecation. Yet the worst outcomes he had envisioned were real and were about to happen—to him. To conjure up the best outcome, one in which he was rescued from this maelstrom, one where he had someone to reach out to, to confide in, someone who wouldn't desert him but help divide the danger into small pieces, was not now and never would be attainable.

All day long he had a feeling that something bad would happen, and now it had. Fire crawled up his throat and spewed a burnt-sienna liquid down the front of his uniform, coating his silver badge. Minutes, maybe many minutes, passed before he felt how wet the ground under him was. He never understood that he was pissing. And the wetness kept on snaking down his leg, one long slither.

He considered the idea of crawling to the nearest tree line. He reasoned that whatever he could have done didn't matter now; everyone was dead. So why take up the mantle of the hero? He bowed to fear; it was a god that promised safety and life after this death. That was all he ever wanted: to be secure. And there was no chance of security for a hero; the only thing certain was that the hero would die.

Tinnin rocked faster when it occurred to him that whether or not he was a hero, he was still going to die. There was nothing he could do to change that.

He looked at the revolver he held in his right hand. He tried to shake it off, but it seemed stuck. He didn't want the gun now. People who had guns acted as if they were listening, not to the firing of the weapons but to some mythical piper whom they beseeched to keep playing and playing so they could keep shooting and shooting. He attempted to wiggle his fingers, but they wouldn't move, frozen around the black handle of his nickel-plated .38 special. All of a sudden, his breathing revved, and what eyesight he had telescoped on the gun. He stared so hard that it took a minute to recognize the silence beyond him. His eyelids fluttered like a candle flame bent on fending off its extinction in a breeze. He told himself now was the time to escape into the woods. When he didn't respond to that suggestion, he told himself to peek through the hole he had drilled to see what had happened.

Immediately, he asked himself, *Why? For what purpose?* He scoffed at the spectacle of him coming out into the open to settle accounts. He now convinced himself that it was Boggs who had forsaken him, not the other way around. Besides, by now, Sasser had probably gunned down Boggs. Tinnin couldn't believe that Boggs had brought him along. Sasser was probably the franchiser. And Boggs stood at the man's side, at the side of the real killer, thinking the two were comrades in arms. Boggs was a fool, and Tinnin was an even bigger fool for ever listening to him.

There it was again—that ornery voice that claimed to inform him of everything but left him knowing nothing, nothing except that he was lost and would not be found; that he was a chance taken too often; that what happened to him was accidental, and there was nothing he could do about it. He was in a hell of his own doing because of what he hadn't done. He hadn't stopped the killings. Billy Blake was just the first in a progression whose end he couldn't fathom.

In the silence that prevailed, he thought he heard new voices but denied their existence, their source. The only voice capable of speaking was a gun.

He cursed himself for not bringing his walkie-talkie; he could have called the Rock for help. But then the thought of a rescue party descending on the area unhinged him further. He knew that no one would ever believe him; he had no proof of anything. No, the sheriff would be there pointing a finger at him; he would be the culprit. From there, it was a simple matter of criminal charges, a quick trial, and a guilty verdict. The prosecutor and judge would conspire to revive the death penalty, and once on death row—

Just then it came to him that capital punishment was already in play. How could he have forgotten? He told himself to shut up, that he was thinking too much, too fast.

For some inexplicable reason, Tinnin rose up and peered through the peek hole. What he saw he disbelieved: the sheriff put a bullet in the chest of the fallen Wynne. He, a deputy, saw the high sheriff put a bullet in one of his own men. Tinnin scanned the area, seeing the prostrate remains of Sasser. He assumed Boggs was also down, although he couldn't see the body. That the sheriff was speaking to someone out of sight confused Tinnin. He asked himself who was left but didn't have an answer.

No sooner had he squatted back down than he condemned himself for not doing something to protect Boggs. He was a deputy sheriff after all, sworn to protect and uphold. First, there was Billy and then Wendy and Sasser, whoever he was, and now Boggs. Deaths weren't adding up so much as multiplying in weight so great it entombed him. And he would have to—he wanted to say—live with it for the rest of his life, but then it came to him that he didn't have very long to live.

The bodies out there stood as straight-backed witnesses to just what a shirker he was. He agonized over the fact that people in Random would remember him as a failure and a coward, a man who tried to escape his fate and let a good man die because of his cowhearted inaction.

At that moment, the image of a fallen Sasser, an image that only now presented itself to him, surfaced in the form of a question mark. If shot dead, how could he be the franchiser? How could he be in cahoots with Wynne? Who was this guy? Had he been wrong to harbor suspicions?

He always had his suspicions about Boggs and his two-beat whistle, as if anyone under pressure could whistle. Boggs's plan was as useful as a steering wheel on a mule. And Boggs's idea of him coming out from his blind to confront the bad guys and even up the odds was dumber than a sack of rocks.

Out of the thinning air came the recognition that there was so much he wished he had done in his life. Other people always seemed to have better outcomes than he did. And no matter what he did to reverse the trend, to change course, it left him wanting. His pledges to reform, to study, to go on a diet, to be a better lawman—they disappeared with the first prick of hunger. And he had all kinds of hungers. And he had left so many things unsaid and undone, all the while knowing that he never once strove to right any wrong. His preference was to keep everything under wraps in the hopes that they would just go away before too long, and sometimes they did.

In considering the sins of being fat, of not advancing his education, of not applying himself to his job, Tinnin appropriated the concept of tricks; in this case, the trick was kin to a possum playing dead. He called himself a sinner, when in fact he should have simply regarded himself as a miserable failure. He was a loser incapable of even affecting a decent sin.

Sinner or not, if he died now—and he surely would—only hell awaited him. His transit would be quick as a flash, which he believed wasn't nearly as horrible as waiting to die.

The more he thought about waiting, the angrier he became. He started inhaling through his nose and exhaling through his mouth. The exercise reversed his exhaustion. Now time ceased, replaced by an irrepressible sense of urgency. He must do something. Exactly what eluded him. He had choices, all of which chilled him to the core. But Boggs was dead, Sasser was dead, and Wynne was dead. The sheriff killed the captain twice; he had witnessed the execution. He must do something, he repeated over and over, but when he tried to move, his legs were solid stumps. He had no feeling below the waist or, for that matter, above it. He rose up again and peeped through the hole.

# CHAPTER THIRTY-FIVE

Harris stepped up beside the skinny deputy. His eyes bored in on Boggs. "You said you owed me a favor, J.B." Boggs held up his hands as if to indicate a truce. At the same time, he inhaled through his teeth and tried to whistle. The flat air that sputtered out was no louder than a sigh.

"And I do." He waved the long pistol as if pointing a finger and told the deputies to handcuff Boggs. "We've got ourselves a murderer, boys." To the biker he said, "See what's in that bag."

Boggs allowed the hooked-nose deputy to snap on the cuffs, all the while watching the biker hunker down on the heels of his black boots and examine the contents of the bag. He removed one of the plastic bags swollen with a white power. He licked his finger and dipped it inside. He tasted the extract, his tongue flickering. "Cocaine! Damn, it's cocaine. A half pound maybe."

While Hook Nose pushed a complacent Boggs around to the front of the station wagon, between the sheriff and the ponytailed agent, Boggs muttered to himself, "Sugar, my ass."

Harris laughed without mirth. "Well, this does change things. We've got no ordinary murderer here, boys." He gnawed at the corner of a sneer. "No, I'd say we've got ourselves one of the biggest busts in the history of this county. And to think the head of my vice squad was involved. Damn fine police work, wouldn't you say, judge?"

Hardy pulled himself away from his stare at the dead bodies but didn't reply.

"Seen ya kill him, sheriff. Seen it all." The hidden voice had such an emotional register that everyone whirled to see Deputy Tinnin come into the light. Disheveled though he was, he still donned his campaign hat.

By coming on the scene, Tinnin told himself it was time to rewrite the history of a coward. He had watched and waited, even whispered, but Boggs never saw nor heard nor thought about him. So he crept around the rubble and through the grass, unaware of what he was doing until he stood and walked with a measured pace toward the sheriff. He held his service revolver but pointed it down. He heard himself tell a lie and believe in the lie. "I seen it, seen and heard it all, sheriff. I heard Wynne tell Boggs how y'all was behind the drugs and all. Behind the killings. You and the judge there." He pointed to Hardy with his handgun. "So I'm bound to place y'all under arrest."

"Why you lard ass—"

"Just you shut up and drop the gun," said Tinnin, surprising himself.

Harris grunted and stomped over to Boggs. With stunning quickness, he locked Boggs in a choke hold and jammed the circle of the pistol barrel into Boggs's sweaty head. "Shoot, Tinnin," the sheriff yelled. "I said shoot."

"J.B.!" cried the judge, his white hands fluttering in front of his drooling mouth. "I said no more—"

"Shut up, John." Harris glared at Tinnin who was now well within the full strength of the light. "Now you shoot if you've got the nerve, boy."

"Wait 'im out," Boggs muttered. He tried to say more, but Harris cinched his hold.

Tinnin's grimace twitched, but he remained steady in the face of the agents fanning out, their weapons leveled. In almost a whimper, he said, "I done told you it would come to this."

"I can hear his heart racin'," Boggs gasped.

The sheriff bit down on his lower lip, rose on his toes, and smashed the barrel against Boggs's skull. Boggs crumbled at the knees. The sheriff held him for a moment and then let him drop, pushing him aside with a kick.

As soon as Boggs hit the ground, gunfire erupted from the northeast tree line. The biker buckled and fell. Before anyone could react, there was a second crack. The ponytailed agent staggered and croaked as if to vomit. Hook Nose fired wildly into the dark. Harris and the judge scrambled behind the station wagon.

Hook Nose crouched, fired twice, and then ran. After two strides, he stumbled and lunged, releasing a wail that made the report of the sniper rifle that much louder. He bared his blackened teeth like a mad dog as a fourth bullet plowed up dirt in front of him. He howled, letting his head fall back as his hands clutched the massive tear in his left thigh. The fifth shot was mercilessly slow in coming. It ripped through the right shoulder, flipping him, silencing him.

Tinnin, huddled behind the rear of the station wagon, rocked and moaned, covering his confused ears to the uproarious silence. He was unaware that the sheriff and the judge were at the opposite end.

A silence Tinnin had no way of measuring lasted until he heard a revolver click. With an involuntary jerk, he sprang away from the sound, scampered around, poised on all fours like a cornered animal. The sheriff's right eye glowed behind the silver barrel. Harris was less than two feet away, kneeling behind the door of the wagon. "Call 'im off," he hissed.

The deputy sat back on his heels in a matter of worship. "I don't know who it is. Honest."

"Do it."

"You gotta believe me." He started to sob. "Please."

"Stand up."

"No, sheriff. Honest. I don't know who it is." Despite his refusal, he came to his feet. He held up his hands as if to keep back a crushing weight. Tears streamed over a greasy glaze of sweat. His voice cracked, and a sniveling murmur of protest followed.

"Move on out there and call him off."

He straggled into the open. His chest heaved so fitfully that he could scarcely wave his arms over his head. He stammered, "Hold your fire. Don't shoot ... don't shoot."

The sheriff snarled, "Tell 'im to come out."

Tinnin looked back. "Who?"

"Tell him, you idiot!"

Trembling, he looked about at the strewn bodies that seemed pitched from heaven and frozen in their free fall to hell. His mouth opened as he peered into the night and struggled to form the words. "C-c-come on—"

The shush of footsteps through the grass stilled him.

Will Blake advanced into the light, his rifle cradled in his right arm. He looked half-savage, without shoes or shirt, a grizzly stubble, unblinking eyes, and matted hair.

"Will, he's—he's got a gun on me."

In a prone position at the corner of the car, Harris whispered, "Tell him to drop it."

"Says for you to drop the rifle, Will."

"He do," said Blake with a croak of a laugh.

"It's the sheriff, Will. He's got a gun on me. Now, c'mon, drop it." After a moment he added, "Please."

Will tossed the rifle. "Won't need it for the likes of him noway."

Imitating a chimp, the sheriff scrambled back to the front of the wagon. He popped up over the hood, his weapon trained on the two men. He rose slowly, his mouth curling into a sneer once he recognized Will.

"On your knees. Hands behind your head."

Tinnin dropped to his knees in one painstaking flop. Seeing Will still standing, he had to tug on his arm. Will wrenched his arm away. "I ain't—"

"Get down, boy. Down." The sheriff smirked.

"Knowed you wasn't for nothin'," said Will to the sheriff. He folded his arms, refusing to kneel.

Judge Hardy crept out from behind the front wheel. He laid his hands flat on the car to brace himself. Even while the right side of his mouth twitched, he glared with narrowed eyes at the sheriff whose long strides put him in front of Will and Tinnin. When Harris raised his pistol at the pair, the judge gained a sudden strength and rushed around, hollering, "No!"

The sheriff looked back, saying, "Get the rifle and shut up."

Hardy stopped short, uncomprehending. He stared at his sneakers, all the while fribbling with the bottom button of his shirt. It took a moment, but then he scanned the area, spotting the bolt-action gun. He stepped up cautiously, as if the barrel would morph into a moccasin and strike. He snatched it and backpedaled. He handed it to the sheriff and then moved back.

"Leave me one in the chamber, did ya?" asked Harris to Will.

"Ain't left you—"

The judge screamed, "There's to be no more killing, J.B!"

"Just how do you propose to keep them quiet?" The sheriff forced his pistol in Hardy's right hand and ordered, "Now get your shit together, John."

Stepping closer, the sheriff took an easy aim; being so close didn't call for marksmanship. "I'll take wild man here; you got the fat boy." All at once, he noticed the condition of the deputy's uniform, the pissed-on pants, puked-on shirt, and the dirt around his mouth as if he had been eating it. The sight along with the pathetic, penitent look Tinnin wore infuriated him. "Why're you wearing—you're a disgrace. Why you wearing that uniform, boy? Ain't like you know anything about law-enforcing."

Shaking his head in disgust, Harris turned back to Will. He positioned the long gun just above the waist. At the same time, Judge Hardy let his weapon drop, but then it came back to level, swaying so that it never really threatened Tinnin.

Boggs stirred, his moan causing more havoc than a cracked twig. Harris pivoted, pointing the barrel at the fallen man.

Judge Hardy fired the only shot.

The sheriff doubled over and gurgled. The rifle slipped from his hands. With bulging eyes, he beheld the judge as a stranger. His head drooped as he keeled over.

The revolver spun downward and slid through Hardy's splayed fingers. His shooting hand reared back as if it meant to fly away. He caught it and studied it with a shudder. He cried out and wilted slowly, his cry soon softening to a blubber, and then bundled himself in an ever-tightening ball.

Despite the carnage before him and the scrambling sound of an ambulance, Will remained planted in a defiant stance. Tinnin made the arduous climb to his feet and stopped gulping air. He said, "Hope it's just an ambulance. How we—"

Staring straight ahead, Will said, "Agnes musta called."

"What're we gonna tell 'em?" Tinnin was nearly hysterical.

"Who?"

"What're we gonna say? Who's going to believe this?" After a second, he said, "I didn't kill nobody."

"Got me my share. Wished that man there left the sheriff to me."

"That man? Know who that man is? That's Judge John Hardy. That's a judge, Will. The chief district court judge. Who's gonna believe he shot the sheriff?"

"Ain't none of my concern."

"Judge," said Tinnin, "Judge, you'll tell 'em what happened, won't you?"

A whimper was the only response the deputy got.

Boggs moaned louder and rolled to his side. Tinnin rushed over and patted his colorless cheeks. Frantically, he fanned the man's face with his campaign hat. Boggs's eyelids trembled. With a timid stroke, Tinnin slapped his face and shouted his name. Boggs settled on his back, spewed air, and blinked in quick succession.

Soon Boggs was sitting and demanding to know what had happened. The last he remembered was being trapped under the car. Tinnin lost the thread of his disjointed account when Agnes silently stepped into the light. She had already surveyed the scene from a distance, noting first that her husband was unharmed. She had recognized Tinnin but was at a loss as to who lay on the ground. The only importance she placed in the fallen men was that they were dead. She marched up to Will, the six-inch .38 at her side in stark contrast to her frilly apron. "See the good ones is all right." Will patted her shoulder. She wrapped her free arm around his waist.

With a jerk of his jaw, Will pointed to the judge, saying, "Shoulda killed that one there 'cept the deputy here thinks it's a good thing he's alive. He'll vouch for what we done."

Boggs lowered his pounding head onto his knees and told Tinnin to remove the handcuffs. As Tinnin fiddled with his key, Boggs asked Will to see if Sasser was alive. Even though the ambulance's red, rushing shrill juiced the battlefield, Will was in no hurry. He loped over to the body and nudged it with his foot. The body resisted. Will kicked it over. He batted his red eyes. His brow beetled. His face drew in, giving it an even sharper cut. He stooped and muttered, "Andy?"

Agnes gasped, dropped the pistol, and rushed over, sliding in on her knees and nearly knocking Will over.

# CHAPTER THIRTY-SIX

Boggs stomped on the rubber mat as if daring the automatic doors not to swing open. But the hospital doors weren't what preoccupied him; he scrutinized the two deputies with balefully slung eyes. The taller of the two, the one with a thick black mustache, was posted outside the emergency room entrance under its metal canopy. The second was just inside the doors, standing at a sloppy attention with his thumbs hooked in his utility belt. Who ordered these men here wasn't as important as why: who or what were they guarding? The only answer Boggs came up with was Simon Sasser, a.k.a. Andy Blake.

Boggs glared at the second deputy as he walked past on his way to the reception desk. Although no one was visible, he bent down to speak through the metal disc in the window.

"In there," said the deputy before Boggs had a chance to speak.

Boggs turned. The deputy's nod pointed to the waiting room, a darkened rectangle that appropriated the dinginess of a bus depot: cold floors, sticky in spots; barren and scarred walls of cinder block; four vinyl-covered couches, slashed in places and duct-taped together; crumpled junk food bags overloading the knee-high ashtrays; torn magazines scattered about.

In the deep recesses of the room sat Will Blake. He was silent and still. He remained without shirt or shoes, his hairy arms crossed but not as a measure against the chill of the air conditioning.

Boggs sat beside him, waiting in the ponderous silence for Will to acknowledge him. Will was stone stiff. The only movement was the slight rhythmic flare of his thin nose. His profile was so petrified that Boggs almost expected to see something crack if he turned.

"They wouldn't believe us," Boggs began without any sign Will was listening. "Even with the judge in there confessing as far back as Cain. They gave me and Tinnin the third and fourth degree … about to lay the fifth on when a detective comes in from where they had the judge and announces that the judge wants a lawyer. They believed us then."

He hesitated a moment in search of a reaction from Will.

"Tinnin's still down there," he continued. "He's trying to reconstruct the whole thing. But the way he tells a story, startin' somewheres in the middle and going nowhere fast, they'll probably be there all night and half the mornin'." His laugh faltered almost as soon as it began. "Probably begin with his cigarette butt theory and have 'em all so confused they'll make 'im start over four or five times."

He looked down, shaking his head in an admiration bordering on affection for Tinnin. "Time well spent when I gave you a call. We sure did need ya out there."

He searched the stone that was Will's face. "Anyways, they done called in the SBI. Reckon it was too much for them to handle, what with their own sheriff dead, gunned down by the judge, and their entire vice squad dead."

Boggs shivered as he touched the lump on his head. "Damn if someone wasn't looking out for me when I got knocked on the head. I can't tell them nothin' because I didn't see nothin' 'cept the sheriff finishing off Wynne. That man's as cold as a well digger's ass. Never seen that side of 'im. But talk about pain and suffering. I got enough right here on my head for some kind of lawsuit against the county. And let's not forget duress. I mean, here I was sufferin' with the knowledge of who the killer was … and then there's this concussion I have, one of them permanently disablin' kind. Oh, man, but do I have a load of troubles." With an exaggerated grimace, Boggs fingered the head wound. At the same time, he probed Will's brooding gaze. He saw no indication of cognition.

"Hey, maybe I ought to go in there and get some stitches? That would sure enough solidify my case."

He waited on Will. Still no sign of comprehension. He went on, "But, damn, if we weren't lucky the judge was left standin'. You'da gone and killed everyone, who'da believed us then?" He waited until he tired of the isolation in the silence. "They called in the SBI. … But I done told ya, didn't I?" He frowned. "So how's Sasser?"

"Who?" Will cut his narrowing eyes over at him.

"Whatever his name is."

"Alive."

"He your boy?"

Will canted his head and nodded with a blink.

"Wondered all along what he was up to. He wasn't out to avenge the girl as much as his brother. Makes sense." He added hurriedly, "Don't figure they'll charge him. Ain't no one but me saw him shoot Wynne. Tinnin was hotter than a hornet about how he didn't see much of anything. Says it was all on account of me, how if I woulda given the signal, he'da come forward. Tried to tell him it was all part of my grand plan, him coming out when he did. Anyways, it all worked out because—the way I see it—Wynne drew down on him. Your boy was just acting in self-defense."

Boggs stopped short, picturing Wynne's Glock holstered in the belt. "Damnation!"

He looked to Will to see if he would respond. He didn't.

"Why didn't I take that gun out of the holster?" He cursed and then added, "Aw, what the hell. The sheriff's boys were the first on the scene. We'll accuse them of—of redecorating their fallen hero."

Boggs drummed up a cough. He stood, shifting his bulk from one leg to the other. He winced suddenly and pressed the heel of his hand against his right temple. "I'd best call Dr. Allen. Ya know, it ain't been but five, six hours since I left this dump. And wasn't I a picture of health then? Tell ya what, when you've got your health, you've—your wife here yet?"

When there was no response, Boggs patted Will's shoulder, saying he was leaving and would check back to see how his son was.

He looked back at Will and said, "Ya know, I wonder ... what with the judge spilling the beans and all, you think my standing in town, at least with the law enforcement crowd, will improve? I mean ..."

His voice fell off and after a moment, "Naw. Forget about it. Doesn't matter one way or another what anyone thinks."

On his way out, he passed the gift shop and on impulse decided to go inside. Once he set eyes on the floral cooler, he went over and picked out a bouquet of carnations for his wife.

# CHAPTER THIRTY-SEVEN

About five minutes after Boggs left, the attending physician came. Agnes was right behind him, her eyes red, the rims swollen. Her hands tumbled over one another. She scarcely bore any resemblance to the determined woman who earlier had charged through the automatic doors, taken one look at Will, and barged into the emergency room despite the sign saying Authorized Personnel Only. She trembled now like a resistant oak leaf in a winter wind.

The doctor was so short and slim that his long smock fitted as well as an overcoat on a child. His youthful complexion denied any approach at taking him seriously.

Will remained rigid, apparently unaware of their advance toward him until his wife called him. He rose. "He gonna make it?" He looked to Agnes for an answer.

Agnes seemed to cringe, not knowing how to respond. At first, the doctor, this boy doctor, said there was every reason to believe that Andy would live, just as years ago the army at first said there was every reason to believe that Andy was alive. And then the boy doctor finished his examination and told her that Andy had a better than a fifty-fifty chance. He offered no explanation, only asking her again to leave. The boy doctor and the two nurses resumed their work while Agnes stood back, paralyzed. Her boy was so different, and yet behind all the difference, she saw him as she remembered: the lanky boy shuffling through the dust of the drive. Still, she was afraid, not only for him but also of him because he had come back from a thirteen-year grave, arisen all of a sudden on August 20, 1982, as a stranger with a new life about which she knew nothing and might never know unless this boy doctor saved him, saved her. Andy wasn't dead, but he might be dying now that new and extraordinary hopes, plans, and dreams emerged without prompting—possibly to be dashed as the old ones had and her with them. In the face of all this risk-without-reward, the boy doctor acted so calmly, not frantically as she expected. But that was just it: she didn't know what to expect anymore, what with one son in the ground beyond even the rumor of life that had shrouded her oldest son for so long, and then to have that rumor, that hope, come to life with blood on it, bleeding red. She didn't know what to say, what to ask, how to pray, or to whom.

The doctor pressed his hands deeply into his lab coat pocket and explained in an earnest, almost solicitous, voice that Andy had to have surgery. A bullet had pierced his shoulder and lodged in his right lung. He said Andy's breathing was weak but acceptable, and his blood pressure and pulse were stable. Nevertheless, the bullet had to come out as soon as possible. The boy doctor added that a surgeon was on his way in to perform the operation.

"He awake enough to talk?" asked Will.

"Yes, but we'll be prepping him in a minute. If you'd like, you can see him. But only for a minute."

His eyes low, Will replied, "Hadn't seen him in thirteen years till tonight … out there on the ground."

The boy doctor ushered them down an aisle banked by curtains, some open and some closed, past rolling tables and machinery. The three slipped through a closed curtain. Under a much brighter light than that in the waiting room, all that was metallic shimmered and winked. Boxes blinked and beeped, and tubes of varying sizes came from all directions and plugged into Andy as if he were an overloaded Christmas outlet.

Once the half-naked Will was dressed in a gown, the boy doctor motioned the couple forward to the bedside. He cautioned them not to excite their son.

For Will, the walk was interminable with chunks of those thirteen years of never-knowing impeding each uncertain tread. He craned his neck like a dog trying to understand. In the back of his mind, he expected some cruel trick to befall him.

Andy appeared peaceful, his eyes shut without strain, his mouth gently parted, but the tubes taped into his nose told the truth about his innocent repose. Will followed Agnes around to the side of the bed clear of medical contraptions. He plumbed the boy's face for some telltale sign of what had happened all these years, where he had gone, what he had done, and what had driven him away from all that he had ever known. Will suffered an insupportable sense of loss as he confronted Andy. He sensed a guilt engulfing him, a guilt borne of every dark cause that he either championed or imagined, the guilt of the blasphemous silence, of the intractable never-knowing. "Andy?" he gulped and cocked an ear. "Andy?"

His son's eyelids trembled before opening.

"Andy, it's me, your pa."

Andy's unfettered arm slipped out from under the covers, and his hand groped to touch. Will flinched, almost jumped clear back to the curtain. Agnes seized it while Will's bloodshot eyes crashed on it as though it were magically sourceless, all that was left living of his son. Tentatively, he reached for the living hand, and once he touched it, he eagerly folded it and his wife's hand into his. He squeezed, at once powerful and powerless.

"You've come back," whispered Agnes, petting the hand. Her eyes devoured the sight of her boy's face.

"Didn't ... didn't know ... I ... ever ...," he gasped. His cloudy eyes met Agnes's. "Didn't—"

"We thought you was dead, your momma and me."

Andy drew in a raspy breath. "I—"

He swallowed hard. "Wendy ... she wrote a ... letter—"

"Hush now, son," said Agnes, stroking his forehead. "We can talk later."

"About Billy ..."

Another swallow caught in his throat. He coughed, pain menacing his mouth and eyes. "Just his name and—"

Agnes put her finger to her boy's lips. "Hush now, son."

Will gripped the joined hands tighter, thrilled to hear the only voice that could have breached the long silence, the inscrutable walls built by never-knowing. "But you was gonna let us know, right?" The welled-up tears spilled in quick succession. He felt a tug on his hand and watched himself and his wife fall toward their beckoning son.

# CHAPTER THIRTY-EIGHT

The radial lines around the corners of Agnes's eyes deepened as she looked behind the bed at how lifeless and deflated the machines were now. When she struggled against the thought that her son might die, they had provided noise, not sounds of life, just noise to distract from the absence of sounds of life. Their silence now opened the way for her son to speak, to show he was no longer reliant on the machines that just hours ago breathed for him, that blinked when his eyes couldn't, that had lines and blips running every which way instead of his words. That clothespin of a clamp on his finger, the nosiest of them all, had been eliminated.

Fewer tubes snaked across the bed now—only the one into the back of Andy's left hand and the thin line that looped into his nose. The electrodes and wires had been removed. The catheter and the bag that collected his piss were gone, so too was the bag that accepted drainage from the wound. A gaping gash, a small cut, a major breach? Agnes couldn't tell what it looked like because of all the bandages, so many in fact that had Dr. Allen not given her some assurance, she would have thought the worst.

Agnes watched as Andy spoke. She didn't listen to the words, just the sound of his voice, its cadence that she had memorized way back when he cried as the doctor laid his sticky, squirmy body on her belly while he cut the umbilical cord. Now he was back in her life; now he was real, touchable, and capable of touching, no longer a figment lurking behind the letters *MIA*. Soon he would be walking down the dusty drive in his bare feet. He already brought out that smile that won hearts and weakened minds. She couldn't get used to the glasses though; they were something she had never pictured him wearing. But they made him look distinguished, a professor or a professional.

Her boy a professional! To make it real, she alternately smoothed and stroked the unbandaged shoulder as if it were one side of Aladdin's lamp. According to Boggs, Andy was in shipping and stationed in Asia. What he did exactly she didn't know, but based on what Dr. Allen had told her about the trips he had taken with Wendy, he must be rich, what with going off on a whim across an ocean to Mexico and then speaking the language like a native. This transformation from missing in action to being a man of action, a man of the world, frightened her. He had apparently become a person of considerable standing without her, without Will, without a background like Random. But he had come home; he had returned to avenge his brother's death. Distance was of no count when it came to roots, to family, to love.

A cross between joy and jitters softened her wet eyes. She watched Andy tell Will about Vietnam. She wondered why Andy wanted to discuss the war. Neither she nor Will had asked about it; they were more curious about why he hadn't come to see them when he arrived in Greensburg. They knew now why he had come—because Wendy Allen had mentioned Billy's murder in a letter. It was almost a footnote in the description of how her training runs had taken her past Billy's trailer and how on the day of the murder, a pickup truck had come barreling out of the property and forced her to dive into a ditch to get out of its fishtailing path.

Agnes thought of how horrible it must have been for Andy to learn of his brother's death in such an oh-by-the-way fashion. However shocking, the news must have galvanized in an instant his resolve to come home and seek retribution. She wondered how many times her boy had read that letter; hundreds, she guessed.

On the one hand, Agnes could understand the stratagem Andy employed in his return, but on the other, she questioned the boy's love for her. After thirteen years of separation, he was capable of not making any effort to see her, not so much as a secret rendezvous to which even Will would not have been privy. But since that never happened, Agnes had to believe he had other plans—perhaps killing the killers and then leaving Greensburg for a few days only to return and announce his homecoming. His plans notwithstanding, how they ended suited her just fine. That he was here and would soon be well almost made her whole.

By the intensity of her son's voice, Agnes believed she knew why he launched into an explanation about what had happened overseas. It was a festering boil that had to be popped in order for him to get better, and this was the worst kind of boil, one lodged deep in the heart, a dark abscess that sometimes wasn't even cured by the first purging. Sometimes a fouler infection set in, and many thought remedies such as alcohol were required to fix it. But that only pitched one sickness on top of another. She prayed that Andy would be rid of the debility with this lancing. She saw signs that suggested as much. He began to slow down his speech. At first, it just poured out like the topmost water out of the spout of her watering pot; when it got about halfway down, the flow slowed, losing some of its hurry.

"And listen to this, Dad; we built the road they sent us in to clear. It was as if we built it for them, so they could kill us sooner, and then I hear how they extolled our combative spirit. What a crock of shit! We built a road that enabled them to better bring the fight to us. There is no way on earth anyone can make sense of that."

"But …" Will began, his voice trailing off into a nowhere. He suddenly found himself positioned behind the tricks that life had played on him, behind the scenes where he could see what he could never explain. And what he saw stunned him: nothing. Nothing was there. No sputtering, blinking, burping machines like the ones that kept Andy going until he could get going on his own. No presence, no phantom, no devil behind the scenes manipulating life's twists and turns. No one was there. Not a single thing. Just empty and waiting.

Will now understood that life didn't single him out to be the victim of its tricks. No, life was life. Circumstances, planned events, and routine matters such as farmwork made up life, specifically his, and the circumstances and events that went awry were not planned. They happened because … Will didn't have an answer. But after a moment, he told himself that they happened because they happened. That was all there was to it. Life didn't add diabolical attributes to a situation; in fact, it made sure qualities and characteristics were stripped from an occasion. It was up to Will to add the descriptive nuances to whatever took place. And what a challenge that was. For a man of his disposition, it seemed impossible to place a glowing account on any event. The best he could do was indifference. Why this was so, he didn't know. For a moment, he pitied himself until it occurred to him that if he had made himself this way, then he could change who he was, change his outlook. And he planned to start right then, with his—he wanted to say new—new son, Andy. The new Will studied the boy's face, marveling at how well it performed; his speech was that of an educated man, his reasoning that of a thinker, his experience in Vietnam that of modern man who was thrust into an absurd situation and had to think his way clear of it.

Andy was saying, "I can't think of an analogy to describe it. But now I do business with the Vietnamese; it's as if nothing had ever happened. My God, can you explain any of this to me? I am doing business with them, these so-called communists. Who was lying to whom? Wasn't the rallying cry that we had to stop communism in southeast Asia or else see it spread all over the world? And where is communism today? Defunct. And yet we killed tens of thousands of our own men and God know how many of theirs. For what?"

Will looked to Agnes, conveying with his runny eyes how the years of never-knowing had finally ended, how that dark time of questions without answers and answers that never answered anything had vanished, expired in the wake of a triumph, an achievement that washed over him and, he assumed, over his wife as well. Smiling, he looked down at Andy, who was saying, "The lieutenant sent out the brothers first—he always did—and they knew they were in for it. What we didn't know was that the path we had taken was a trick. It was so easy to take it rather than hump through walls of jungle with sawtooth elephant grass and thick stands of bamboo. The trail was perfect; it funneled us right out into an opening where Charlie waited. He had set up these perfect fields of fire and lit them up once the entire company was out in the open. When we advanced, we hit Bouncing Betty mines. It was like Custer at the Little Bighorn. We formed a circle, and within minutes a dozen men were down. And remember now we hadn't even gotten to Route 547 ..."

So there were tricks, Will mused as Andy continued, but they were the work of men, not of life. A trick led Andy into an ambush. It startled Will to think that even he crafted tricks, such as the time he killed the dog to lure the buzzards. He concluded that a man who practices guile will ultimately be beguiled. Tricks abounded, but they were not as large as life itself.

As strong as the urge was, Will refused to succumb to the notion of a trick when he did the math: a while ago he had no sons; now he had one son. Two sons minus two deaths equals zero. How he got to one from zero was not a trick. There never was a zero, only he didn't know it. It took time for the knowing to happen.

For no discernible reason, Agnes began to shiver. She removed her hands from Andy's shoulder lest he feel her tremors. She couldn't understand this talk about jungles and an enemy called Charlie, but she had seen a movie about Custer's Last Stand. It horrified her to think of her son in the middle of so much death, among men dying under a blasphemous sun.

Andy continued, "It was a tactic of theirs. Fight and then fall back. They let us go. I wasn't about to ask why. Maybe they knew what was about to happen."

He asked for a glass of water. Will filled a plastic cup and restored the lid with the flexed straw inserted in it. As he handed it to Andy, his hand shook even more than Andy's as he grasped the container.

Watching the IV line rise as Andy's hand did brought to mind a puppet on a string. Agnes shivered at the thought. The sensation vanished with her sudden concern as the straw shimmied over the dead skin covering his dried lips. With a crumbled tissue she dabbed the spittle seeping from the side of his mouth.

Andy handed back the cup and rested his head on the pillow. He looked at the ceiling and blinked once. He brought his eyes down to focus on Will's expectant expression.

"I wasn't a coward, Dad. I did my share of fighting; I didn't back away from killing. I accepted every rotten assignment they gave us even though none of them had a rational reason. The art of war is the invention of chaos.

"My last fight was the perfect example. Charlie retreated, like I said. Who knows why? But once we got our guys medevaced, we slogged our way to this so-called highway, which wasn't much better than any one of those old wagon roads running through the county.

"And as we were taking up our positions, in comes a gunship, one of our Cobras. It swoops down, firing at us. At us! In seconds two guys near me, one being the lieutenant, I hear them say, 'I'm—' They never got the rest of it out: 'I'm hit.' They said we had thirty killed or wounded by our own guns." After a moment, he added, "Wasn't much left of us after that."

Andy eased his head back on the pillow. It was as if the telling exhausted him. His body seemed to collapse onto itself, his arms and hands inert, his eyes riveted on the ceiling fan.

"Andy?" said Agnes, nudging his shoulder. "Want us to call the doctor?"

Andy didn't reply.

Without being asked, Will brought the water cup up to Andy's lips. It hovered there for a moment, and then Andy guided it to his mouth. His gulps were loud.

Agnes repeated the question as her eyes followed Andy's bobbing Adam's apple.

"No," he whispered, "I want to forget. Now that you know, maybe I can forget."

"Please, honey, put it behind you," said Agnes, bending over to whisper in kind. "We don't care. The onliest thing we ever cared about was you comin' home alive."

Andy reached up to take her hand. "Momma, I couldn't come back, not to the country that sent me into that madness. It was all so absurd. Being killed by your own men. Fighting, dying without purpose. That battle I was in, they said we won. We took some godforsaken mountain only to abandon it a few days later. I don't know how many were killed. Hundreds, maybe thousands. And they fought for no ultimate purpose. The North Vietnamese moved right back in after we left. I ... I can't—"

Agnes hushed him by placing a finger to his lips. She looked up to Will as if to say, "Do something."

Will gripped the bedrail. Watching Andy close his eyes so slowly unnerved him. "Son, we never took you for no coward. That war made no more sense to me than it done to you. But back then, you sorta believed that the folks you sent to Washington had better sense than you did, that they was actin' on your behalf to make things better. We know different now."

"But, Dad, you don't understand. I deserted. Just walked out of that hospital at Bien Hoa, walked over to the airfield, got on a plane, and got off in Bangkok. No one ever stopped me. No one ever questioned me. It was just all part of the madness."

"Hospital?" Agnes tried not to shout. "You were wounded? You were in a hospital? No one ever told us that."

"I was bound to be," he tried to laugh, but it sounded more like a cough. "Between the copter and Charlie, I didn't stand a chance."

Will said, "If you were wounded, that meant you woulda come home, right?"

"Yes." He swallowed, not water but air in gulps. "You can thank Wendy. She appeared one day out of nowhere, and when I found out where she was from, I understood she was my guiding angel."

Agnes asked, "Then why'd you go to Mexico with her 'stead of here? Why didn't you two come here? She was from here."

"In my case, it just took a little longer to get home."

Will hesitated before he asked, "Was it on account of the words we had before you left? Cuz if it was, I didn't mean 'em. I didn't mean to say such ugly things. Can you forgive me, son?"

Andy swallowed. "I don't remember what you said. But I never took anything you said to be mean-spirited. You were just being a father."

"Think your brother can forgive me for what I done told 'im just before he died?"

"Billy … Billy never would hold anything you said against you. He has nothing to forgive, Dad."

# CHAPTER THIRTY-NINE

The weather prediction Boggs made to Andy Blake, a.k.a. Simon Sasser, was off by a week. Fifteen days after all the killings, the false fall collapsed under a withering spell. The peculiar vengeance Boggs spoke of was right on the mark, for it did seem that a month of swelter compressed itself into one week. What breeze there was only served to spread the heat out more evenly. The agriculture extension office issued warnings of heat stress on livestock. At The Store at night, the men unbuttoned their shirts, pushed back their caps, and loosened the laces of their boots.

Shufflin' Sam, his legs outstretched, tapped the tips of his brogans together and said, "Heard talk the Legion's fixin' to have a Columbus Day parade."

The remark broke Shine's supine repose. He straightened up and said, "Ain't they got rid of that barbecue by now?"

Before Sam got around to answering, Coonie broke in, telling how he had called the Greensburg radio station, WGRB's noon swap-shop, and offered to exchange his wife for a pickup in good running condition.

"Get any takers?" asked Shine.

Coonie worked the Rose Bud chew and spit into the tin can he kept under his seat on the bench. "The man wouldn't let me tell the phone number before he hung up. But my wife's sister, she called. Don't know how she knowed it was me."

Sam said, "S'pect she gave you an earful?"

"Done her like they done me."

"She call back?"

"Weren't even time to say hello for her talkin' like she never knew I hung up."

Shine said, "I reckon that lost boy of Will's got hisself some medical bills, bein' in there the better part of two weeks … him or Will, one."

"Ain't more than I got," cried Coonie. He spit and missed the can. He let the drool run. "But I ain't signed no paper or nothin'. Won't neither."

Sam asked, "Will's boy stayin' on?"

"Agnes said they're fixin' to go to Singapore once he gets his papers straight with the army." Shine added after a spell. "Don't see how Will's got the time what with auction, but Agnes says she's goin' even if he don't. The boy's payin' for it all. Must have more—"

"It possible for a woman her age to still be growin'?" asked Coonie.

Sam said, "No tellin' what a lost coin'll do to ya when it finally turns up."

"Kinda strange, ain't it?" said Milt.

"I'll say this for Will," said Coonie. "Mess with him, and you messed with too much. He won't stop till he settles accounts."

"Weren't for that private detective fellow, ain't none of it come to satisfaction, the way I hear," said Milt.

Sam said, "Ya know, my daddy was all the time sayin' how dang smart them federal generals was. They just took to the burnin' and left the killin' to us." He went on after a moment, "We always been right good at killin'. Don't nobody feel obliged to help us out there."

"Gettin' time to kill the hogs," said Coonie after deliberating on Sam's remark. "Well, not any time soon … but soon."

"What hogs you got to kill?" asked Shine.

"Onliest ones with any hogs is the Legion," said Milt.

Shine said, "Pigs and parades."

Coonie laughed so hard it looked as if an imaginary hand reached out of the dark and yanked at the waist of his pant. He straightened after a while and said, "Don't reckon Judge whatever-his-name-was will be asked to head up the parade."

Shine said, "The court will be in session, only he won't be on no bench."

A brief silence fell on the group.

"Always heard Judge Hardy was a hardworkin' man," said Sam.

"And the sheriff never did fool with my business none," put in Shine.

"Goes to show only the poor is honest," said Milt. "Because the onliest thing we got plenty of is patience."

Coonie stamped his feet and slapped his thighs. After a laugh he said, "Yeah, but Shine ain't poor, and he's honest. Never cheated no one on his liquor."

"I was accused once," said Shine. "I was the winter of '72 or '73, one; when we had that gosh-awful ice storm, and then come on top of it a snow, a foot or better. And my cousins Euliss and Carlton from up near Yanceyville was down gettin' themselves a load but couldn't get out on account of the ice. They didn't want to be runnin' liquor and have no accident, so they settle in at my place like it was home, just sittin' and sippin' till I come to find Carlton been sippin' so much he plum' passed out with his boots parked on the stove and his feet in 'em. He passed out all on his own because me and Euliss was down closin' up the garage, and when we come on back, we find Carlton's brogans, the hard sole part of 'em, done melted clean off so that there was just the points of these little tacks stickin' out." Shine laughed lightly, but it turned into a deep cough. He thumped his chest, and eventually order was restored.

"So when we seen what happened, Euliss let out a holler, and Carlton shot up. When them hot tacks hit the sides of his feet, he liked to jump clear out of 'em, 'cept he couldn't, laced like they was. So he started doin' a dance like he was on that TV program the James City station shows. Ya know, the one they call *Soul Train*. Only Carlton was takin' the express and every time burstin' one of them blisters on the bottom of his feet. Tell you what, that boy did a real fine jig, till finally Euliss tells him, 'Run out in the snow!' He done it, and sure enough the ice smarted even worse.

"Well, I got so dang tired of them boys, 'specially Carlton moanin' all the time like he done. So come the next mornin', I told 'em to leave. There was only four, five inches on the ground then, and the boys packed up—believe it was a Rambler—and headed down the road wavin' good-naturedly. I'm standin' on the porch and just about to turn back inside when the Rambler goes skiddin' off into a ditch. Well, in no time, they're back on the porch grinnin' like they just done arrived and like I was glad to see 'em. So Euliss and me, we drive on over to Will's to fetch his tractor. I promised Will a jar if he'd just get those boys gone, and Will come, but 'fore we even got the chains on, Euliss directs him right into the ditch, sunk the tractor clean up to the axle. So then Will's mad as fire for havin' no more sense than to listen to Euliss who's about half-drunk. To kinda calm the waters, I invited all 'em in cuz by then it was snowin' good. Now, Carlton, he's already inside doing his best to burn his feet again because he's so drunk and cold he couldn't keep 'em away from the stove and liked to burn the bandages off. And Euliss, he ain't no better, apologizin' up a storm for gettin' Will stuck but making no sense at all, only making Will that much hotter. So I sent Euliss out to get some jars and pulled up some chairs because, of course, Carlton was occupying the good one with his big snowball feet stretched out all over it and only a half an eye open.

"So we sat around for a while, and a while got to be a day, and come nightfall weren't none of us fit to go nowhere, just sittin' there like a balancin' act. So we done what we could, which was nothin', and the next day we done a little less than nothin' 'cept to send Euliss out to the car for more liquor. But the third day, come the third day and in comes Agnes with the sun, walked right through the door like it weren't there and sayin' how we was so sorry we'd sell the Lord's Last Supper for a drink and how we weren't fit for decent people to even see. And mind now, she wasn't talkin' about Carlton and Euliss when she said decent folks because, boy, they sure looked a sight mean. And 'fore she carried Will on home she run 'em off. I reckon it was three, four days later that Carlton and Euliss come to find we done drank all the liquor they bought, and they ain't got nothin' to show for it but one pair of good boots between 'em and heads what felt like they been poleaxed."

After Shine adjusted his butt he continued, "Never did trade with them no more. Claimed I cheated 'em. And Carlton, he ain't never been right in the head noways. He claimed I owed 'im a new pair of boots and got so slapdab crazy about it, he drives on down to Greensburg to the magistrate, 'cept the magistrate had him locked up for drunk and disorderly. Spent thirty days in the jailhouse and thirty more cuz he had a fist fight when Euliss come to see 'im."

The listeners looked into the night, shaking their heads as if in agreement. Coonie developed a slight rock, which came to an abrupt halt when the story ended.

After a time Sam said, "Ya know, when I was growing up down on the river, it was winter when we got to be neighbors with them on the other side. The river froze over, and we could cross. Have a woodchoppin' and such and wouldn't never see 'em again till next winter. Somethin' to be said for winter—the cold, the ice, the snow when we gets it. It brings folks together. You can get on with bein' neighbors."

www.ingramcontent.com/pod-product-compliance
Lightning Source LLC
Chambersburg PA
CBHW020841260626
47169CB00003B/1075